Raves for

A CLEAN KILL

A PERFECT LIFE

"Already one of my candidates for the best books of 2005 . . . This is a book for readers, but it should also be loaded into the backpack of any young person who aspires to be a crime writer." —*Chicago Tribune*

"Laced with page-turning tension and memorable scenes . . . Rich details and smart use of dialogue help make this a near-perfect ride." —*Publishers Weekly*

"Thrillers are supposed to be twisted, tortuous, perplexing. But Mike Stewart's *A Perfect Life* is more raveled, roiled and contorted than most."
—*Los Angeles Times*

"This is the kind of read that keeps you up at night. The action is fast, the writing is smart and the story is excellent. . . . Stewart's plot twists are persuasive and surprising enough to keep you guessing."
—*Birmingham News*

"A compelling thriller . . ."
—*Atlanta Journal Constitution*

"Mike Stewart knows how to wring every bit of suspense out of a story, so don't expect to get much sleep once you start reading. . . ." —*Peninsula Post*

Also by
MIKE STEWART

Dog Island

Sins of the Brother

A Perfect Life

Mike Stewart

A Dell Book

A Clean Kill

A CLEAN KILL
A Dell Book

PUBLISHING HISTORY
G.P. Putnam's Sons hardcover edition published January 2002
Dell mass market edition / June 2006

Published by
Bantam Dell
A Division of Random House, Inc.
New York, New York

Library of Congress Catalog Card Number: 2001031851

Dell is a registered trademark of Random House, Inc.,
and the colophon is a trademark of Random House, Inc.

ISBN-13: 978-0-440-24134-8
ISBN-10: 0-440-24134-0

Printed in the United States of America
Published simultaneously in Canada

www.bantamdell.com

OPM   10 9 8 7 6 5 4 3 2 1

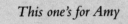
This one's for Amy

The invisible worm
That flies in the night,
In the howling storm
Has found out thy bed

WILLIAM BLAKE

Prologue

THE SOFT GLOW from a gas carriage light played across the Volvo's door as it rolled to a stop alongside the curb. The Baneberrys had a two-car garage under the house and at the end of a downward curving driveway, but Kate was bone tired—physically and mentally exhausted by a solid week on jury duty. She didn't want to contend with a temperamental garage door. She wanted to be inside her house. She wanted to eat and sleep and have a weekend to forget about lawsuits and lawyers.

Kate Baneberry stepped out into the damp November night, swung the car door shut, and pulled her boiled wool topcoat tight around her shoulders. In the moonlight, her blonde hair shone white above startlingly blue eyes that seemed to gather and reflect light wherever she looked.

On the small front porch, she jangled her keys to find the one that fit the door, slipped it into the lock, and turned the dead bolt. She paused to reach inside the black box next to her door and pull out a handful of mail.

Inside the neat two-story colonial, Kate set her purse, her mail, and a white paper bag on the deacon's bench in the entry hall. She peeled off her coat, draped it over the backrest, and carried the mail and the paper sack into the kitchen, where she flipped on overhead lights.

Outside, through the window over the sink, the last gray smudges of dusk disappeared into black. Tension flowed out of Kate's neck and shoulders and dissipated into a tingling chill along her spine.

Her gaze drifted from the window to the blank screen of a small television on the counter; then she turned away as if changing her mind about something. She took a blue-tinted tumbler from the cabinet next to the window and filled it from the cold-water dispenser built in to the freezer door. She drank deeply as she crossed back to the granite-topped island and pulled two fast-food roast beef sandwiches from the bag. She began to flip through the stack of envelopes and holiday catalogs.

And she froze.

The rush of Kate's own heartbeat and quickened breathing filled her ears. She pulled in a deep breath, and she listened as a domino line of thoughts tumbled through her mind. She could have sworn she had heard a sound—maybe the soft brush of a foot on carpeting or the whispered friction of a man's pant legs as he walked—only she couldn't be sure she'd heard anything, and she wondered if it was possible to somehow sense noises too slight to hear.

Standing under bright kitchen lights and framed by the empty window, she stood perfectly still and tried to focus. Her perception of the thing that had made her heart race seemed to hover somewhere between sound and premonition. It was neither, exactly. But whatever it was had filled her with the uneasy sense that she was not alone.

She had been holding the holiday Williams-Sonoma in one hand, thinking vaguely of starting her Christmas shopping. She dropped the catalog on the counter and walked to the back door. As she closed her fingers around the knob, a small scratching noise—a rodent noise—seemed to come from the hallway off the living room.

She shook her head from side to side and said, "Oh, good Lord," out loud. Kate walked back into the entry hall and through the living room and down the short hallway to the bedroom she shared with her husband. As she went, she flipped on lights as her fingers found familiar wall switches without her needing to look or think about what she was doing. And, all the while, she listened for squirrels on the windows or mice in the walls. She smiled to convince herself to smile, but the same strange sense still hung heavy in the house. And, in her bedroom, she caught the barest whiff of some vague, indefinable scent. It wasn't unpleasant—just foreign and, it seemed to her, masculine.

A clicking sound startled Kate, and her heart popped hard in her chest. Someone was in the kitchen.

Painted walls and pale carpeting blurred as she rushed through a familiar jumble of rooms and hallways. She was just outside the kitchen door and still moving fast when the realization hit that she was hurrying *toward* the noise and not running away. Maybe she was angry. Maybe it was territorial. She was standing on the tiled kitchen floor before she had time to think about it. And she was alone.

For the second time that evening, Kate crossed the room and closed her fingers around the backdoor knob. She twisted the cool metal to make sure the door was still locked; then she turned and hurried back through her house, jiggling outside doors, scanning windows for open locks or broken glass, and finally peeking out front to make sure her station wagon was still parked by the curb, still visible in the glow of the gaslight.

She stopped in the small foyer and listened. Seconds ticked by. She forced her breathing to slow. The thumping in her chest subsided and then faded away. A few seconds passed, and Kate had convinced herself that nothing more ominous than squirrels in the attic or bats in the chimney had prickled her already frayed nerves. And she began to feel foolish.

She walked back into the kitchen, where she clicked on the television to feel less lonely. An ad for a BMW convertible flickered across the screen. A silver sports car swerved through curves on the California coast, and Kate thought how glad she would be when that awful trial was over and she and the rest of the jurors could get back to their lives. The whole thing, she thought, was making her a little nuts.

As she dragged up a wrought-iron stool next to the center island, the commercial ended and Channel Five started a news story about a road-rage shooting on the Daulphin Island exit ramp off I-10. The male anchor introduced the pretty blonde reporter with the great laugh—the one Jim, her husband, had a little crush on—for a background piece on gun control.

Kate squirted packets of red sauce inside her sandwiches. She stood and poured her water into the sink, refilled the glass with ice cubes, and then covered the ice with cold tea from the refrigerator. She felt a second wave of tension melt away as she sipped the comforting, bitter brew flavored with bright green mint leaves from her garden. She climbed back onto the stool and ate dinner.

Twenty-six hours later, Kate Baneberry—an attractive, middle-aged housewife who heard noises and sensed danger and ate roast beef sandwiches for dinner—was pronounced dead at Bayside Hospital.

One

TWO LITTLE BOYS with blond bowl cuts were playing in the yard. Over and over, one tore across the lawn, holding a football overhead like the skull of an enemy, and then dove into a pile of dead leaves. The second kid piled on and they rolled around in the leaf pile, fighting like wild dogs over the football; then the victor would pick up the ball and take off for another running dive into a new pile. I remembered doing pretty much the same thing twenty years earlier in a different small town with my brother.

Some things are eternal. Young or old, rich or poor, human beings love to beat the hell out of each other.

I sat down on the brick front steps across from a pretty blonde woman, balanced a plate of food on my knee, and watched. She smiled, and I motioned at the kids. "Are they yours?"

She shook her head. "No. I think they're Sara's." I didn't know Sara, so I arranged some turkey and dressing and cranberry sauce on a fork and put it in my mouth. She said, "Looks like they're having fun."

I smiled and nodded and chewed.

"Relative or friend?"

I looked at her. "Of?"

She laughed. "Sorry. Of our hosts."

"Oh. Friend."

She kept looking at me with her eyebrows raised, as though I wasn't through talking.

As a general rule, I try not to fill in conversational blanks. At worst, it can get you in trouble. At best, well, it's just babbling. But it was Thanksgiving. *And,* I thought, *what difference does it make?* "The woman I would have been with today just moved back to the Midwest, and my elderly parents are on a holiday Caribbean cruise for elderly parents." I pointed my empty fork at the sky. "So, here I am."

She took a sip from a mug of coffee. "Oh, I know who you are. You're Tom McIntosh, aren't you?"

"Close. I'm Tom McInnes."

"Oh, sorry. Nice to meet you. I'm Sheri Baneberry. Our hostess, B.J., said I should talk to you."

Sheri had really large, spectacularly white teeth. Other than that, she was a perfect compilation of mediums—medium nose, medium build, medium-length hair. The overall impression was of a pretty, twentysomething woman completely devoid of sexuality—sort of a universal, upper-middle-class mom-in-waiting. Of course, I realized it was entirely possible that I wasn't turning her crank, either. Anyway, that's what I was thinking when a bloodcurdling scream pierced the crisp fall air, and I spilled gravy on my pants.

The slightly smaller bowl cut was wailing and cupping a tiny hand under a nose streaming blood from each nostril. I started to stand, but the hurt little boy didn't wait for help. He sprinted up the bricks between me and my dinner companion, holding his nose and crying and screaming for his mother. The bigger kid froze for two beats and then hightailed it around the back of the house.

I blotted at the gravy on my pants with one of those hand-embroidered linen napkins that pressure guests to struggle through the meal without actually having to wipe their mouths. I nodded in the direction of the little boy who had just galloped up the steps between Sheri Baneberry and me. "Dinner theater."

She smiled. "Which one were you?"

I stopped to think about what she meant. "I guess I was the nose breaker, since I was older. But my little brother wouldn't have run for Mom. He'd have gone to find a baseball bat."

She laughed. "Do you two still have the same loving relationship?"

More than a year after his death, I still missed a beat before saying, "His name was Hall. He died last year."

"I'm sorry."

"Thanks. Me too."

Sheri Baneberry turned sideways on the steps and pointed her knees at me. "But in a way it brings me to the thing I wanted to talk to you about. My mother passed away, well, it'll be two weeks ago this Saturday."

I told her I was sorry for her loss.

She just nodded and went on. "It was some kind of food poisoning. She was just forty-six, which surprises people. But she had me when she was twenty-one, which is younger than most people have kids nowadays, and she was pretty young-looking. So . . . anyway, Mom checked into Bayside on a Saturday afternoon. She'd been sick all morning with the kind of stomach and intestinal problems you get with food poisoning. And the short version is that something went wrong and she died that night."

I set my plate on the bricks between my feet and folded my thirty-dollar napkin to hide the gravy smear. "I'm sorry, Sheri, but I don't do malpractice, if that's where you're heading. I *do* go to court—I'm not a green-visor, transactions kind of lawyer—but I tend to represent clients who're involved in business disputes. An argument over a contract, something like that."

She flashed those big teeth, but it didn't seem friendly. "So you're not a slimy plaintiff's lawyer?"

"No, that's not what I'm saying. There are some bad doctors out there, just like there are bad lawyers and bad Indian chiefs, I guess. And there are good lawyers who do that sort of thing. It's just not what I want to do. So I don't."

"And B.J. tells me that if you don't want to do something, you just don't do it."

I looked into her medium-brown eyes. "Sounds almost unflattering when you say it."

She forced a small laugh. "Sorry, I guess I'm not at my best. It's just that I need someone I can trust to look into what happened to Mom. I was talking to B.J. inside, and she says that even though you can be kind of . . ." Sheri hesitated, and a rose blush crept up either side of her neck.

"The last time I checked, B.J. was a friend of mine. So it couldn't be that bad."

"Well, she just said you're kind of headstrong. Maybe a little difficult sometimes. It was nothing much worse than that. But she also said, quote, 'Tom McInnes is as trustworthy as a Boy Scout.'"

I didn't really know what to say to that, since I wasn't sure it was true, so I just looked at her.

"She also says you're supposed to be...well, 'smarter than God' is the way she put it."

I smiled. "That's what I keep telling people."

"Anyway, my father's on the warpath. You know. He wants to sue everybody and their uncle, and I don't want a lawyer who'll look at him and see dollar signs."

"Are you asking me to talk your father out of something? Because I can't do that."

"No. Definitely not. I'm looking for someone I can trust to take a look at what happened to my mother and give us an honest report." Sheri took a sip of coffee from her mug as her eyes darted around our Thanksgiving hosts' front yard. "I guess it's obvious I don't think Dad needs to sue anyone. Just putting the whole thing behind us is what I'd like to do. But if one of the doctors or the hospital did something god-awful, then, you know, I guess we need to know that."

Across the lawn, what had been a series of neatly raked and rounded piles were now jagged circles of brown and red and yellow leaves. I turned back to examine my new client's face. "Okay, Sheri. As long as you know what you're getting and what you're not getting. At this point, all I feel comfortable agreeing to do is analyze what's there and give you a report, but the way we're talking about doing this won't be cheap. A regular plaintiff's lawyer would take it on contingency, which means he or she would only charge if you win. I don't work that way, especially since I wouldn't be investigating with the goal of collecting a big verdict at trial. What I do is charge two hundred an hour, which is not unreasonable around Mobile. My investigator gets seventy-five. And this could take a while."

Sheri turned to look out at the yard and slowly, almost imperceptibly, nodded her head.

"And," I said, "as I already explained, if this thing goes to trial at some point, I would not want to handle it. You and I would both be happier if I handed it off to someone who tries cases like this every week."

Sheri Baneberry smiled her pretty smile again. "Lawyers usually get a retainer or something, don't they?"

I nodded.

"Is five thousand okay? That's what B.J. suggested."

Now I smiled. "Five thousand's fine. But let me talk to your father first. It may be the kind of thing that only takes a few phone calls. If it looks more complicated than that, you can give me the check. I'll put it in a trust account and bill time and expenses against it."

I looked down at my plate of cold turkey and dressing smeared with congealed gravy. "Sheri, do you happen to know where Bill and B.J. keep the scotch?"

"Follow me."

The Monday morning after Thanksgiving, I sat watching silver raindrops explode and collect into rivulets on the panes of my window. My office was in the Oswyn Israel Building in Mobile—an old place where plaster is plaster and not Sheetrock and the windows actually have panes. Down the short hallway, I could hear the soft patter of a computer keyboard as my secretary, Kelly, typed something.

I was watching the late-November rain and thinking a little about reasons the INS should allow one of my clients to stay in the country, when the phone rang. I picked up the receiver and said hello.

"Is this Tom McInnes?"

I said it was.

"This is Jim Baneberry. You talked to my little girl, Sheri, on Thanksgiving about handling a lawsuit for us."

"No. Not exactly. I agreed to look into things for the family. To more or less analyze the case and report back to you and your daughter."

"Well, we don't need you."

"That's fine. You mind if I ask why?"

"I got a *real* law firm to take it. Not some guy out on his own. And they didn't try to hold me up for a five-thousand-dollar retainer."

I took a breath and reminded myself that the man had just lost his wife. I'd always heard that there are stages of grieving. Apparently, I'd caught Sheri's father dead center in the anger stage. "That's not what happened, Mr. Baneberry."

"I know what happened. I wasn't born yesterday. Somebody's mother dies and you come swooping around like a...I won't say it. But you aren't gonna pull that on my family. Like I said, I've got a *major* law firm on this now. And if you bother me or my daughter again, I'll tell them to come after you, too."

I took a couple of breaths and turned back to gaze at raindrops puddling like lines of mercury along the bottom of each windowpane. In the distance, the rippled lead of Mobile Bay stretched out beneath fog and rain. As evenly as possible, I said, "Mr. Baneberry? Which 'major firm' did you hire?"

And he hung up on me.

I fished out a business card Sheri Baneberry had given me and punched in the number. She answered her own phone.

"Sheri?"

"Yes. Is this Tom?"

"Yeah. I just got a call from your father."

"I was afraid of that." Her voice sounded tight and hoarse. "I talked myself red in the face last night trying to get him to understand why I hired you. I don't guess it did much good."

"Not much."

"Are you still going to help me?"

"Yep."

"Dad's going to gum things up, though."

"It looks that way, Sheri. After the doctors and the hospital get a load of your father and his trial lawyers, well, they're not going to be in a very cooperative mood, to say the least. So, considering all that, what we need to do is move fast and find out as much as possible before they start gumming up the works."

"I'll call Mom's doctor and see if she'll talk to you. I've known her forever, and I think she'll be normal about it." She sighed. "I guess your job just got complicated." Some of the stress had sifted out of her voice. "I'll go ahead and send you the check, you know, the retainer we talked about."

I told her I'd send over a runner that afternoon with a contract of representation. "By the way, Sheri, which law firm *did* your father hire?"

"Just a minute." I heard scuffing sounds, and she came back on the line. "Here it is. I don't have the lawyer's name, but the firm is called Russell and Wagler."

"Shit."

A second passed before Sheri said, "That bad, huh?"

"Depends on which side you're on."

Two

LUSH LANDSCAPES STREAMED by in shades of charcoal, stripped of color by heavy clouds and pouring rain. I was just north of Daphne, headed south from Mobile. The gray-tone groves and rolling pastures grew more manicured, the houses backed farther away from the highway, and suddenly I was in town. I turned off Highway 98 and headed east.

A blinding flood of fat raindrops swamped the windshield. I reached down to flip the wipers on high and switch from low beams to fog lamps. I could now see lower, if not better. But I kept the halogen bulbs burning. They were highlighting gusts of rain and throwing shimmering zigzags across wet pavement.

Inside the Jeep, the heater puffed hot air on my feet as Dean Martin sang "Silver Bells." December was still two days away. I switched off the radio and listened to the pulsing whisper of wind billowing across the blacktop, making the Jeep sway a little as it went, and to the soft steady swoosh of water passing beneath my tires and washing over the windows.

When I had spoken with Dr. Laurel Adderson by phone, she had been subdued yet concerned—maintaining a perfectly measured professional distance. Yes, she had been Mrs. Baneberry's longtime physician. Yes, it was a terrible loss and most unexpected. And no, of course she wouldn't mind meeting with me if it would help ease the family's pain.

She had asked me to meet her just outside Daphne, which almost made sense. It was, after all, the town where Dr. Adderson lived and practiced medicine; and it was where Kate Baneberry had lived and died. So it would have been the perfect meeting place if only Dr. Adderson hadn't insisted we meet at the Mandrake Club. She knew that in her offices I might have been tempted to ask to see medical records. I tried suggesting that we meet at the hospital. But that was where the treatment and death records were stored. So, without arguing, Dr. Adderson had simply said, "No."

We would meet at her club, where coffee, hospitality, and sincerity would no doubt be the only things offered the visiting lawyer. And where the good doctor could stand up and leave—or even have me politely expelled—if the conversation grew uncomfortable.

Dr. Laurel Adderson was handling me a little, keeping me at bay. And that was fine. Handling and being handled are activities that take up most of a lawyer's day. Besides, if I was going to do my client any good, I desperately needed to meet with Dr. Adderson before Russell & Wagler got at her.

And it was on my way home.

If you want someone to do something your way,

make it easy for them. I was making it easy for the doctor by driving to her hometown for the meeting, and she was making it comfortable for me by inviting me to drop in at her warm and welcoming club halfway through a rainy-afternoon commute.

We were jockeying for position, like two kids fighting over a football in a pile of dead leaves. And we both knew it.

As I left Daphne behind, the drenched and shimmering blacktop wound through orchards and across horse farms with long stretches of white fence and occasional farmhouses too large and too perfect for farmers. Lightning flashed to the south, and, like a child, I counted the seconds until hollow barrels of thunder rolled across the sky.

Seven miles outside the city, a paved road interrupted a line of white fencing. Next to the road stood a monument—no more than six feet high and three feet wide—constructed of old brick and sheltered by copper roofing. Bolted to the brick and safeguarded from the elements by a center-pitched roof was a bronze plaque that read THE MANDRAKE CLUB.

I turned in and followed the road around a sharp curve, where the pavement split around a walled gazebo. I stopped and rolled down my window. A security guard stepped out. The club's name was stitched on the front of his cap. Water cascaded from his visor, and a see-through gray raincoat covered his uniform.

"Yes, suh?"

I told him my name. "I'm here to see Dr. Laurel Adderson."

"Yes, suh. Just a moment, suh." The guard stepped back inside the structural embodiment of his authority and checked my name against a clipboard. Then he leaned out of the door and, using a slow karate-chop motion, signaled for me to proceed down the road.

After rounding another hard curve, the clubhouse came into view and I realized two things. One, the road had been purposefully designed into an S-shape to hide both the guardhouse and the clubhouse from nosy peasants on the county highway. And two, Dr. Adderson belonged to one hell of a nice club.

Nestled into a grid of hundred-year-old pecan trees, the Mandrake Club looked at once old and new. Like the sign monument out by the highway, the main building was constructed of ancient brick and the steep roof was sheathed in seasoned copper. Atop the second-story roof and centered over the main entrance, an octagonal turret with a pointed roof supported a weathervane cut in the shape of a prancing horse.

Except for the pecan trees, nothing about the place was really old. But it had the too-perfect weathered ambiance that only big money can afford and only old money knows enough to want.

The road circled in front of the clubhouse—no doubt designed for dropping off Southern belles—and then curved down and to the side, where a parking lot lay hidden by thick rows of longleaf pine.

I stepped out into the waning rainstorm, locked the Jeep's doors just for spite, and followed a brick walkway through the pines to a covered catwalk that ran along the building to the front entrance, where I got *yes-suh*'d again.

The uniformed doorman pulled open the door as I approached and, not being a rube myself, I glanced at his nameplate before saying, "Why, thank you, Harvey."

I glanced back to see if Harvey was impressed, and he closed the door.

Inside, the floors were hardwood, the walls were made of brick and dark paneling, and the rugs and furniture looked middling expensive. Someone's budget had tightened by the time the furniture was put in, but it was still, as I said, one hell of a nice place.

At 4:20 on a Monday afternoon, no one was in evidence in the entry hall. I started out on my own to find "The Gun Room," where Dr. Adderson had said we would meet. Whether by some flaw of character or streak of useless genius, I walked straight to the club bar and quickly found someone who I assumed was the bartender.

A muscular, ethnic-looking fellow with hollow cheeks nodded hello.

I asked where The Gun Room was.

The bartender's face remained immobile.

I tried again, "Excuse me..."

"It's at the other end of the building." His deep voice was thick with accent—something like the way a French-Canadian would sound if he had learned English in Brooklyn. And it occurred to me that I'd heard that jumbled dialect somewhere before.

I said, "Thank you," and he just held my eyes. He didn't look angry. He looked like he was thinking deeply about...something.

I glanced back as I left the room. The bartender had vanished.

Two minutes later, I found The Gun Room and Dr. Adderson, both of which looked rather old and well built. She rose from a table covered in white linen and walked across the room with her hand outstretched.

"You must be Mr. McInnes."

I said it was nice of her to meet me, and she said, "Nonsense. I just hope it wasn't too much to ask you to drive way out here in this rain."

Dr. Adderson knew full well that her club was no more than ten minutes out of my way, and I knew that she knew. But she was setting a courteous tone. Nothing wrong with that.

She turned back toward her table. "Come over here and we'll get you some coffee or something."

I followed and took a seat across from hers. After I had ordered a large latté from the waitress, I took a minute and looked around the room at a pretty amazing collection of fine English and American double shotguns hung from sets of brass stirrups. It was beginning to dawn on me that there probably was not a golf course out back.

I turned to the doctor. "What kind of club is this?"

She smiled. "The kind for people who agree with Mark Twain, that the game of golf is nothing but a good walk ruined. We've got enough land here for a course, but no one wants it. The club started out as a stable for hunters, what most people would call jumping horses. Now we've got stables and some riding trails, and we've contracted to ride on some of the adjoining properties. There's a pool, of course. The room we're in is a tribute to the gun group, which is where I fit in. We've got a sporting clays range and a kennel with some of the best pointers and retrievers in the state. Just north of here we have a tract of land under lease for quail hunting and dove shoots."

Something was tugging hard at a childhood memory. Finally, I asked, "What's that smell in here? It smells kind of like an old hardware store."

Dr. Adderson smiled again. "It's gun oil. Hoppes Number Nine. I like it."

"Yeah. I didn't mean it wasn't pleasant. It's just not your usual tea-room smell."

"I'm not sure most of our members would like hearing this called a tea room, but . . . I agree it's a nice background scent. To me, it always smells like my father's den." She motioned at the walls. "You can't have all these antique side-by-sides in here without spreading a little gun oil around to fight corrosion."

I was looking over the doctor's head at what appeared to be a heavily engraved L. C. Smith double from around the late 1920s. "Well, I'll give you this. You're sure not trying to put on the poor-country-doctor act for the lawyer."

Laurel Adderson didn't smile. "Sheri Baneberry tells me you're not that kind of lawyer. I was led to understand that you couldn't care less how much I'm worth. I was led to believe that you wanted to find the truth."

"I didn't mean to offend you. It's just that I assumed you wanted to meet here instead of your office or the hospital so I wouldn't be tempted to ask for medical records."

No bullshit from this one. She said, "That's right."

"So you'll have to excuse me for expecting some bobbing and weaving."

The waitress brought my coffee. As she put it down, Dr. Adderson said, "You're excused. Now what can I do for you?"

"Tell me about Mrs. Baneberry. I need to hear everything you know about the food poisoning and her death. But first, let me just go ahead and ask you: Does it make any sense at all for a healthy, forty-six-year-old woman who has sought hospital treatment to die of simple food poisoning?"

"Salmonella poisoning."

"Okay," I said, "does it make any sense for Kate Baneberry to have died of salmonella poisoning under those circumstances?"

Dr. Laurel Adderson took a delicate sip of tea from a china cup and said, "No, Mr. McInnes. It doesn't make any sense at all."

Three

AT ITS SOUTHERNMOST TIP, Alabama drops down next to the Florida Panhandle and splits into two short prongs or legs. The water between those prongs is Mobile Bay, and the City of Mobile sits at the apex, or the crotch, of that split. Some—referring to the city's sea-faring history and its location—claim that Mobile is the place, literally the birth canal, through which much of the deep South was born. Others—who are less impressed with the city's Mardi Gras societies and unyielding social climate—say its founders prophetically placed Mobile exactly where an asshole should be.

I loved the old place, or I wouldn't have located my practice there. But, at the end of the day, even I headed south to live on a more tranquil part of the bay, a place where slipping bare feet into worn boat shoes is considered dressing for dinner.

Highway 98—the road I had taken into Daphne—

runs down the Eastern Shore of Mobile Bay through Daphne and Fairhope to below Point Clear, where it cuts across the right foot of Alabama and crosses into Pensacola.

I followed the rain-washed highway as far as Point Clear, where I turned onto the familiar crunch of my gravel driveway a few minutes past seven. Inside the beach house, I placed a call to my mother to see if she and Sam had returned from their Thanksgiving cruise. It was something one of them had dreamed up to avoid another holiday spitting contest between my father and me. I got their machine and left a message. Next I punched in Sheri Baneberry's home number with the intention of reporting on my meeting with Dr. Adderson. I talked to another tape recorder and hung up.

Finally, I tried Susan Fitzsimmons's new number in Chicago.

Susan and I had a complicated relationship. Fall of the previous year, I had manipulated Susan into helping me find my brother's killer, who took exception to our efforts, stabbed Susan, and shot me. Obviously, we both survived. Six months later, she and I became *involved*—the post-college euphemism for affection and sex—during my efforts to help a young friend of Susan's who had witnessed a murder. Our relationship had lasted almost six months.

But Susan missed what she wryly called "the safety of Chicago."

As she had become increasingly involved in my life, Susan had come to believe that I was attracted—"almost driven," in her words—to dangerous people. I, on the other hand, wondered why so many dangerous clients and situations seemed to be attracted to me.

Susan said I was in denial.

I said, probably so.

She then suggested that maybe I had spent my life seeking out life-and-death battles to prove my worth to an overbearing and unforgiving father.

I suggested that maybe she'd been watching too much *Oprah*.

Now she had moved to Chicago, and her phone had rung fifteen times. Maybe she hadn't found time to buy a machine or hire a service. Maybe it was easier to avoid calling me if I couldn't leave a message. Maybe the world didn't revolve around me, and Susan was just out having a life.

Fifteen minutes later, I was microwaving leftover chili when my phone rang. I walked into the living room, grabbed the mobile receiver, and said hello.

"Tom? This is Laurel Adderson."

"Oh."

"Did I catch you at a bad time?"

I shook my head, which wasn't all that helpful to someone on the other end of a phone line. "No. Not at all. I just thought it was going to be someone else. What can I do for you?"

"Well, Tom, I've been thinking. And I've been talking to the hospital's in-house lawyer."

"I thought he might want a report on our meeting."

"Wouldn't you?" Dr. Adderson sounded unfazed. "Anyway, I convinced him that you and Sheri aren't out for blood. And—don't make me sorry I did this—but I also convinced him that it might help resolve the family's concerns about the death if he let me go over some of Kate Baneberry's records with you."

This was unexpected. "From the night she died?"

"Yes. If you can get her husband to sign a waiver of doctor-patient confidentiality, then I can show you something that's been bothering me about the progression of her illness."

As the doctor talked, I had walked back into the kitchen. I pulled the chili out of the microwave and reached for an onion. "How about this? Sheri's father, Jim, is . . ."

"Angry."

"Well, yes, he is." I grabbed a chef's knife from a wooden block on the counter and began peeling the onion. "As I told you this afternoon, he's got his own lawyers. If I ask him to sign a legal waiver, red flags are going to go up and we'll be buried in pinstripe suits. So, how about if I ask Sheri to get her mother's medical records from her father? He has the right to access those records, and he can't very well object to letting his own daughter look at them." I stepped on the trash can lever and dropped the crinkled-gold onion skin inside. "Since I'm her attorney, she can let me see the file without his permission."

Dr. Adderson let a few seconds go unfilled. "But that doesn't give me the all's-clear to discuss her condition with you."

I made horizontal cuts through the onion. "At the risk of sounding insensitive, Kate Baneberry no longer has any confidentiality to protect. She's dead. And besides, we already discussed her this afternoon."

The line went silent, and I thought I may have offended her. Then she said, "Do you shoot?"

"Yeah. I guess. I go bird hunting about twice a year." I separated three thick slices of onion and chopped them up.

"Come to the club Wednesday at one. We'll eat and go over the records. Two o'clock is my usual tee time at the clays range. We'll shoot and talk."

I thanked her for calling and got no response. "Dr. Adderson? This may sound crazy, but something's been bothering me all afternoon. I got directions today from a guy in the bar at your club. He was . . . he was intimidating as hell is what he was."

"Charlie? Charlie's big but he's not what I'd call intimidating, especially not to a man like you."

I put the knife down and turned to lean my backside against the kitchen counter. "This guy was about my age or a little younger. Black hair. Gaunt cheeks. Build like a fighter, like somebody who works out for strength, not bulk."

Laurel Adderson laughed. "That's not Charlie. Our bartender's tall and round, with a big red beard. The guy you described . . . if there is someone like that who works at the club, I don't know him. And he doesn't sound much like he'd be one of our members."

"No. I'd say this guy would scare the living hell out of the membership committee. Thanks anyway."

"Sure. See you Wednesday."

I punched the off button on the phone, dropped it on the counter, and scooped chopped onions off the cutting board and dumped them on top of my dinner. The chili, a cold bottle of Guinness, and I went into the living room, where I parked my food on the coffee table and then walked to the front hallway.

I peered out at the driveway, where I could have sworn I caught a flicker of movement in the shadows, but then there was nothing there. I locked the door and set the alarm. And while I was doing each of those things, the muscular stranger at the Mandrake Club stood silent watch from the back shadows of my imagination.

As I plopped into a chair and reached for the remote control, I started to feel a little embarrassed by my reaction to the hollow-cheeked stranger. I glanced up at the blank stare of the big beachside window that now showed only night.

I examined my pale reflection, then shook my head at the two-dimensional ghost in the window. "What a wuss."

Four

I COULD SMELL whisky on her breath.

Sheri Baneberry's smiling features looked blurred, like a smudged photograph with a thumbprint over the face. Her blonde tresses poked and twisted this way and that, I guessed, from riding with her window down. Out in the driveway, over my client's shoulder, I could see some kind of sea-green Japanese SUV. The motor was running, and I could see a dark human form inside the vehicle.

Two hours earlier, just before five o'clock Tuesday afternoon, Sheri had called my office to say she'd gotten her mother's medical records from her dad. I'd offered to stay late and go over the records with her, but Sheri hadn't wanted to deal with rush-hour traffic in Mobile. Instead, she had suggested that she could bring them to my house, and I had agreed.

Now I had a drunk blonde on my front porch.

"Come in. You must be cold." My client was wearing shorts and a sleeveless turtleneck on November 30.

"I never get cold." She brushed by and left me standing alone in the entry hall.

I thought, *Half a bottle of Jack Daniel's has that effect.*

I followed and found Sheri standing in the living room. She held out a brown accordion file folder. "Here it is."

I took the folder and thanked her.

Sheri said, "Swelcome," then walked over and sat in an upholstered chair facing the beach windows. She waved her left hand at the folder. "Whatcha looking for?"

I sat on the sofa and dropped the folder on the coffee table. Sheri wasn't in any shape to help me go through the file, and I wasn't in any mood to try to make her. I lifted the edge of the folder and peeked inside at my bedtime reading. "I'm not sure yet. I just wanted to go over the records before I see Dr. Adderson tomorrow. See if anything jumps out at me."

Sheri kicked off her sandals and put her bare feet up on the coffee table. "I can tell ya what Dad's lawyers said."

I waited while she looked around the room. "Okay."

"You got anything to drink? I had a bourbon before I came over, and just one drink always gives me a headache."

If she'd had one drink, it was in one hell of a big glass. I said, "I don't drink."

"You drank at B.J.'s on Thanksgiving."

"I'm turning over a new leaf. What'd your father's lawyers say about the medical records?"

Sheri Baneberry sighed. I, clearly, was an inadequate host. "They said Mom was doing good all afternoon, and then she just got sick and died."

"That's some kind of in-depth analysis. They must be very proud."

Sheri shrugged. "They've got a paralegal who's a nurse."

"That would explain it."

"Listen. You want me to hang around and go over the records with you? I got a friend out in the car, but she'll wait if you need me."

"No, that's fine. We can talk later. Just tell me this . . ."

Someone knocked on the front door, and Sheri said, "Must be Bobbi. Guess she got tired of waiting."

I stood and walked to the foyer. Sheri followed.

When I opened the door, Bobbi stepped into the house and stopped in the entry hall halfway between Sheri and me. Bobbi was a tall, athletic brunette, who wouldn't have looked out of place as a girls' tennis coach at any high school in the country.

Sheri introduced us, and Bobbi Mactans said, "Hi."

I motioned in the direction of the living room. "Would you like to come in? We'll just be a couple more minutes."

Bobbi peered into my eyes as though she was trying to see through them. Her irises were so dark that the pupils were indistinguishable from the surrounding color. "No, thank you. Sheri and I really need to get going." And without taking her eyes from mine, Bobbi said, "Sheri, are you ready?"

"Sure."

I held up my hand. "Sorry, Sheri. Just one more thing. Who was with your mother that Saturday? Did anyone stay with her?"

I was looking at Sheri, but I could see Bobbi trying

to hold my eyes with hers. Sheri said, "I was there. Most of the time, anyway. Dad called around two Saturday afternoon to tell me they were headed for the emergency room. I got to the hospital around three-thirty and stayed until dinnertime. Mom was getting better when I left."

"Was your father there the whole time?"

Sheri looked bored, like maybe she was losing her buzz. "I think so."

"Was he there when you left?"

Bobbi cut in. "She said he was. Look, Sheri, we need to get..."

I interrupted, but tried my best to sound pleasant. "Bobbi, your friend's paying me a lot of money to ask these questions."

Bobbi's hard black eyes narrowed, and she walked out onto the porch. I turned to Sheri. "Well, was your father with your mother *in her hospital room* when you got there *and* when you left?"

Sheri was growing blurrier by the second, but wasn't the least bit irritated by my cutting off her friend. "Yeah, Dad was there when I got there. And he was still around when I left."

"Still around the hospital or *in* your mother's room?"

"Oh. Uh, he went to the cafeteria."

"Did you see him come back?"

"Unh-uh. He was still gone when I left."

I put my hand on the small of Sheri's back. "You need to get your shoes." Sheri walked into the living room and slipped painted toenails into her sandals. As we walked back toward the open front door, I said,

"Okay, thanks, Sheri. I'll call you tomorrow after I talk with Dr. Adderson."

Just inside the door, she turned to face me. "I'm a little bit drunk."

"I figured that out."

Tears pooled in her blurry brown eyes. "I'm sorry, Tom. I really am serious about this, and I appreciate what you're doing. It's just... it's funny how awful it is to lose your mother, even if, you know, you're a grown-up."

I glanced through the open door and met Bobbi's black-eyed glare. She and Sheri were both in their twenties, but I wasn't sure I was in the presence of any actual grown-ups.

Sheri stepped gingerly toward the open door and closed it between us and her friend. "Tom, can I tell you something about my mother?"

"Anything you want."

She leaned against the door and rocked the back of her head against the painted wood. "I was in the fifth grade—I guess about ten years old—and I'd seen a Bela Lugosi movie or something 'cause I decided I wanted to be a vampire for Halloween." Sheri squeezed her eyelids shut and tears rolled down her cheeks. She swallowed hard. "So anyway, I tell Mom that that's what I wanna be. And I've got a pretty unrealistic picture in mind of the costume I want. I want a cape like Dracula's. You know, black with red satin lining. One of those things cut in a half circle so it would hang in folds and I could hold it in front of my face and give people the evil eye.

"Anyway, I'm rambling on about all this, and Mom just listens. Later, when she couldn't find a costume like

I wanted, she went to the fabric store and bought black and red satin. She was still working with my father then—working as hard as he did—and she stayed up every night for a week after he went to bed. Mom designed and sewed a cape and a vest to go with some black pants and a shirt I'd picked out. She even went out and bought a three-dollar wig and cut it into a widow's peak like Bela Lugosi had because I didn't wanna run around acting like a demon in a little blonde pageboy.

"Do you understand what I'm telling you, Tom? I had this childish fantasy of what I was going to look like on Halloween, and my mother worked herself ragged to make the fantasy real for me." Sheri still had her eyes closed tight, and her lips trembled as she spoke.

I reached out and took her hand. "I understand what you're telling me, Sheri."

She raised the back of her head off the door. She opened her eyes and nodded. "Well, guess what. On Halloween, at school that day, I found out all my friends were going to hang out at the carnival and make fun of the other kids. These three girls that I thought were so *cool* were already laughing about the losers in the class who were going to dress up like little kids that night.

"So," she paused to take a deep breath, "when school let out at three o'clock, I ran home in tears and told Mom that I didn't want her costume, that I was too old for it, and everybody would make fun of me." She paused to wipe at her face. "You know what she did? She told me not to worry about it. She helped me pick out something else to wear, and that was it. She never even mentioned it again."

I nodded. It was the kind of story that every kid,

every lucky one, has about their mother or father. And, like all such stories, it was ordinary and maybe even trite—except that it wasn't.

I squeezed her hand. "Are you going to be okay, Sheri? Do you need anything?"

My inebriated client smiled a little. "I'll be fine."

"Just one more thing. Do you know if your mother had any ownership interest in your dad's construction company?"

Her eyes rolled back and seemed to scan the crown molding. "Maybe. I'm really not sure." She paused and lost interest again. "Good night, Tom."

"Good night."

Sheri opened the door and stepped out onto the porch, and Bobbi slipped her arm around Sheri's waist to help her down the stairs. And I thought, *Well, she's drunk.* Then Bobbi kept her arm around Sheri all the way to the car. And I thought, *She doesn't want her tipsy friend to trip and fall in the dark.* Then Bobbi opened the passenger door, helped Sheri inside, and reached across to fasten Sheri's seatbelt.

Bobbi backed her Isuzu Trooper around, dropped the transmission into drive, and spun gravel down the length of my driveway.

I locked up and wandered into the kitchen, where I found a cold bottle of Foster's in the refrigerator.

Kate Baneberry's medical record was a two-beer file. And—as far as I could tell—Jim Baneberry's lawyers were right. Kate Baneberry had been responding to treatment, getting better, even eating a little dinner. Then she just died.

I picked up the phone and punched in my investigator's number. No answer. I briefly considered calling his pager but realized that what I wanted could wait. I punched in another number, and my secretary, Kelly, answered on the second ring.

"Sorry to bother you at home, Kelly."

"No problem. I'm just sitting here watching *NYPD Blue*."

"Whose butt are they featuring tonight?"

Kelly laughed. "No bare bottoms so far. What can I do for you?"

"I wanted to let you know I'm not coming in tomorrow. I've got to meet Kate Baneberry's doctor in Daphne for lunch, so I'll just work here until then. You can put any calls through. I'll be here at home till around noon."

"Okay."

"Do me a favor. Joey's not answering. Could you please call him in the morning and ask him to check out some people for me? And, Kelly, I don't want these people to know they're being checked out. You understand?"

"Absolutely. Who are they?"

"The first one is Dr. Laurel Adderson. I need to know about any malpractice claims filed against her in, say, the last five years or so. And tell him to do a general background check."

"Okay. Got it. Who else?"

"The second is a woman named Bobbi Mactans." I spelled the name, then gave Kelly the tag number of Bobbi's Isuzu Trooper and hung up.

Five

"THE BIGGEST CONCERN with food poisoning is dehydration." Dr. Laurel Adderson and I had finished lunch and were lingering over coffee while we waited for our spot on the clays range. The club's cavernous dining room was outfitted with a cathedral ceiling, distant waiters, and a linen-draped buffet table covered with really good, really fattening food.

Dr. Adderson went on with her explanation of Kate Baneberry's condition. "Kate checked into emergency at Bayside just after two Saturday afternoon. She reported that she had awakened around four that morning with stomach cramps and that she had been experiencing severe diarrhea and vomiting since that time. When I saw Kate, she was seriously dehydrated. I immediately ordered her put on a glucose IV to replace fluids, and we administered meds to control the nausea and diarrhea. And Kate was responding. Her nausea and diarrhea had pretty well run their course anyhow, which is what you want. If someone has eaten tainted food, what you want is to let the body throw the poisons off before you interfere. But, like I said, the nausea had run its course, and we had medicated Kate to settle her stomach." Dr. Adderson's voice sounded normal, her speech professional and unhurried. But I noticed her hands gripping the armrests on her chair, twisting sticks of carved mahogany like twin screwdrivers locked into rusted screws. "Of course, we verified that salmonella was the culprit, and we ran other, standard tests that came back perfectly normal for someone battling food poisoning. Her electrolytes were elevated, but there was nothing to really concern us. So the treatment was to replace fluids, keep her comfortable, and monitor her condition. I called in from home at seven and was informed that Kate had improved enough to have a light supper."

Our waiter appeared and spoke quietly. "They're ready for you on the sporting clays range, Dr. Adderson."

"Thank you, Simon." She turned back to me. "Are you ready?"

"Sure."

We exited through double glass doors at the rear of the dining room, crossed a stone veranda, and descended a wide fan of stone steps.

Parked on a small asphalt path, a golf cart waited with our shotguns already stowed vertically in a gun rack that took the place of the usual golf-bag stand on the back.

Dr. Adderson nodded at my Beretta. "Is that your Silver Pigeon?"

"Yeah. I checked it when I got here."

She shook her head. "That's a good gun, but you're going to miss some clays shooting a twenty-gauge."

As we climbed into the cart, I said, "I'm going to miss some clays anyhow. I've only done this once before."

"Aren't you interested in winning, Mr. McInnes?"

"Right now, I'm interested in finding out what happened to Kate Baneberry."

She gave me a look.

I smiled. "I'm used to the gun, and I put in a couple of Briley extended skeet tubes to open up the choke and cover as much sky as possible. I'll be fine."

Dr. Adderson returned my smile. "I had a feeling."

She stepped on the accelerator and we started off with a jerk. The cart path wound around the side of the clubhouse and cut through a hundred yards of old-growth hardwoods before we came to the first station. Two carts were ahead of us. On the wooden stand, a CPA type who looked like his mother had dressed him with one of everything from L.L. Bean was blasting away at spinning orange targets.

"It'll be a few minutes." Dr. Adderson turned to me. "There are ten stands. Before you shoot, the trapper will release 'show birds' so you can see where they'll be going. All this varies, but generally you'll have two clays released in different directions. You shoot singles first, then two report pairs, which means the second clay is released when you shoot at the first one. Then you'll get two true pairs. Shoot the one farthest away first."

I looked at her.

"You got that?"

"I'll figure it out." Now the CPA's partner—a little

round guy with yellow glasses and a bald head—stepped up onto the stand. "You're pretty serious about shooting, aren't you?"

Dr. Adderson nodded.

That was enough small talk. "What happened to Kate Baneberry after dinner that night?"

The doctor stepped out of the cart and fished what looked like stereo headphones out of a canvas-and-leather bag. She tossed them to me and pulled another set out for herself. As she hooked the hearing protectors around her neck, Dr. Adderson said, "What happened *appeared* to be a weakened heart."

"From the food poisoning?"

"No. The food poisoning *may have* been the triggering mechanism. But the organic susceptibility—the arrhythmia that *may have* resulted in cardiac arrest—*may have* been a time bomb waiting to happen."

The CPA and his bald buddy pulled away, and two women stepped out of the cart in front of us. "You said on Monday that her death didn't make sense. Now you say it could've been her heart. And you're using an awful lot of 'may-haves.' "

Dr. Adderson didn't comment. She looked off into the distance and worked the muscles at the points of her jaw.

Okay. I tried a different tack. "You were Mrs. Baneberry's physician. I assume she had yearly physicals."

The doctor put on a pair of amber shooting glasses and looked at me. "She did, and no abnormality was ever detected. Unfortunately, though, patients often don't tell their doctors about heart palpitations, which could indicate a history of arrhythmia. And unless the patient tells the doctor about them, or she's so scared of the doctor's office that her heart starts fluttering, there's really not much way to know the problem exists. And, if that's what happened in this case—*if* that's what happened to Mrs. Baneberry—the stresses of salmonella poisoning could have brought on arrhythmia and cardiac arrest."

"Couldn't you tell from the autopsy?"

Dr. Adderson hesitated before answering. "The autopsy showed that she died of cardiac arrest. Nothing out of the ordinary."

She was holding back, and I was getting a little frustrated. "Okay," I asked, "then was there *something else* that could've accounted for the sudden heart attack?"

The doctor's eyes were trained on the woman shot gunner ahead of us. "*If* Kate had been under an unusual level of stress, that *could have* been a contributing factor. But she didn't mention anything."

The second woman was shooting now. It would be our turn in another minute or two. "Well, if you don't know what happened, what did you want to tell me about 'the progression of her illness'?"

"I've already told you."

I looked at her.

She dropped her eyes to the leaf-covered ground. "I'm going out on a limb here."

The trapper called out. "Dr. Adderson! Your party is up."

She didn't move. "I think it's *possible* that some outside substance was introduced into Kate's system after she entered the hospital. And—*if* that happened—I don't think it was a doctor or nurse or any other hospital employee who introduced that substance."

"What are you talking about? What kind of 'substance'?"

She lifted her Krieghoff twelve-gauge out of the cart rack and propped ten thousand dollars' worth of shotgun on her hip. "Tom, do you remember a few years back there was a serial killer the newspapers called the 'Black Angel of Death'?"

"Is that that nurse who killed a bunch of intensive-care patients at different hospitals?"

"Yes. But I'm not talking about him being a nurse."

The trapper called again. "Dr. Adderson!"

She turned and, with the timber of, for example, a doctor addressing a nurse, said, "Just a moment!" Then, in a softer tone, she added, "Please."

I decided it was time to cut through the bullshit. "Are you telling me that you think Kate Baneberry's husband killed her?"

Dr. Laurel Adderson emptied a box of shells into the pocket of her vest and turned toward the first station. "No. I'm just telling you that . . . I don't know, that I think *something* happened. A patient with no history of arrhythmia dropped dead from heart failure. And she didn't die while she was under real stress from the salmonella poisoning. She dropped dead at a time when she should have been—and was—getting better. Her husband was there. My people weren't. If they had been, none of us would be talking about lawsuits now." She stopped walking but didn't turn around. "But—let me make this very clear—I am not, generally or specifically, accusing anyone of anything. As a lawyer, you should understand that."

And, as a lawyer, I understood precisely what the doctor was telling me.

* * *

By four that afternoon, Dr. Adderson had thoroughly whipped my ass and my ego on the clays range, which only confirmed my earlier impression that she was an extraordinarily competent woman, on many levels. The stations had been automated, with little remote-control devices locked inside military ammo boxes that were mounted on posts at each stop. Dr. Adderson had driven the cart; she had allowed me to shoot either first or second, depending on how I felt; and she had shown me how to launch clays with the remotes. I was a little surprised when she handed the remote to me when it was her turn. I half expected her to launch the clays with one hand and shoot with the other.

Still driving the electric cart, the doctor dropped me at my Jeep, waited for me to load my Beretta and shells into the back, and then pulled away with an invitation to "come back anytime."

She was enjoying my discomfort, while I obviously wasn't. It wasn't that I didn't like losing to a woman. I'm even more politically incorrect than that. It's losing to anyone that I can't stand.

I dragged my wounded pride into the Jeep and drove away through the increasingly chilly December afternoon. As I passed the guardhouse, I raised my index finger in the universal Southern-driver's salute. The guard smiled and nodded.

Winter solstice was only three weeks away, and daylight was already fading as I turned onto the county highway and began debating whether to drive into Mobile, whether to put in an appearance at the office. The road had dried out from the previous day's deluge, and I pushed the speedometer to seventy-five on the lonely stretch of highway. The engine warmed. The heater clicked on and sprayed hot air across my feet.

I suddenly felt exhausted. I would go in to work tomorrow, or maybe I wouldn't, or...something. I couldn't remember what I thought I would do. My thoughts lost focus and substance and swirled together like ribbons of smoke in a warm summer breeze. White fences along the roadside blurred and doubled and crossed in front of my headlights. I slammed on the brakes as a horrible diving pitch racked the Jeep. The undercarriage jumped and spasmed and jumped again, as if rolling over a series of logs and gullies.

And while this was happening, while the Jeep roared and plunged and buckled, I began to fall through a black tube. Velvet walls spun by an inch from my nose, and a cacophony of creaking, slamming metal dissolved into the whispered rush of wind through trees.

And I was gone.

Six

MY BRAIN HAD GROWN thumbs—thick, coarse digits that fumbled thoughts and jabbed at my temples with each heartbeat. The tang of copper and salt mixed with saliva on my tongue. I spat blood and opened my eyes. Pale, odorless smoke hung inside the Jeep, and I was jarred into full consciousness by a pure and primitive terror of burning.

I grabbed the door release and yanked, but the metal was buckled shut. And I seemed to be stuck. *Stop and think.* I shoved at a flaccid air bag in my lap and found the seatbelt release. Somehow, my knees were up on the seat. I gripped the bottom of the driver's-side window and shot through the shattered opening.

Hard ground slammed into my right shoulder. Sharp bits of rock tore at my knees and palms as I rolled and scrambled on all fours to get away from the smoking Jeep. I found my feet and sprinted twenty yards before spinning around to look for the fire that wasn't there.

All I saw was the white-trash coat of arms—a demolished vehicle on a field of grass. The Jeep's front end had smashed through one side of a concrete horse trough and then collapsed against the other side. The front wheels sat inside the trough. The grille had been hammered to within two feet of the windshield, and the arched hood stood like a crumpled pup tent between them.

I breathed deeply to clear my head, and something hissed deep inside the mangled heap.

Powder-gray shards of concrete speckled the ground. I glanced up at the evening sky and then scanned the empty horse pasture for...someone or something. I didn't quite know who or what. Heavy clouds had moved off to the east now, and a late-harvest moon cast the empty pasture and surrounding trees in stark, silver-print contrasts.

Suddenly the night seemed far too quiet.

"Tom! Tom!" A woman's voice cut through the night.

And, for some reason, I didn't want to answer. Then I saw the feminine form of Dr. Laurel Adderson scrambling across a grassy knoll, running toward the Jeep. I yelled, "Don't."

She turned my way. "Tom?"

"Don't go near it. There's smoke. The gas tank could blow."

Dr. Adderson was already hurrying toward me. "Are you hurt?"

I rolled my shoulders and flexed my back the way you do to check for injury after taking a bad hit in sports. And that's what it felt like—like a musclebound linebacker high on monkey juice and attitude had blindsided me. "I'm all right. Just banged up some."

She was in front of me now, putting her hands on me, holding her face close to mine, stepping inside my personal space the way doctors do. She held my head in her hands and pulled my eyelids open with her thumbs. "Are you seeing double? Any blurring?"

I shook my head. It made me uncomfortable for her to stand so close, but her soft, capable hands felt good on my face.

"Can you walk?"

I stepped back. "Yeah, I can walk. I'm fine."

She looked unconvinced but nodded her head. "Air bags. Just a few years ago, no one would have walked away from that." She motioned toward the smashed Jeep with her chin. "Come on. We need to get you to the hospital." She saw me looking at the still-smoking Jeep. "It's not on fire, Tom. That's talc. Everybody thinks their engine's burning when the bag deploys. It's packed in talcum powder so the folds of plastic won't stick together."

I looked at her.

She took my hand. "It's okay. Now come on."

We climbed a hill, and the doctor's Mercedes came into view. Its high beams pointed in the direction of the Jeep, but the pasture dropped down from the highway, so the halogen beams shot over the top of my wrecked vehicle and highlighted a line of treetops across the pasture.

Smashed bits of white fencing littered the ground. We crossed a drainage ditch and climbed up onto the blacktop, and my new brain-thumbs began to thump again at my temples. Dr. Adderson opened the passenger door for me.

I stopped to look at her. "How'd you find me?"

"Get in the car. We can talk on the way."

I stood where I was. "You can't see the Jeep from the road."

Dr. Adderson's eyebrows arched. "Are you . . ." She

took a deep breath and shook her head. "I saw where you crashed through the fence." She pointed. "Look."

I turned and looked at the demolished length of fence. And, even in the moonlight, the Jeep's tire tracks—parallel strips of churned black earth—stood out against a roadside carpet of pale winter grass. I nodded and stepped inside the car. She walked around and climbed into the driver's seat.

Dr. Adderson dropped the idling Mercedes into drive, punched a button on the steering column to turn on her flashers, and swerved onto the highway.

I examined her profile in the soft glow from the instrument panel. "I want a tox-screen."

She knitted her eyebrows and glanced over at me. "Mind if I ask why?"

"Because either I've got a brain tumor all of a sudden or somebody drugged me."

The doctor paused. "When was the last time you ate or drank something?"

"Lunch."

"That was four or five hours ago." She cocked her head to the side and, once again, glanced over at me. "Doesn't really seem to make sense, does it, Tom?"

A gas station bathed in fluorescent light came over the hill as we entered Daphne's outskirts, and Dr. Adderson turned toward the hospital.

I thought back to the black tube with velvet walls, to the rushing wind that enveloped me even before I crashed. "Just do the tox-screen. Okay?"

At the hospital where Kate Baneberry died, the same doctor who had treated her turned me over to a lab technician with instructions to draw blood and do a complete lab workup. Fifteen minutes later, Dr. Adderson returned and led me to a hospital room, where she placed a clear plastic mask over my nose and mouth.

"You've had carbon monoxide poisoning. It's what I suspected. CO binds to red blood cells and displaces oxygen. You passed out because there weren't enough unaffected cells left to carry sufficient oxygen to your brain. Crashing, by the way, may have saved your life. When the windows broke, fresh air flowed into the car. That's why you woke up." She pointed at the mask. "This is just oxygen. We're going to basically flood your system with oxygen to help you throw off the carbon monoxide."

Through the plastic, I mumbled, "How long do I have to stay here?"

"I'd rather you stayed the night."

I shook my head no.

She rolled her eyes. "Give it an hour or so."

"Doctor, I know a heater can sometimes push an exhaust leak inside the car, but I didn't know it could put somebody under that fast." It felt goofy trying to talk though the plastic shield. "I hadn't gone more than five miles, and the heater had only been on a couple of minutes."

Dr. Adderson shrugged. "Can I call someone for you?"

She was avoiding my question, but doctors tend to do that anyhow. "I guess my secretary, Kelly. But I hate to bother her just for a ride home."

"Don't worry. I'll take you home. I just think it's a good idea to have someone who can call and check on you. You're going to feel pretty lousy in the morning."

I gave her Kelly's number, and the doctor left me alone to snort oxygen.

★ ★ ★

Lingering cloud cover had thickened, blacking out the full moon and the bright streaks of stars that had jeweled the sky earlier in the night. Trees spun by in shades of black. Dr. Adderson watched the road. She didn't speak. She concentrated on maneuvering over miles of country blacktop.

When we pulled into my driveway around 8:30, I spotted Kelly's little ragtop parked by the front walk. I turned to Dr. Adderson. "You didn't tell her to come over tonight, did you?"

"No. Of course not."

As the doctor's Mercedes rolled to a stop, Kelly swung her car door open and popped out. On the other side, my investigator, Joey, unfolded out of the tiny sports car like a giant on stilts exiting a clown car at the circus.

Dr. Adderson had the normal reaction to my giant friend. "Who's that?"

I smiled. Joey stands about six-foot-six. He has white-blond hair and piercing gray eyes, and women tend to be favorably impressed. "He's a friend of mine. Big, isn't he?"

All she said was, "Good Lord."

Outside the car, I made quick introductions. The doctor told me to stay home and rest the next day, and she pretty much ordered Kelly and Joey to check on me periodically; then she climbed back into her car and drove away.

I mounted the steps and paused just outside the front door.

Joey said, "What's wrong?"

I sighed. "My keys are still in the Jeep."

Joey laughed. Kelly stepped up and fitted a key into

the door. I'd forgotten she had one. Joey said, "I've already got a man out there looking around. He'll get your keys. Don't worry about it."

Inside, Kelly said, "You should sit down, Tom. Do you want a Coke or maybe something to eat?" She was in her mother mode, which is particularly amusing on someone who's about the size of a healthy twelve-year-old.

"I'd like a drink."

She shook her head. "Nope. I don't think that's a good idea."

I said, "Probably not," and plopped down on the sofa. As Kelly walked toward the kitchen, I added, "You do remember that you can't cook, don't you?"

She waved me off over her shoulder.

It took fifteen minutes for Kelly to make a ham sandwich and put it in front of me. It took about fifteen seconds for me to eat it.

While Kelly was puttering in the kitchen, I had been bringing Joey up to speed. He listened quietly, asking only two or three pointed questions, and nodded his head. I knew he already had someone checking out the Jeep before some wrecker service could haul it away, which was exactly what I wanted. I wasn't sure what I wanted him to look for, other than my keys and shotgun. I left that up to him. Joey would know a hell of a lot more about investigating possible tampering than I would. So all I did was fill him in on the Baneberry case and share a few theories. Finally, I asked if he knew anybody who might make me a deal on a new Jeep. He promised to bring over something for me to drive until I could get to a dealership.

By 9:30, my Mutt-and-Jeff nurses were gone. I locked up the house, set the alarm, and climbed into bed.

I slept like a rock, which was surprising considering how much pain I was in when I finally woke up. The bedside clock read 10:23 A.M. My shoulders, my back, and my legs ached so badly that I barely noticed the headache.

Two extra-strength Tylenol and a long, hot shower helped. I scraped at the stubble on my chin, dabbed Neosporin on a few wreck-related cuts, and dressed for a day off in jeans and a polo shirt. Combing my hair in front of the bathroom mirror, I thought I looked pretty good for someone who'd careened unconscious into a concrete horse trough. But then, anything this side of dead under the circumstances was, it seemed to me, looking pretty good.

I padded downstairs and hung a right with the intention of heading through the living room to the kitchen.

And I froze.

My living-room sofa and two club chairs had been shoved against the back wall. An oak table from the kitchen squatted in the middle of the living room. On top of the table stood two dining chairs facing away from each other. Across the tops of the chairs, someone had balanced the coffee table, and on top of that was a tall crystal vase from the entry hall with a basketball perched on top. It was all my stuff, but none of it was exactly, or even remotely, where I'd left it.

I ran to the front door and jiggled the knob, then reached into the front closet and pulled out a softball bat. A quick search of the house yielded nothing. A more thorough search inside closets, under beds, and inside major appliances had the same result.

The doors and windows were locked, and, most disturbing, the alarm was still set.

Shit. I picked up the phone and punched in Joey's cell number. He answered on the first ring.

"Joey? You're not going to believe this." I filled him in on the makeshift sculpture in my living room.

He didn't say anything. He was thinking.

I broke the silence. "Have you found anything useful on the Jeep?"

"Not yet." Joey was quiet for a few seconds before saying, "I guess I'm statin' the obvious, but it's pretty clear that somebody wanted you to know the wreck last night wasn't an accident."

I didn't answer. He didn't expect me to.

"Why do you think they did that, though? What's piling up a bunch of crap in your living room got to do with anything?"

I looked up at the Rube Goldberg sculpture. "Actually, if someone is trying to send a warning, it's a pretty smart way to do it. Think about it. If I get the cops out here, they're going to take one look at this and treat the break-in like a prank. And if I told them I totaled my Jeep last night and this pile of stuff is a warning...they'd probably give me a ride back to the hospital so I could get my brains unscrambled."

Joey said, "Somebody wants to play."

"Looks that way."

Joey's an unusual guy. You never know what's going to get to him. "Fine. Somebody wants to play, we'll fuckin' play." He paused. "Why are you so quiet?"

"I didn't know I was."

Joey thought about that. "You're gettin' pissed off, aren't you?"

"Yeah, I am."

Seven

MY MIDNIGHT VISITOR had shoved a glass-topped table over by the window to make room for his sculpture. Now, morning sunlight bounced off the tabletop and angled up to shine dead center on the vase that formed a crystal column between the precariously balanced coffee table and my ancient basketball. The vase threw a shimmering, cut-glass rainbow across the ceiling. And I wanted very much to kick the whole damn thing over. Unfortunately, the whole damn thing was made out of some of my favorite stuff.

By the time I had wrestled the oak table back into the kitchen and shoved my living-room furniture into place, I desperately needed food. Either inhaling carbon monoxide or crashing into a concrete slab had unsettled my insides, and my empty stomach felt as though it were coated with dryer lint.

Twenty minutes later, I had already polished off two bowls of Cinnamon Toast Crunch and was pouring a cup of coffee when Joey knocked on my door. I found him standing on the front porch. He looked especially proud of himself.

The smiling giant glanced over my shoulder. "Where's that pile of furniture and stuff you told me about?"

"I put everything back."

Joey shook his head. "You got no sense of the absurd. I wanted to see it."

"What the hell are you so happy about?"

"Just trying to cheer you up." Since our phone conversation, Joey had shifted into his cheer-up-the-sick-guy mode.

I smiled. "Yeah, well, I don't want to be cheered up."

Joey raised his eyebrows, shook his head theatrically, and made *tsk-tsk-tsk* noises. Then he stepped away from the door and swept his hand out toward the driveway. The Vanna White move didn't really suit him. "And look what I brought you."

I looked. Squatting on my white gravel drive was . . . I didn't know what it was. But it looked like a great-white-hunter vehicle, like the kind of thing John Wayne and Red Buttons would have used to chase a wildebeest across the Serengeti in *Hatari!* The sand-colored 4×4 had a spare tire bolted to the hood, a huge winch welded to something that looked like a cattle catcher in front of the grille, and a metal luggage rack running around all four sides of its roof.

"Okay." I looked back at Joey's smiling face. "What is it?"

"It's a Land Rover, bubba. And not one of those pussy SUVs stockbrokers buy to haul their kids to soccer games. This is a serious off-road vehicle. A Series

2-A Safari. Somebody told me Land Rover only sold 'em in Africa and South America."

"And you got this one . . . ?"

"It was a fee. I managed to locate something you don't wanna know about for a client you *really* don't wanna know about. The guy was in the kind of business where you're rich one day and indicted the next. Give him credit, though. The government attached his liquid assets, so he paid me off with this."

I looked from Joey to the Land Rover and back to Joey again. "You sure you don't want to keep it? It's got all those memories for you."

A classic red GTO convertible pulled into my driveway. "Loutie's here. Gotta go." Joey tossed me the keys. "Check it out. The guy I got the Rover from blew a wad of cash on it. Brush guards, steel-mesh headlight covers. Leather seats and a CD player, a phone, everything you could want. Bought it from some place in California that restores 'em to like new."

"Does it have airbags? I've developed a real fondness for airbags."

"Yeah, I think so. If you wanna keep it, I'll let you have it for what the guy owed me in fees. Be a hell of a deal."

As Joey trotted out toward Loutie's car, I said, "You're a prince."

Joey yelled back, "Ain't that the God's honest truth."

Loutie Blue—a gorgeous ex-stripper who for years had been Joey's best operative—smiled and waved, and they were gone.

I glanced down at the key ring in my hand. It held two remotes, two sets of keys, and a gold disk about the size of a half-dollar. Each side of the medallion bore the likeness of a cannabis leaf—and I thought I understood what kind of business Joey's client had pursued before his unfortunate incarceration.

Bright blue skies belied near-freezing temperatures, but it felt good to get out of the house and drive through the countryside. After Joey and Loutie Blue left, I had piddled around, typed a few notes on my laptop, and made some lunch. By one o'clock, I couldn't stand it any longer. Now I was heading north toward Bay Minette, the county seat, to talk with a friend at the courthouse. I knew that I was probably wasting my time, but I was out of the house. And I was doing *something*. Someone had tried to stop me It was important to keep going.

I followed County Road 104 through Silverhill to Highway 59 and turned north. It was a workday, and I passed half a dozen log trucks and that many more refrigerated vans hauling seafood. Every few miles, an entrepreneur with a pickup truck had set up either a firewood or a Christmas-wreath stand by the side of the road. One old guy was selling both. I met two Volvos and one Jeep with Frazier firs roped to their roofs.

Around 2:30, I pulled Joey's safari vehicle into a metered space next to the Bay Minette town square. Baldwin County long ago erected a gorgeous courthouse with character and architectural detail to burn; so, of course, they tore it down. Instead, I followed a concrete walkway to the side door of the kind of government building people build nowadays, which is say square and ugly. Inside, I walked the familiar ways of justice to the Office of the Clerk of the

I had called ahead, and Janie—the clerk's se

greeted me by name. "Tom! What in the world happened to you?"

I'd forgotten the spiderweb of shallow cuts on my forehead. Apparently, the air bag had protected most of my face during the collision, but the Jeep's windshield had splattered my crown and forehead with tiny glass projectiles. I smiled. "I ran my Jeep into a horse trough."

"That doesn't sound like a good idea. Are you okay?"

"I'm fine. But you're right. It was a terrible idea, especially for the Jeep. Is Curtis in?"

Janie stood and walked back to a door and leaned inside. "Curtis? Tom McInnes is here to see you. You got a minute?"

A booming voice said, "Sure I do. Tell him to come on in."

Curtis Krait is one of those men who continues to insist in middle age that he wears a forty-regular suit, because that's what he wore in college. Every time I saw him around the courthouse, I cringed at the sight of starched cotton digging into his neck and expensive wool suits that pulled and puckered across his expanding vanity. But it was a harmless vanity, to everyone except Curtis.

As I stepped into his office, I saw that Curtis had shed his coat, and the only apparent discomforts were the contrasting and painful-looking cinches at his neck and waist. The county court clerk stood and held out a soft brown hand. And I had to smile. Everyone likes Curtis. You can't help it. He's one of those natural political animals who radiate likability, even on those occasions when he's otherwise irritating the hell out

Following a few concerned questions about my encounter with a horse trough, we moved on to basic Southern pleasantries about each other's jobs and families. I only had the former; Curtis had both. In the real South—which is to say, not Atlanta or South Florida—if you ever decide to skip the small talk and go straight to business, well, you're just an asshole is what you are.

Finally, I got around to why I'd come. "Curtis, I'm trying to dig up information about a woman who was on jury duty here three weeks ago. It would have been the second week in November."

Curtis squinted his eyes behind smudged, horn-rimmed glasses. "Does she have a complaint about something?"

"Well, she's probably not real happy about being dead."

"God, Tom." Curtis chuckled, then said, "Oh! I bet you're talking about that woman . . . What's her name?"

"Baneberry."

"Yeah, Kate Baneberry." He reached up to push his glasses up the bridge of his nose. The round horn-rims immediately returned to half-mast. He seemed not to notice. "I remember her. I guess you're working for the family."

"Why would you remember one sick juror?"

" 'Cause of the case. Don't you know what case she was on?"

I shook my head and tried to look ashamed.

Curtis pushed at his glasses again. It was a nervous habit. "That was the Federal Life case. The plaintiffs got fourteen million dollars out of that thing."

"Okay. Yeah, I remember seeing something about it in the paper. Bad faith."

Curtis nodded. "Woman got most of her skin burned off in a car fire, and Federal wouldn't pay."

"Was she covered?"

He shrugged. "Who knows? The jury thought so. What's going on here, Tom? Are you getting into plaintiff's work?"

"No way. I'm just looking into Mrs. Baneberry's death for a family member. And why I'm here is really kind of a long shot. It's just that Kate Baneberry's doctor told me that stress could have played a part in her death. Now that I know what case it was, I can see where she probably was under a lot more stress than she was used to."

Curtis just nodded.

I studied his face. There was something there. "Curtis, you've got hundreds of jurors filing through here every week. Is there any *other* reason you remember Kate Baneberry?"

He folded his hands, formed an arrow with his index fingers and bumped it against his lips. He was thinking. I shut up and let him.

Finally, he said, "You quote me on this and I'll tell people you're a lying SOB."

"Okay."

"Tom, you know how bailiffs are. It's a relatively boring job. Herding jurors around and fetching lunch, guarding folks who really don't need to be guarded. Basically, it's a lot of standing around waiting. So, they tend to entertain themselves by gossiping like a bunch of old biddies. And, since they're stationed outside the jury room where they can hear most of what's going on, they usually have plenty to gossip about."

I nodded. Every lawyer knows that, if they like you,

bailiffs can be an invaluable source of information about which way a jury is leaning.

Curtis went on. "Well, when this Baneberry woman turned up dead, the bailiffs were laughing—well, not laughing, but you know what I mean. They were talking about it because they claimed Baneberry was the sole holdout on the jury."

Now he had my attention. "You're telling me that Kate Baneberry was the only juror standing between the plaintiff and fourteen million dollars?"

He laughed. "Worse than that. She was the only thing standing between Russell and Wagler and forty percent of fourteen million dollars."

"What?"

Curtis got up and walked around me and closed the door. "I'm serious now. You going to keep this to yourself?"

I nodded.

"Well, the bailiffs were saying that, one other time about three months ago, a holdout juror on a Russell and Wagler case got sick and had to be replaced by an alternate. They claim that in that case too, after the sick juror left, the jury ended deliberations early and returned a plaintiff's verdict." Curtis reared back in his chair and laced his fingers behind his head. "Tom, you know as well as I do that stuff like this gets better in the telling. But, true or not, it's kind of getting to be a running joke around the courthouse. You know, stuff like Russell and Wagler should come with a surgeon general's warning: *Disagreeing with this firm can be hazardous to your health.*"

"Do you think there's anything to it? Other than gossip, I mean."

"Tom." His light-brown eyes scanned my face. "I

think it's just a bunch of bored guys trying to stir up a new courthouse legend. I'm not taking it seriously, and you shouldn't either."

"It is interesting, though."

Curtis nodded and his glasses slipped further down his nose.

"Who was lead counsel?"

"Chris Galerina was first chair for the plaintiff." He pushed at his glasses. "Is any of this helpful?"

"I'm not sure yet."

"Well, good, bad, or indifferent, that's all I know. I'm sorry to rush you out, but I've got to get some work done."

I stood to leave. Curtis followed me to the door and put his hand on my shoulder. "You owe me one."

I opened the door and stepped out. "Any time I can help, Curtis. You know that."

Curtis held my eyes. "I know. That's why I'm talking to you." He smiled and closed the door.

Whether it's the Office of the Clerk of the Court of Baldwin County, Alabama, or the hallways of the U.S. Senate, politics is politics. Information is swapped for favors, and favors beget even better information. Curtis was good at it. He knew who to talk to, who to bullshit, and who to ignore. But he *still* talked when it suited his needs, which is precisely why I hadn't told him that Jim Baneberry had now hired Russell & Wagler to bring suit in connection with a death that had already benefitted that firm to the tune of about six million dollars.

It was beginning to look as though—just maybe— Jim Baneberry had the fox guarding the henhouse, and I wondered if he knew it.

Eight

THAT EVENING, I was home by five. I was still too banged up to take a run, but a long walk along the shore helped work the kinks out of sore muscles.

A couple of neighbors had strung tiny white lights along the lengths of their docks. One had perched a Christmas tree on a small, free-floating platform in the bay and decorated its branches with strings of those big green, red, and blue bulbs you don't see much anymore. As I turned onto the pathway to my back door, I was beginning to feel better—more than a little overwhelmed, but better.

I ordered Chinese from a new place in Fairhope.

After dinner, I was hunched over my laptop making notes on the meeting with Curtis when I sensed someone or something stirring in the shadows outside. Enough was enough. I retrieved a Browning nine-millimeter from the gun closet, flicked off the interior lights, and stepped out into the cold December night, locking the door behind me.

Heavy cloud cover shrouded the moon as I moved through deep shadow, scanning the yard and beachfront for any hint of movement, for any unfamiliar form or sound. Vague, lavender-edged shapes floated across the sky. Leafless trees rustled in the frigid air. And I was in the mood to shoot something. But I could find nothing that needed shooting.

Still, when I finally stepped back inside the empty house, my heart raced. My fingers fumbled with nervous energy as I twisted the dead bolt into its slot. And the imagined shadow, the sense of unseen movement, remained.

I slept that night with pots and pans stacked in front of the doors. I scattered wadded newspapers in the hallway and on the floor around my bed. Then I burrowed deep inside cool sheets and beneath the down comforter, where I thought of how much more ingenious and streetwise the wadded-newspaper thing had sounded in *The Maltese Falcon*.

When I awoke, the house was just as I had left it. The shadow had disappeared with the night. I showered and dressed. I put away pans and stuffed newspapers into black plastic trash bags.

But outside, on the hood of Joey's Land Rover, I discovered the rigid, furry-gray corpse of a squirrel. And sitting in that off-road tank, parked on my own driveway at nine o'clock on a bright December morning, I found myself hurrying to lock the doors.

* * *

By midmorning, I was in my Mobile office and had found refuge in the familiar comfort of my cracked-leather chair. Kelly had cleared my schedule following the wreck, so I had nothing much to do. And I found my thoughts consumed by echoing images of a deceased rodent.

Squirrels die. And, when they die, it's not unheard of for them to seek out a warm place, like the hood of a car, to do it—especially on a cold December night. But I knew that wasn't what had happened. I was certain that the tiny reminder of mortality on my hood wasn't natural. And I knew it the way you know someone you've just met has had hair plugs or a boob job.

Human intervention leaves an imprint.

The squirrel's rigid posture didn't quite form to the hood; the tiny cadaver had been too perfectly centered between the spare tire and the windshield; and the glassy stare of its dead-rodent eyes was directed too precisely at the driver's seat.

Someone—some subtle, intelligent asshole—wanted to either scare me off the case or split my attention. I was being discreetly violated—gingerly mind fucked—and there wasn't a whole lot I could do about it. Calling the cops to report a dead squirrel would have been even more laughable than reporting a stack of furniture in my living room.

But what had I done instead? I had searched the beach with a loaded handgun. I had set the alarm. I had scattered kitchenware and reading materials throughout my house. It was embarrassing.

I glanced at my watch. It was close to eleven. I

needed something useful to do, something else to think about. I fetched a fresh mug of coffee and called Sheri Baneberry to set up a meeting.

She told me I couldn't come to her place of business.

"I'll wear a suit and everything."

"My boss doesn't like us taking care of personal business here in the office. I'll come by your office at lunch, if that's okay."

I always prefer talking with clients and witnesses in their natural environs but, since I wasn't given a choice, I told her that was fine. "By the way, what is it you do in that office where no one can come see you?"

"We're a marine insurance firm. I'm an actuary. I compute risk profiles for international maritime shipping."

"Ouch."

"I like it." She sounded defensive.

"What did you tell me your father does for a living?"

"Oh. Uh, construction. He and his partner are general contractors."

I thought about that. "I've got a client who builds shopping malls. Guy's rich one year and broke the next."

"That's the business. But Dad's been mostly pretty lucky."

I told her I'd see her at lunch and hung up.

Under the heading of coddling the recently wrecked, Kelly brought me a cup of coffee. Now I had two. I read the newspaper.

At 12:10, I heard the front door ding-dong. A few seconds later, Kelly stepped into my office. "Sheri Baneberry is here with a friend who won't tell me her name."

"Her name's Bobbi Mactans."

Kelly smiled. "Did you see them come in, or have you already had the pleasure?"

"The second one."

"I'll show them back."

"Kelly? Tell Sheri I want to see her alone."

My petite secretary raised an eyebrow. "Ms. Mactans already seems irritated to be here. I don't think excluding her from the meeting's going to help."

"I think *irritated* is Bobbi's natural state. The hell with her. I need to talk with my client."

Kelly nodded. I heard argumentative tones from the front room, and Kelly returned with Sheri Baneberry. Sheri's face flushed pink, and she flashed a bitter smile. My client was one of those women who, for some reason, smile when they get mad. I'd seen other people do that—mostly women—and I'd always wondered what kind of cheerfully brutal parenting trains a person to strangle anger with a fake grin. Maybe women aren't supposed to get mad the way men aren't supposed to cry. "Supposed-to" screws up a lot of people.

Her teeth were too big. She had to put them away to talk. "I thought you worked for me."

From behind Sheri, Kelly caught my eyes and rolled hers. I smiled, and Kelly left the room, closing the door behind her.

I shifted my attention back to my client. "I do work for you."

"Then I want Bobbi in this meeting. And, in the future, I don't expect you to order my friends to cool their heels while you summon me to your office."

"Cool their heels?"

Sheri glared at me.

"Have you ever hired a lawyer before?"

She pointed her chin at me and shook her head.

"Well, let me explain how I work. I do, indeed, work for you. But I'm not Pépé the houseboy. I won't do whatever you say, whether it makes sense or not. You're paying for my advice. And my advice may include things you don't agree with, like not having your girlfriend listening in on privileged conversations."

Sheri's face reddened again but not, I thought, from anger.

"In fact," I went on, "if I *did* let Bobbi listen in, what I told you would no longer be a privileged communication. Did you know that?"

She swiveled her head, but it was a grudging admission.

"Then that's a good example of what I'm talking about. I'm not just making up rules to irritate you, Sheri. There are legal protections that I want to make sure you don't inadvertently waive."

"What if I don't care?"

She wasn't making sense. I waited.

"I mean, what if I want her here anyway?"

"Then we'll call her in, and she can sit in that chair over there while I tell you what I know."

Sheri studied my face. "But if I don't take your advice, you're not going to keep going—you're not going to keep working for me—are you?"

"No, I'm not. But Sheri, I'm not trying to be a prima donna. It's just that you're paying me to advise you regarding your mother's death. If you're not going to take the advice you're paying for, I think it'd be better if you found another lawyer. Or, I could give you the names of a few private investigators in town who'll investigate their asses off, without trying to advise you about anything."

Sheri gazed out at Mobile Bay through the window over my shoulder. Very quietly, she said, "Maybe." Then she focused on my face. "First, tell me what you've learned so far."

And I did. Because everything I had learned, I had learned while Sheri Baneberry was pumping two hundred an hour into my bank account. So, she had the right to know everything I knew. I told her about Dr. Adderson's suspicions, about my own carbon-monoxide-induced wreck, and all about my meeting with Curtis Krait at the Baldwin County Courthouse. I only purposefully left out two things. I didn't tell Sheri I had asked Joey to do a background check on her friend, Bobbi Mactans. I also didn't tell her about my visit from the midnight furniture stacker, since I had no real way of knowing whether the appearance of a table-chairs-vase-and-basketball vertical construction in my living room was tied to her case. At least, that was how I excused my decision not to tell her.

It didn't even occur to me to share my dead-squirrel story.

I was just finishing with the details of my meeting with Curtis when the front door ding-donged again, and I heard a tangle of excited male and female voices.

Kelly burst into my office. "Tom, there's a man out front demanding to see you." She motioned at Sheri with a nod. "It's about Ms. Baneberry. He says his name is Jonathan Cort."

I glanced at Sheri, who suddenly looked like a teenage girl caught buying a personal massage device.

But, in this case, I had a feeling that I was the forbidden prick.

"Who's Jonathan Cort?"

Sheri met my eyes. "He's my father's business partner."

Great. I headed for the waiting room. When I got there, I found an angry Bobbi Mactans and an even angrier fifty-year-old man who looked like a construction foreman. Jonathan Cort was about my size. He had dark hair, black eyes, and a leathery face that had been creased and hardened by decades of wind and sun.

I asked, "Can I help you?"

Cort looked over my shoulder. "Sheri! Come on. We're leaving."

I turned to look at Sheri, who had stopped in the hallway three feet behind me. She seemed to be frozen in place—except that I noticed the front of her silk blouse, where it draped between her breasts, was vibrating. My client was trembling with fear.

Cort walked toward me. The big man reached across his chest and put his hand on my shoulder with the intention of sweeping me aside.

"Move!"

"I don't think so."

Cort locked eyes with me, and his stare reminded me of someone else who had recently tried to bore holes through my eyes. He said, "Move, or I'll move you." But he was already tugging at my shoulder, and I didn't think he had a lot more in him.

Without looking away from Cort's eyes, I said, "Kelly, call the cops."

From the hallway, I heard her say, "I already have."

Cort stopped tugging, but he continued to grip my

shoulder. "What? You're gonna call the cops 'cause I want Sheri to leave with me?" He shook his head and grinned. "What're you gonna tell 'em? You gonna tell 'em I scared you?"

"No. I'm going to tell them you barged in here and committed assault and battery."

Now his expression changed, and I could tell he was thinking about something other than grabbing Sheri, which was what I wanted. "You're full of it. I didn't batter anybody."

"As soon as you tried to shove me out of the way, you committed legal battery. And I've got three witnesses who can testify that I didn't aggravate you or fight back. But, if you try to get past me to Ms. Baneberry, I'll be forced to stop you . . ."

"You think you can?"

". . . and press charges on her behalf and mine." I paused. "Now, get your fucking hand off me."

Jonathan Cort dropped his gaze to my chest and paused while logic overtook anger; then he spun and walked to the door. As he snatched at the knob, he snapped over his shoulder, "This isn't over."

I said, "Good exit line."

He slammed the door. And, for the first time since Cort had stepped in front of me, I noticed Bobbi, my client's choleric companion, standing in front of the big double window. She was red-faced, breathing heavily, and bowed up like the toughest kid on the playground.

I turned and walked into the hallway, where I stood very close to Sheri with my back to the waiting room and Bobbi Mactans. I spoke softly. "You know Bobbi probably called him?"

She nodded.

"What do you want to do? Do you want me to keep going on the investigation?"

When she spoke, she whispered. "Keep going."

"Okay. But I have to ask. Somebody has already tried to put me out of commission for looking into your mother's death. Are we going to have any more problems keeping my investigation, *and* our discussions, private?"

Sheri Baneberry shook her blonde head no and repeated, "Just keep going."

I convinced a purple-faced Bobbi that Sheri needed to remain in my office for an indeterminate period. I suggested to Bobbi that she might not want to wait, and she glared at me. I told her I'd make sure Sheri got back to work, and she glared at me. Finally, I just told her to leave.

Bobbi stormed out. A few minutes later, I escorted Sheri Baneberry out of my office, down the service elevator, and through the parking deck to a waiting cab. When she was well away, I walked through the lobby and stopped just inside the glass front doors.

It took a few minutes to spot them. Bobbi Mactans and Jonathan Cort sat in a silver BMW at the end of the block. They were watching the front of my building.

Nine

I WAS READING back over the newspaper—checking out celebrity birthdays, running down the crossword clues to see if I knew anything—when Joey strolled into my office carrying a leather shotgun case and a file folder. It was 2:05. Sheri had been gone for more than an hour.

Joey grinned. "Busy?"

I folded the paper and tossed in on the desk. "I'm convalescing."

"Poor little fella." Joey leaned my wreck-recovered shotgun against the wall and plopped into one of the tufted client chairs. "Did you know that *Mizzz* Bobbi Mactans is sitting in a silver convertible up the street staring a hole in your building?"

"As a matter of fact, I did."

"And that there's a man with her?"

"I knew that too."

"Then I don't guess I need to tell you who he is."

"Jonathan Cort, moderately tough guy and business partner of Jim Baneberry."

Joey raised his eyebrows. "And?"

"And what?"

"And Bobbi Mactans's father."

"What?"

Joey grinned. "Unh-huh. Not as smart as you thought you were, are you?"

"They do look alike."

Joey grinned. "Yeah, I bet you were just about to put it together."

"What's with the different last name? Has she been married?"

"In case you hadn't noticed, Bobbi ain't exactly the marrying kind. No. She petitioned the court last year to change her last name from Cort to Mactans."

"Oh."

"I saw the paperwork at the courthouse. And I have to say: damn, Tom. Where do you find these fuckin' people? Your friend Bobbi went on and on about how women are government-sanctioned slaves who acquire the names of their masters after marriage. She even put it in the petition that she chose 'Mactans' 'cause it's part of the scientific name for a black widow spider." He shrugged and shook his head. "I think it's fair to say that Bobbi has *issues*."

Joey could always cheer me up.

He tossed the file folder on my desk. "Here's what you asked me for. It's got some more background on Bobbi Cort Mactans. And the stuff on Dr. Laurel Adderson is in there." He pointed at the folder. "The bottom line on malpractice, though, is Adderson has been sued twice in five years. One claim was dismissed on summary judgment. The other was settled. From what I could see from the court records, both cases looked like bullshit to me." Joey leaned back in his chair. "By the way, we got something on the wreck."

I waited. "And that would be?"

"Bubba, someone who does *not* love and admire you connected a carbon-monoxide canister to the heater in your Jeep."

"You actually found it?"

"Yep. Took a while, but we got it. There was this piece of what looked like rusted tailpipe in the drainage ditch next to the road. Whoever rigged the Jeep went to a lot of trouble. The canister was glued inside the rusted pipe with foam sealant and fitted to the heater intake with wax. When the heater kicked on, the canister filled the Jeep with carbon monoxide in less than a minute. At least, that's what the engineer said who I had look at the thing."

"Why wax? That seems weird."

"Yeah, that struck me too. But that's where this dickweed got real professional. You see, the wax sealed the canister onto the air intake. But as soon as you slammed through the drainage ditch, the wax popped loose and the pipe fell off—'cause that's what it was designed to do. This old piece of pipe with the canister hidden inside was a good seventy feet from the wreck. Hell, if I hadn't had a mechanic crawling around on the ground collecting every little screw and doohickey, nobody would've ever found out about it.

"And here's what I guess is the smartest, or maybe the scariest, part, depending on how you look at it. If, for some reason, the whole rig hadn't worked, the heater would've eventually melted the wax and dropped the pipe on the highway, where nobody would've ever looked at it twice. So, whether it worked or didn't work, there wasn't gonna be any evidence either way that somebody had tampered with your vehicle."

I turned to look out the window. "Somebody knows what they're doing."

Joey grunted. "Yeah. And whoever it is has got a blue-steel hard-on for you, bubba."

In the distance, an oil tanker cut a vague, wavering "V" across the harbor. I turned to face Joey. "Have you got some time this afternoon? I need you to help me take care of something that's been getting on my nerves."

Joey leaned forward in his chair. "I don't know. I guess. What is it?"

An hour later, when Joey finally walked out of my office, I picked up the phone. I needed to go somewhere and see someone, and I needed to call the state bar association and find out where and who.

The receptionist at the Alabama State Bar connected me to Member Services, who turned me over to Lawyer Assistance, who put me through to Ethics and the Law, who finally patched me through to a young woman named Beth, whose responsibility was Emerging Issues in Legalmetrics. No shit. That was the name.

"Beth, this is Tom McInnes in Mobile. How are you today?"

"Fine."

"Can you help me with a jury research issue?"

"What is it?"

"I'm looking for someone who can analyze, or at least fill me in on, juror health issues."

Silence.

"You know, like what percentage of jurors leave jury service due to health problems. That sort of thing."

Silence.

"Hello?"

"I'm looking it up." More silence. "Here. Try Dr. Kai-Li Cantil at Auburn University." She spelled the first and last names. "Dr. Cantil is . . . let's see, an assistant professor of psychology looking into," the cadence of her voice grew stilted, the way people talk when they're reading out loud, "'the effects of jury duty on the emotional and physical health of jurors.'" She paused. "Is that what you're looking for?"

"Sounds like it. But I'm curious how you knew about her."

Beth sighed. "We keep records." I waited. "We're one of the funding institutions for her research, and we keep records. If we're going to give a researcher money, we expect our members to get some benefit from it. So we keep records for people like you *who need help.*"

It may have been my imagination, but I could have sworn that Beth had unnecessarily emphasized the last three words. I said, "Nice to know our dues are being put to good use. Do you have a number for Dr. Cantil?"

"You can call Auburn information for that number. Is there anything else?"

"That's it. Thank you, Beth."

She managed to squeeze out "sure" before hanging up.

I called Auburn University information. I called the School of Behavioral Sciences. I called the Department of Psychology. Finally, I found someone with Dr. Cantil's number, which eventually yielded a conversation with the assistant professor's bored secretary.

The doctor was out torturing undergraduates with the last final of the semester. But, she said, Dr. Cantil would be happy to see me Monday afternoon for a mere hundred dollars an hour.

I thought of Sheri Baneberry's dwindling funds in my trust account. "Wouldn't I get a break on fees since I'm a member of one of the associations sponsoring her work?"

"No."

I made an appointment for 1:00 P.M. and hung up.

Time to go play with Joey.

I sent Kelly home early and locked up the office. Joey was supposed to have already checked out the Land Rover. I climbed in, maneuvered through the concrete deck, and pulled out into light Friday-afternoon traffic. Bobbi and her father were still parked down the street.

I made the block and pulled up next to their silver BMW from behind. I waved and rolled down the passenger window. "Still waiting on Sheri?"

Bobbi glared. Jonathan Cort nodded just once without looking at me.

"Sorry it's taking so long. She's still up there going over medical records with my paralegal." Of course, I didn't actually have a paralegal, but they didn't know that.

Cort said, "Fine."

I smiled. "Shouldn't be more than another hour or so. Have a nice weekend."

This time the daughter spoke up. "Fuck you."

Cort smiled. He must have been very proud.

I am easily encouraged. Something kicks in, something like a runner's high, when the facts of a difficult case start falling into place. Not everything needs to be there. I only need enough to push me in the right direction, to give me the sense that I'm sneaking up on a dragon and not a windmill. And, finally, that's how I was feeling as I headed south toward Point Clear.

The rain had cleared, and it was going to be a bright, cold weekend. I cracked a window to let in some fresh air. Soon, I passed straight through Point Clear and continued south for thirty more miles, where a small shrimping village cluttered the roadsides. The place didn't really have a name. It wasn't incorporated or anything. It just had docks and shrimp-processing plants, two cafés and a bar—things shrimpers need.

I checked the rearview mirror and wheeled the Land Rover off the road. The mud grips dug into sand and trash as I slid to a stop behind a maroon Dumpster. And still, I seemed to be alone.

After making sure my wildebeest-chasing safari vehicle was visible from the road, but not *too* visible, I sprinted around the rusted remnants of a chain-link fence and ducked inside a diner that was, as nearly as I could tell from the sign outside, named "Diner." A counter covered in swirls of green linoleum stretched in front of a row of those chrome soda-fountain stools that are bolted to the floor and swivel when you sit on them. There was a wall clock behind the counter. *Barber's Milk* was printed in red on its face, and someone had duct-taped the cord to the wall between the clock and the painted and soiled electrical outlet in the baseboard. It was just after 4:30. I climbed onto a stool and ordered a burger and a Coke from an old woman with coal-black hair and grocery-sack cleavage. As she passed through a swinging door into the kitchen, a gush of hot air escaped bringing with it the homey aroma of beef tallow flavored with day-old fish.

The cook wasn't in a hurry. Neither was I. Twenty minutes passed before I dropped a ten on the counter and left through a screen door next to the restrooms in back. The alley smelled like the diner, times ten. Cardboard boxes and giant, commerical-sized vegetable cans cluttered the sides of a narrow service drive that stretched from their Dumpster, on the right, to a short wooden fence on the left.

I sprinted to the fence, put one hand on top, and jumped up to balance on top for a second before springing hard to the other side. After stopping to look over my shoulder, I ducked into the back of a tavern. And that's where I waited. Frozen just inside the back door of a bar that never closed, I waited and listened.

A cracking sound, followed immediately by a thick splash, was my signal. I stepped into the alley just in time to hear a quiet voice say something that sounded like, "Fuggin merde." And there was the dark, hollow-cheeked stranger from the Mandrake Club, sitting up to his waist in a pit of black water swarming with fish guts and shrimp heads. Joey was standing next to the ancient barbeque pit with a .45 automatic pointed at the man's head.

Joey smiled. "Hello, asshole."

The man sprang up onto his haunches in the muck, and he did it much too quickly and effortlessly to make me happy.

Joey cocked the hammer on his .45. "Unh, unh, unh. Calm your ass down. You don't wanna get shot, and I don't wanna shoot you." He smiled very becomingly at the man. "Well, maybe I do, but I'm not going to unless you make me."

The man nodded his head. "Put de fuggin gun down. We can talk 'bout dis." There was that strange accent again.

Joey shook his head and motioned at a Styrofoam cooler next to the back fence. "Tom, it's in the cooler."

I crossed over and pulled off the lightweight cover. Inside was Joey's Nikon autofocus thirty-five-millimeter with a short-focus zoom lens and a padded strap. I didn't know what would happen when I turned around to play photographer, so I checked to make sure the thing was on and the lens cap off before I lifted it out of the cooler.

Fortunately, the stranger who was marinating in Joey's homemade gumbo had his eyes trained on the .45 automatic as I stood and pointed the lens at him. Unfortunately, when I pressed the shutter release, the quick-fire, metallic chirping of the motor drive caused Joey to glance my way.

Through the lens, I saw the stranger put one hand on the side of the pit and pivot his legs parallel to the ground like a break-dancer. I dropped the camera from my eye and yelled as the man executed a ballet-like scissor kick between Joey's knees and put my giant friend flat on his back.

I tossed the camera back into the cooler and rushed forward. The stranger was on his feet now and moving fast. As quickly as he had started, the man stopped and spun in midair, aiming a roundhouse kick at my temple. I stepped inside the kick, speared his thigh with my elbow, and aimed a straight right at a head that was no longer there.

He was by me. I spun in time to see him grab the Styrofoam cooler in one fist and dump the camera into his open hand. *The pictures.* I charged, and he swung the camera at my head by the leather strap. Instead of ducking, I clamped both arms around the camera and took the blow on my shoulder. Bending double and twisting, I felt the strap break, and I was somersaulting toward Joey. The stranger rushed again, and, lying on my back like a downed kid in a playground fight, I nailed him in the chest with my right heel just as Joey swung his .45 at the man's head.

And he just disappeared.

I popped up in time to see my nightly tormentor swinging his legs to the side to clear a six-foot fence like a gymnast on parallel bars. Two seconds later, he appeared again as he topped a second, taller fence at the end of the alley.

The dark stranger glanced back just as Joey raised his gun to fire.

I shouted, "No!" and clamped my hand over Joey's wrist to lower the gun.

Joey cussed.

The stranger met my eyes, just for a fraction of a second. His eyes narrowed, and I could have sworn he looked confused. Then he dropped to the other side of the plank fence and was gone. Joey charged through the bar to try to catch the man out by the road. But I knew he wasn't going to catch him—not somebody with that kind of head start, not somebody who moved like that.

I didn't wait for Joey. It was my job to disappear. I picked up the broken camera strap and located Joey's blue Expedition parked on the other side of the alley. His keys were in the ignition. A nylon sports bag full of my clothes lay on the passenger seat. I could get the pictures developed in Auburn. I'd have to call Joey about who I could get to check the strap for fingerprints.

I left heading north, speeding away from a lightning quick, demonically creative stranger who I hoped was too consumed with running away from a white-haired giant to worry about where I had gone.

Ten

DUSK HAD SETTLED by the time I hit I-10 and turned west toward Mobile. Most of the heavy traffic was meeting me—people headed home at the end of the workweek, people who were worn out and hungry and looking forward to their weekends. I mostly shared the westbound lanes into the city with truckers and a few road-soiled cars with out-of-state plates.

The interstate twisted through urban jumble. I turned north on I-65, humped over a couple of suspension bridges, and struck out through the night toward Montgomery. I set the cruise control on seventy-five and hit the SCAN button on Joey's radio. Jarring bits of talk radio and country blues, classic rock and white-boy hip-hop crackled through the speakers, sounding like a Rod Serling journey through the space/time continuum.

I caught a snippet of familiar notes and pressed the button again to lock onto the signal. Some small-town

station along the roadside was playing one of my favorite Christmas songs, "Clyde the Camel." It's about a
camel who saves Christmas à la Rudolph. And it's awful. Terrible. Embarrassing. But it reminded me of
Christmas when I was ten years old, and that makes up
for just about anything. So I sat there in Joey's huge
four-wheel-drive, cruising over an ever-vanishing,
never-ending ribbon of gray interstate and singing
what little bit of the song I could remember.

The song ended. I clicked off the radio and realized
I was high with relief at having slipped away from the
stalker from Louisiana.

Oh.

It had been in the back of my mind. I just needed
space or relief or maybe Clyde the Camel to pull it
out. The accent—French-Canadian with a Brooklyn
brogue—was classic South Louisiana Cajun, what people who are looking for an ass-whipping call coonass in
that part of the world.

I pulled my cell phone out of my jacket and flipped
it open. Joey answered.

I asked, "Did you catch him?"

"Hell, no. Sonofabitch runs like a rabbit with fire up
its butt."

"Didn't much think you would. Gave me time to
get away, though. Thanks."

Joey didn't respond.

"Anyway, listen. It just came to me. The guy's either
a Cajun or somebody who grew up around Cajuns.
The first time I heard his voice at the Mandrake Club,
I wasn't really paying attention because I didn't know
he was anybody I needed to remember. But it just came
to me after hearing him talk behind the diner."

Joey said, "Okay." I don't think he was impressed. "You got the camera?"

"Yeah. And the strap he grabbed. I thought maybe we'd get some prints."

"Maybe. I doubt it. It ain't like on television. There's a helluva lot of stuff that won't hold a fingerprint."

I had a thought. "What about the cooler? The Styrofoam's got a hard finish, and he picked it up."

"Aw, shit."

"What's wrong?"

"I was just about home." He cussed again. "I'm turning around."

"You left it in the alley?"

"Hell yeah, I left it in the alley. I had other things on my mind, and it was a fuckin' two-dollar cooler. Don't worry. I'll get it."

I looked down at the Expedition's gas gauge. "What kind of mileage does this bus of yours get?"

"About the same as a bulldozer."

"Okay. I'm going to pull over here and get some gas. I'm at the . . ."

"Don't say where you are. That's a smart little bastard you got after you. While you're, uh, out of town, stick with the cell phone and don't say anything about where you are. I'll talk to Kelly about it."

"That seems a little over the top, but okay." I clicked on the turn signal and pointed the headlights at the first Greenville exit. "Before you hang up, I wanted to ask you something. When we were in my office this afternoon trying to figure out where to trap this Cajun guy, you told me about the fenced-off alley behind the diner. And you told me about the old barbecue pit where, if we did things right, we could trip him up."

"Yeah."

"Well, where did that slop—the rotten shrimp heads and fish guts and stuff—where did that come from? Did you put it in, or had somebody been back there cleaning fish?"

Joey laughed. "The pit already had rainwater in it. And it was already black and nasty-looking where the water had soaked up some old ashes and stuff. That's what gave me the idea. I just looked around the alley and found a ten-gallon lard can full of stuff somebody was probably saving to chum for sharks and dumped it in."

"Why?"

"You know. Just for fun."

I hit Montgomery that night a few minutes before ten and found a room at the Riverfront Ramada, the one near the restored Victorian train station. Dinner was soggy room service. Sleep was fitful. I rolled out of bed at seven Saturday morning, showered and shaved, dressed, and packed. I had planned to stay in the capital for the weekend—resting, convalescing, whatever. I couldn't sit still. I paid my bill with cash, drove to a little café in Old Cloverdale for breakfast, and headed out toward Auburn.

After an hour buzzing east along I-85, a set of huge orange tiger-paw prints led me up an off-ramp and across the overpass. Five miles later, College Street wound past the old brick-and-steeple campus—the one where my father had taken classes forty years ago—and into a downtown of bicycle shops, pizza joints, and collegial bars.

Auburn is a pure college town. It exists for no other

purpose than to surround and support the university, and every business on the street was designed to satisfy some particular want, or imagined need, of a twenty-year-old undergraduate. But now fall semester was over. Most of the student body—and therefore most of the city's inhabitants—had departed for Christmas break with the folks. The little town seemed to be resting.

After pulling into a metered spot just past Toomer's Corner, I stepped out of Joey's Expedition and up onto the sidewalk. Waves of frigid air rolled down the street, ruffling the hair and clothes of a few lonely souls out running errands among the storefronts. I zipped my coat and started walking. I didn't really know why I had pulled over to window shop instead of searching out Dr. Kai-Li Cantil. But I've learned that if some weight starts tugging at my subconscious, it's usually a good idea to listen. Homo sapiens has survived for thousands of years, in no small part, by listening to primitive alarms, by listening to an instinctual intelligence that tells us to run or fight or hide. I didn't see any reason to start ignoring it now.

I stopped at a jewelry store window full of fraternity and sorority pins scattered across rumpled black velvet. Next door was a plate-glass window decorated with snowmen and snowflakes. In one corner, the artist had painted a green Christmas tree surrounded with colored squares that were meant to be presents.

It was a sub and pizza joint. I walked inside. "Nice window."

Three girls in Colorado skiwear worked behind the food counter. The nearest one—a copper-tone red-head with tiny freckles scattered across her nose and cheekbones—said, "Thanks. Take a seat anywhere. We're just opening."

I took a table against the wall and watched. The red-head rang open the cash register and broke rolls of quarters, dimes, and nickels into divided trays. One of the other girls wiped down the counter. The third girl, a vacant brunette, opened a sliding window behind the counter to reveal a middle-aged black woman in the kitchen.

And something still bothered me. I stood and looked at the redhead. "Do you have a phone I can use?"

"Back hallway. Outside the restrooms."

I thanked her, and she smiled. Red had a great smile. But then, youth has a great smile.

I picked up the receiver before remembering Joey's warning. After hanging up the receiver, I punched in Joey's home number on my cell phone and got his answering machine. At his office, I got voice mail. Trying *his* cell phone, I got a lounge-lizard baritone telling me to try again later.

I tapped in Kelly's home number. She answered on the third ring. I said, "Good morning."

"Good morning yourself. Where are you?"

"That doesn't matter. But I wanted to tell you that I'll be out of the office the first couple days of next week." I paused. "Is everything okay?"

"Sure. Everything's fine. Loutie Blue's been trying to get you, though."

"Why?"

"I'm not sure. What's going on, Tom?"

I looked around the empty café. No one to hear. I turned my back to the room and told Kelly about the Cajun stranger.

When I was through, she said, "Call Loutie."

So, when I hung up, that's what I did. Loutie didn't work at an office. I rang her up at the house on Monterey Street in Mobile.

"Tom." It was Loutie's usual greeting, and it always sounded different. She formed the sound to fit the circumstances.

"Good morning, Loutie. Kelly says you're trying to get me."

"Yeah. It's probably nothing..." She paused in midthought. "You sound strange. What's going on?"

"I don't know. Something's scratching at the back of my mind. I'm not sure what it is yet." I turned to watch the redhead place a single carnation in a bud vase on my table. "So, what's 'probably nothing'? Why were you trying to reach me?"

"I can't find Joey."

"It's Saturday. I bet he's sleeping in. Not answering the phone."

"It's more than that, Tom. Joey was supposed to come by here last night, and he was a no-show. This morning, I went by to take him to breakfast. He's not home. He's not anywhere, as far as I can tell." She paused. "And I know that happens sometimes with Joey, if he's on a case or something, so I'm not ready to panic. But I knew he was doing some work for you, so I was wondering..."

I said, "He *is* working," and stopped short.

Suddenly, I knew part of what had been bothering me. Joey had gone back to get the Styrofoam cooler in the alley. And if I had been smart enough to think of going back last night to retrieve the cooler to check for fingerprints, then the Cajun may have been smart enough to know we'd do just that. He also may have been smart enough to have been waiting for Joey when he stepped into the alley. *Shit*. If it had been anyone except Joey, I would have warned him not to go alone. But I was not in the habit of worrying much about Joey's safety. The man can bench-press a Buick.

I told Loutie Blue about my and Joey's adventure in the alley, up to and including Joey's statement that he was going back for the cooler.

"At least now I know where to start looking." Loutie was a practical woman.

"Be careful, Loutie."

"I'm always careful."

"No. I mean it. We had this guy at gunpoint and stuck up to his ass in a puddle of fish guts. All Joey did was look away for half a second. The guy put Joey on his back, grabbed the camera, and was in the process of kicking my ass when Joey got the gun back on him. And he just disappeared. You hear what I'm saying, Loutie? I'm not saying he could take Joey head-to-head. But this guy doesn't come at you head-on. He screws around with your mind and tampers with your car and takes you out at the knees when you're not looking." I realized I sounded scared. I was.

Joey's best operative said, "I promise. I won't take any chances."

And, after years of working around Joey and Loutie, I understood what that meant. It meant that the beautiful ex-stripper on the other end of the phone would shoot my Cajun friend in the knee, or some other part of his anatomy vital to locomotion, the minute she saw him.

I just hoped she'd see him coming.

Eleven

AFTER WORKING MY WAY through a tall cappuccino and most of *The Montgomery Advertiser*, I called ahead from the pizza shop. Dr. Cantil was in her faculty office that Saturday morning and would see me then instead of Monday. She would be grading finals, she said. But I had come a long way, and she agreed to make time. I thought she sounded slightly disapproving of my apparent eagerness, but the perceived disapproval may have been colored more by my expectations than her tone. Or maybe I was put off by the slight British accent—they come with reserve built in.

I paid Red for the coffee and got directions to the nearest one-hour film developer. Tiger Tooth Photo had a place two blocks down. I knew someone would. College is the time to engage in expensive, artistic pursuits that will, in two or three years, gather dust on a closet shelf behind flannel suits and tassel loafers.

The shots of my Cajun tormentor were promised for 1:30 that afternoon.

After backing out of my downtown parking space, it took about four minutes to drive to the professor's building, where I borrowed a reserved parking space next to the back door. Unlike the Architecture and Business schools, Behavioral Sciences resided in the same nondescript building it had occupied fifteen years earlier when I was an undergraduate. It seems that alumni with psychology and sociology degrees do not endow buildings—not that some of them probably don't want to.

Freezing mist stung my lips and cheeks as I stepped out of the warmth of Joey's SUV and hurried across a veneer of ice that had begun to form on granite slabs cascading from the back entrance. I pulled open one of the double fire doors and stepped into a puff of heated air.

My footsteps echoed unpleasantly in the corridor. I cringed at each sharply defined footfall without really knowing why. I found a staircase and climbed to the third floor, where the words KAI-LI CANTIL, PH.D. were painted in black on the frosted-glass panel in the door to room 315. I knocked and heard the British-colony voice from the phone tell me to come in.

I pushed through and found Dr. Cantil sitting cross-legged on the floor in front of her desk. She was surrounded by five stacks of documents, which she had fanned out around her like the arms of a starfish. The assistant professor looked like she was praying or meditating. Her elbows rested on her knees, her thumbs moved in barely discernable circles against her temples, and her fingers overlapped across a bowed forehead as if she were trying to shield her eyes from the light. It didn't look like she was grading papers. But whatever she was doing was her business, not mine.

Without looking up, Kai-Li Cantil said, "I'll be with you in a minute."

I closed the door, leaned my back against the cool glass rectangle, and waited. The professor's straight black hair hung in a shining curtain nearly to her waist, fanned around her shoulders, and fell forward from the sides of her bowed head. She was completely absorbed by the papers in front of her, which meant she wasn't paying any attention to me, which meant I could stand there and unabashedly study her like a model in a magazine.

Her skin held a light tan blush, even in December. But Dr. Cantil wasn't pure Asian or simply an olive-skinned Brit with an exotic name. She was, I decided, a bit of both. Considering the look and the accent, I was thinking Hong Kong.

Finally, Dr. Cantil unlaced her fingers and massaged her eyes with the muscles at the base of her thumbs. She looked up. "Sorry. I was in the middle of something." As she spoke, the professor got to her feet.

Dr. Cantil was tall—close to five-nine—and young. I decided she looked about twenty-eight, but she could have been a year or two older. She had the high cheek-bones and angular features of Asian ancestry, softened by a strong dose of European blood and made more striking by the contrast of bright green eyes. I missed a beat when I met those eyes.

Dr. Cantil looked vaguely amused by my expression.

"Thank you for seeing me," I said. "I got into town early. I would've been stuck here all weekend if we'd had to wait till Monday afternoon to do this."

"No problem. But, as I said by phone, I have no familiarity with your request. I would have gone over my secretary's notes before our scheduled meeting." Dr. Cantil walked around and sat behind a plain oak desk that lived somewhere beneath a foot-thick carpet of faded treatises, scattered photocopies, and paperback journals. She motioned at an inexpensive wooden chair. "Please. Have a seat."

I sat, and all of the professor from the nose down disappeared behind stacks of research. I stood and dragged the chair to the side of her desk.

She smiled. "Sorry. It's the way I work."

I fished a business card out of my pocket and held it out. She took the card and dropped it on a pile of photocopies that lay on her desk in a twisted spiral like cocktail napkins on a bar. She didn't mention hourly rates or business arrangements. It seemed clear that the professor was much more interested in *why* I had come to see her than in how much money she would make as a result.

Those penetrating green eyes were waiting expectantly. I started. "What I've been told is that you are an assistant professor of psychology who's studying the effects of jury service on jurors."

She nodded. "Yes. The physical *and* emotional effects of jury service."

"I understand that the state bar's providing some of your funding."

"Some of it."

"Well, I need to talk with you—as a jury expert—about a case that may go to trial. So I need our conversations, and any documents that may pass between us, to remain confidential."

"Of course. I've worked with attorneys before."

"Okay. I just didn't want it getting back to the bar that I'm investigating another law firm."

Her eyes searched my face. "Is that what you're doing, Mr. McInnes?"

I felt my focus drifting inside those exotic green eyes, and I glanced at my watch to break the moment. When I looked up, I still didn't know what time it was. "There's a, ah, plaintiffs' firm in Mobile called Russell and Wagler."

She nodded. "Serious people."

"Yeah," I said, "top of the food chain. But even for meat-eaters like them, the firm has been just a little too damn lucky with jurors. In at least two trials, Russell and Wagler has gotten a huge verdict after a holdout juror got sick and was replaced by an alternate."

Dr. Cantil leaned back in her swivel chair and put her heels on the corner of her desk. She was wearing jeans and worn hiking boots. "Two sick jurors does not a sample make. You can't logically draw any conclusions without more data."

"Yeah. I knew that much. What I'm looking for is someone who has collected data on juror illness rates that can be tied to specific law firms, and, obviously, I was hoping you're that person."

She nodded and dropped her eyes to her desk. "Let me think about that for a minute."

So I did.

Dr. Cantil glanced around her office as thoughts rolled through her mind, and I watched her do it. I think it was a satisfying exercise for both of us. Finally, she said, "That presents an interesting puzzle. I don't have data broken down by law firm. But, for every trial in my database, I do have fields for the principal attorneys on the cases. Originally, I put attorneys in the database in case I needed to contact someone to learn more about a given jury. But..." She stopped talking and looked at the corner of the ceiling for a few seconds. "I might be able to get something from Martindale-Hubbell," referring to the national directory of attorneys. She stopped again and shook her head as if dismissing the idea. "Does the state bar association publish any kind of directory listing attorneys under the firms they work for?"

"Sure. They publish a directory every year, broken down three or four different ways. Alphabetically, by geographic region, by firm. I can get you a copy."

"No. The hard copy won't do it. I'm trying to figure out how to tease my research for the data you want without wasting *my* time and costing *you* a fortune. What I need is a CD-ROM or a Zip disk with the law-firm directory on it. If the bar association publishes the directory, they'll have the disk they sent to the typesetter. If I can get a copy of that disk, I could write a simple search-and-compare program to match the trial attorneys in my database with their firms in the directory—that's why I need the information on disk. Then I'd be able to pull juror illness rates by attorney. Of course, I'd have to go back and, ah..." She was thinking.

I waited. She didn't say anything else, so I did. "But, after you do all that, you'll be able to determine whether it appears that Russell and Wagler has been manipulating their juries. Is that what you're saying?"

She nodded. "More or less. Assuming that, if they've done it, they've done it more than two times. At least, it's theoretically possible to determine whether the rate of juror disability on their cases is outside the range of naturally occurring events. But are you seriously claiming that this firm is . . . what? Poisoning people or bribing them or something?"

"I don't know. That's what I'm trying to find out."

She paused. "What happened to your head?" Dr. Cantil was looking at the network of cuts on my forehead. The real-world psychologist was overtaking the abstract researcher, and she may have been wondering if she was sitting across from a head-trauma case gone goofy.

I debated how much to tell her. If I told her everything—including the attempt on my life, the stacked sculpture in my living room, and the dead squirrel on my hood—she might throw me out of her office and call the guys with butterfly nets. But if I wasn't forthcoming, I could be putting her in real danger with no warning about what she was getting into.

"I was in a wreck. Someone tampered with my Jeep, and I think the same person who caused the wreck has been watching me. You should know—before you agree to help—that I think the wreck and the surveillance have something to do with this case."

The professor squinted her eyes. "You do know, Mr. McInnes, that you sound a bit crazy."

"That was blunt."

She smiled. "I'm a psychologist. I know crazy when I hear it."

"Do I look crazy?"

"You don't look like a homeless schizophrenic, if that's what you mean. You look like a cute, successful attorney who's probably used to getting his way. But delusional psychosis is a chemical imbalance in the brain. You could look perfectly normal and still be, as we say in the profession, crazy as a loon."

"You think I'm delusional?"

"No. But I do think I'm going to check you out before I spend my Christmas break doing research for you."

I was beginning to like Dr. Kai-Li Cantil. "You want some references?"

Dr. Cantil pursed her lips and shook her chin at me. "I've been doing research on Alabama juries for four years now. Talking to lawyers and judges all over the state. Don't worry, Mr. McInnes. I'll find out about you."

I looked into those intelligent green eyes, and I believed her. And that made me feel strangely unsettled.

With forty-five minutes to kill before my pictures were promised to be ready, I found a sandwich shop called Over the Hump, where I ordered the speciality of the house—a Hump, of course—some chips, and a Coke. There were a half-dozen high school kids out and about on Christmas break, hanging out in the sandwich shop, smoking cigarettes and playing video games beneath the mounted head of an African water buffalo.

Too much dinging and clanging. Too much juvenile bravado. I loaded back into the Expedition with my lunch and drove to the arboretum next to the university president's mansion. I sat on a small, arched bridge, with my feet dangling over a stream, and ate. It was cold but quiet. And it was beautiful. Beautiful day. Beautiful landscape. Nice memories. Sixteen years earlier, on a warm spring night, I had passed an amazing, slightly inebriated midnight hour on that bridge with a little Chi Omega named Cheryl Lansing.

I found myself humming as I ate.

At 1:30, I found a trash can for my sack and cup and napkins and climbed back onto the chilled seats of the Expedition. Ten minutes later, I presented a claim stub to a pale-skinned, long-necked photographer type behind the counter at Tiger Tooth Photo. And he looked at me as though he couldn't fathom why I'd do something so embarrassingly stupid.

I nodded at the stub. "You said the pictures would be ready at one-thirty."

He sighed. "And they were."

"Well, could I have them please?"

He shook his head. Clearly, I was a moron. "They've already been picked up, *sir*."

Something started to claw at my stomach. "What are you talking about?"

"Cindy, the girl you sent in to get them. She came in five minutes after you did and said you needed the prints in a hurry and she was supposed to wait. We gave 'em to her before one o'clock. If you'll just check with her..."

The tiny, instinctual thorns that had prickled my nerves since I awoke that morning in Montgomery thickened into a sinuous vine that squeezed some soft and vital organ just above my stomach. I said, "I don't know anybody in Auburn named Cindy, and I didn't send anybody in here to pick up my pictures."

The clerk's veneer of superiority faded. "She knew your name, uh..."

"Who is she? You said her name like you know her."

He stuttered a little now when he talked. "I, uh, don't, uh, want to get anybody in trouble. Listen, uh, let me give you a coupon for free develop..."

"Who is Cindy?"

"Uh, listen. Why don't I..."

Someone was getting farther and farther away with my hard-won pictures of the Cajun while this idiot was trying to give me a coupon for free film. I walked around the counter and stood toe to toe with the slight, pale-skinned clerk.

"Sir," he said, "you're not allowed back here."

"Tell me who Cindy is and where I can find her."

"Why don't you let me go see Cindy myself, sir. I'm sure..."

I did not have time for this. The clerk needed motivation, and I knew I was going to have to do something unattractive to provide it. "I'm sorry, but if you don't tell me where to find her, right now, I'm going to hit you in the stomach so hard you'll vomit now and every time you eat for the next two days."

"You can't just..."

"There's nobody here but you and me. Like I said, I'm sorry, but I need those pictures. And you warning somebody who stole my prints that I want them back is not my idea of helping." I grabbed the front of his shirt in my left hand and lifted him onto his toes. I wanted to scare the little bastard enough so that I wouldn't have to actually hit him. Next to losing the pictures of the man who'd tried to kill me, the last thing I wanted just then was to beat on some pencil-necked kid making minimum wage in a photography store.

I spun him and pressed his back against the wall. The kid's shirttail had come out when I grabbed him, and his milk-pale stomach quivered in anticipation of what would probably be the first serious punch of his young life.

I glared into his eyes. I was trying for menacing. "Where the hell is Cindy?"

He blinked hard at tears. "Stop. I'll tell you. Please, stop."

I pulled him away from the wall, but kept his shirt gathered in my fist.

He stammered. "Cindy works at the pizza place. She said you had lunch there."

"Has Cindy got red hair?"

He nodded his head up and down. "That's her. Dark red hair. Good-looking. She's got your pictures."

I let go of his shirt and walked back around the counter and headed out. At the door, I turned and came back. The poor guy was shaking. I put a fifty-dollar bill on the counter and said, "Sorry." It didn't fix anything, and it made me feel even more like the miserable, bullying SOB that I was. *Good move*—humiliate a guy and then take away any chance for him to reimagine the encounter as a confrontation of equals by apologizing for humiliating him. That skinny kid was going to hate me for a long, long time.

Just outside the door, I started running. The pitiful kid I had just terrorized was almost certainly phoning a young waitress named Cindy to warn her that a maniac was on his way to see her. I had to get there fast.

Twelve

IT'S HARD TO OUTRUN a push-button phone.

As I charged through the door of the pizza place, I saw the vague brunette waitress holding a headset to her ear. Her head snapped up. Her eyes were wide. She screamed one word. "Willie!"

I held up my palms. "It's all right. I just need to talk to..."

The kitchen door swung open, and Willie stepped into the dining room. He was a short black man, maybe fifty years old, and he had a kinked spray of gray and black whiskers on his chin. He wore all white—shirt, pants, and full apron with pizza stains.

Willie walked quickly through the restaurant and stopped between me and the waitress behind the counter. He put his fists on his hips, and I could see work-hardened muscles and tendons rolling beneath the dark skin on his arms. The whites of Willie's eyes seemed stained with tea, the way some people's eyes look when they're almost pure African.

I spoke to him now. "I'm not looking for trouble. I just need to talk with Cindy."

The brunette waitress had her hand cupped over the phone's mouthpiece. She looked up and said, "Don't let him in, Willie."

Willie nodded at me. "Just go on outta here. No need for trouble."

"I'm not looking for trouble. One of your waitresses, a girl named Cindy, picked up some pictures of mine down at the photo shop by mistake. I just need to talk with her."

"I said just go on. You ain't talkin' to nobody here."

The waitress had hung up the phone. She was watching. I said, "I told you I'm not looking for trouble. But I'm not leaving without talking to Cindy."

Willie nodded. "You figure you gonna come through me?"

"If I have to."

He nodded again. "Maybe. Maybe not." I don't think I was scaring him. "But Cindy ain't here, so I don't guess we're gonna find out."

"She was here just before lunch." I pointed. "She brought me a cup of coffee at that table right there."

"She's gone home for Christmas."

I looked at him.

"*The man,* he come in this morning and give her a three-hundred-dollar tip. It was enough for a plane ticket home. She's gone."

I asked, "How long?" then hesitated. Willie had said *the man.* It was an outdated expression, but then Willie was a little outdated himself. "Are you saying a cop came in here and paid Cindy three hundred dollars to steal my pictures?"

"I ain't saying nothin' about *stealing*. But, yeah, man said he was a state cop. Plainclothes with a badge. So you ain't got no reason to be bothering Cindy or anybody else in here."

The brunette waitress yelled out. "Don't tell him anything else, Willie."

I looked back at Willie. "You let these college girls tell you what to do?"

He shook his head. "*My* place."

"Then tell me what this plainclothes cop looked like, and I'll be gone."

Willie grinned big, showing a front crown rimmed in gold. "You be goin' anyhow. Look behind you."

I heard the door open and turned around. There in the doorway was my quivering friend from the photo shop. He was standing between two uniformed cops, and he was pointing an accusing finger in my direction.

The photo shop kid and I had been hanging out in Auburn Police Headquarters for three hours. He bitched to everyone who'd listen. I sat in a chain-link cage and meditated on the criminal direction my life had taken of late.

Municipal court was in session. If it was like most college towns, the weekend judge would be a local attorney who filled in on Saturdays to give the regular jurist a break from sentencing fraternity boys to community service. I was not looking forward to this. Lawyers are not amused by other lawyers who degrade their profession by beating shop clerks about the head and shoulders.

For most of the afternoon now, the kid had waited in a metal chair by the sergeant's desk, reading magazines, fidgeting, and generally exuding an air of injury. I waited in my cage. At 4:43 P.M., a bailiff opened the chain-link gate that separated criminals like me from polite society and led me through the building to a hallway outside the courtroom. Inside, I could hear a rasping baritone lamenting the wasted lives of old drunks and young. Finally, I was marched into court to face my accuser.

The judge was old. He wore thick glasses with black, World War II—era frames, and he would have had a crew cut if there had been any hair left on top to stand up. He knew I was a lawyer. Even before he'd heard any testimony, I was instructed to be ashamed of myself.

My accuser went first, and he told the truth.

When it was my turn, I told the truth too, only I shaded it a little.

I told the judge that I had been angry about the kid giving my photos to some stranger. I had wanted to know who he gave them to. I had cussed some and grabbed the kid's shirt. I said that I had then apologized for my actions and had given the kid fifty dollars for the name of the person who'd picked up my prints.

When I finished my story, the kid said, "I object," which wasn't exactly the correct use of that evidentiary device, but we all knew what he meant.

I told the judge to check the kid's pockets for the fifty.

The kid blushed. He produced the fifty. The judge ruled.

The kid had to give my fifty back, and I had to pay a three-hundred-dollar fine for misdemeanor disturbing the peace. I started to argue, but the judge gave me a look. And that was it.

The desk sergeant led me back into the holding area, where I recovered my wallet, watch, and belt and found that I had exactly two-hundred-seventy-three dollars and twenty-six cents on my person. And that included the recovered fifty from the photo guy.

I had credit cards. The sergeant grinned. "We don't take plastic."

My wallet, watch, and belt went back into the lock-box. I went back into the cage. The photo kid stopped by to smile and flip me the bird on his way out.

So far, my Auburn trip wasn't really working out.

I called Kelly in Mobile to have money wired. At least, that's what I would have asked her to do if she'd answered the phone. It was close to 6:00 now. I tried a couple more numbers. Joey still wasn't home, and I found myself mumbling into unanswered rings. I think I said something about hoping he was still alive, since that's what I was thinking, but I really just remember indulging in a little aimless mumbling appropriate to the circumstances and surroundings. Next, I tried Loutie Blue without success. I assumed she was still out looking for Joey.

My friends in Mobile were engaged in the circle of life, and I wasn't in it.

I cussed some and placed a call to Dr. Cantil. She was still in her office. I explained my situation.

Her only comment was, "You've had a busy day."

"Will you come?"

"I have to go by a cash machine. I'll be there in twenty minutes."

"You're kidding."

Dr. Cantil laughed. "Didn't you expect me to help you?"

"Actually, no."

It was 7:00 P.M. Dr. Cantil had paid my fine and collected me from the cage without comment. When her ancient Volvo was well away from police headquarters, I asked her to take me to a cash machine so I could pay her back.

She nodded but she had the strangest look on her face.

I kept waiting for her to say something. Finally, I said, "Why'd you come?"

"You mean, why was I willing to bail out a convicted ruffian with delusions of being shadowed by invisible assassins?"

"I guess that's one way to put it. Not the way I would've picked, but..."

She smiled. More than that. She seemed, well, mirthful. "I checked on you. After you left my office this afternoon, I was, quite honestly, concerned about your connection to reality. So I picked up the phone and found a few lawyers I know in Mobile and Montgomery who were in their offices on a Saturday afternoon." Dr. Cantil glanced over at me. "I had some interesting conversations."

"You can't believe everything you hear."

"What I heard was that you definitely are *not* crazy."

"You can believe that part."

"After asking around a bit for someone who knows you well, I spoke with a criminal attorney in Birmingham who has known you since you were both here in university."

I knew who she meant. "Spence Collins."

"Yes. Our networks intersected at Spencer. I've assisted him with jury selection on two capital trials. He told me to believe you. He said that you are drawn to these types of cases."

I'd heard that opinion expressed before, and I didn't much like it. "I don't know if 'drawn' is the right word. This started out as a simple malpractice case. For all I know, that's still all it is."

The professor cut her eyes at me. "We all have at least three images. The person we think we are, the person that others see, and the person we actually are."

"Thanks for clearing that up."

"Spencer was not the only person I consulted who expressed this opinion of you. The way he explained you to me was this: Attorneys—litigators, at least—find themselves in the middle of all sorts of situations that could, if pressed, become dangerous or even violent. Most of them look the other way or resign from the case or simply contact the authorities when things begin to move in a frightening direction. He said that you don't do that. He said that you *just keep pressing*."

"Doesn't make me sound very smart, does it?"

"People are complicated. Spencer, for example, says he's glad he has the sense to stay away from trouble. But he seems to admire whatever it is that makes you barge ahead."

The conversation was turning uncomfortable. I

wanted to go back to being *the person I thought I was*. "Are all psychologists as much fun as you are?"

She smiled. "Sorry. Shrinks love to shrink."

"No, no. I'm glad to finally meet someone who thinks I'm as fascinating as I think I am."

Dr. Cantil pulled into a drive-thru lane at an AmSouth branch. When she pulled up next to the machine, she said, "Give me your card."

I handed her my credit card.

She fed the plastic rectangle into the slot. "What's your pin number?"

I looked at her. "I think you're supposed to keep that secret."

"You are." She was studying my face. I could almost see the shadows of thoughts flickering behind her pale eyes.

"Is this a test?"

She shrugged.

"Okay. But I'm trusting you with a very important number." I looked into her eyes. "It's six, six, six."

She laughed out loud. "Fine. I'll back up. You and Satan can get out and do it yourselves."

I smiled. "It's three, seven, one, nine."

She tapped in the number and, at my instruction, pulled three hundred out of my checking account. Dr. Cantil handed me my card and pocketed the cash as reimbursement for my fine. As she pulled back onto the street, she said, "Interesting number."

"Huh?"

"Your pin number. 'X' marks the spot. That's how you remember it. You just draw an 'X' on the keypad."

I looked over at her profile. She looked proud of herself, which made her appear even younger than her twenty-eight-or-so years. I said, "You're a smart woman."

"I hear the same thing about you," she said, "except for the woman part. By the way, if you don't mind a little driving tomorrow, I found the law firm disk we talked about."

"From the state bar?"

She nodded. "I told Beth it was an emergency. I'm supposed to call her at home tomorrow morning. If you can make it, she'll meet you at our Montgomery campus at noon with a copy of the disk."

"Dr. Cantil?"

"Kai-Li."

"Okay, Kai-Li. Are you convinced now that it's an emergency?"

"Let me explain. You see, Tom...May I call you Tom?"

I nodded. "Sure."

"My family is scattered from Hong Kong to Bermuda to Scotland. I had a long, lonely, boring Christmas break ahead of me. Then this crazy attorney walks into my office with a problem that sounds like actual *fun*."

I studied her face. "But you're not completely convinced that it's the emergency I think it is."

She tilted her head to one side. "Not completely. But it *is* interesting."

Thirteen

I AWOKE IN an uncertain room, a polyester print tucked under my chin. Susan had been out of my life for some time, and I was edgy from having dreamed of her—or someone like her. My night vision of Susan had floated from a true picture of her to someone almost her, someone who kept the shaggy blonde hair and flashing smile but whose eyes had turned an absorbing Asian green.

It was late. Midmorning. I pushed out of bed onto the balls of my feet and walked stiffly across the carpet to pull open heavy hotel drapes. Hard winter light cut at my eyes, and I retreated to the bathroom to shower and shave and finish waking up.

Half an hour later, downstairs in the Auburn Convention Center, I found Sunday brunch being served in the dining room. I ordered waffles and then found a pay phone in the lobby where I placed a call to Joey. He didn't answer. Neither did Loutie Blue.

I returned to my table as waffles and sausage, orange juice, and coffee arrived. Some sort of convention that involved pudgy, middle-aged women seemed to be the hotel's only other business. The women all chose the buffet—it was "all you can eat," and that's what they were having. Maybe it was part of the package.

I ate waffles with maple syrup and watched. After all, someone was watching me. Some guy with a suit and a badge had found me in Auburn and stolen my photographs of the Cajun stranger. And I thought it would be nice if I could catch a glimpse of the person who found me such interesting and easy prey. But unless *the man* had morphed into a chubby, fifty-something housewife—which I was beginning to believe was not outside the realm of possibilities—my stalker wasn't in evidence.

Stuffed with waffles and orange juice, I headed back up to my room to stuff my nylon bag with clothes and toilet articles before checking out. As the door clicked open, I heard the soft wind-noise of the shower running. I'd already started to shut the door, planning to get the hell out of there, when I realized I couldn't do it.

The scariest thing about ghosts is the unnatural fact that you can't see them. I was tired, and I was ready not only to see this one but to kick its ephemeral ass.

I pushed inside. The outer room was empty. I grabbed a brass desk lamp for a weapon and stopped outside the bathroom door. The shower kept running. The knob turned in my hand. I burst inside and snatched the shower curtain aside.

No one was there.

My shampoo was still on the tiny ceramic shelf. The

hotel soap was next to the drain where I'd dropped it and left it. I turned. On the fogged plate-glass mirror above the sink, someone had used what looked like a finger wrapped in a washcloth to draw a smiling happy face. Beneath the drawing my visitor had written a greeting: HAVE A NICE DAY, ASSHOLE.

Ten minutes later, a few minutes after 10:30, I pulled out of the hotel's parking deck and headed for the interstate. It was not a pleasant drive. I found myself repeating a pattern of speeding recklessly and then slowing in a useless effort to force calm.

Kai-Li had said that Beth, the state bar association's voice of Emerging Issues in Legalmetrics, would meet me at Auburn University in Montgomery—she called it "A.U.M."—to deliver a disk containing the state bar directory broken down by law-firm affiliation.

A.U.M. is on the Auburn side of Montgomery, four or five miles outside the city limits, and the trip took less than an hour. And if someone was following the big blue Expedition, he or she was better at following than I was at spotting followers.

I was there early. Beth was waiting when I arrived. She had gelled hair, heavy makeup, and razor-thin eyebrows, and she was standing outside the entrance to the Student Life Center. As I approached on foot, she did something with her face that was intended to approximate a smile.

"Tom McInnes?"

"Yes, Beth. It's nice to meet you in person." We were face-to-face now. "Thank you for coming out on

Sunday morning like this. I know it's beyond the call of duty."

"Dr. Cantil said it was an emergency. And, anyway, I'm meeting some girlfriends just down the road at one." She had a Zip disk in one hand, and she tapped it against her thigh as she spoke. "We're going Christmas shopping this afternoon."

I smiled and nodded and looked at the disk.

Beth smiled and nodded and looked hard into my eyes.

Oh. I asked, "Can I pay you something for your trouble?"

Beth made the smile-face again. "I would usually say no. But I've gotten away from home this morning without any cash. So, you know . . ."

"Sure. Absolutely." I reached into my pocket. "How about fifty dollars to help with Christmas shopping with your friends?"

She continued to look at me as if I hadn't said anything.

Okay. "Sorry, I wasn't thinking. There's not much you can get these days for fifty dollars."

She shook her head. I took out five twenties and held them out. Beth made her smile-face, and I got the disk.

Beth went inside the Student Life Center for some reason I didn't know. I cut a diagonal across the central green and headed toward the gymnasium parking lot, where I'd left Joey's Expedition. As I made the outside corner of the gym, I saw two young guys in golf clothes lounging against my vehicle, which seemed fine. It was, after all, a college campus, and they looked like college students. There was symmetry there.

I walked up to the giant Ford and popped the locks with the remote.

One of the guys, a big, athletic-looking kid with a Marc Anthony haircut, spoke up. "Are you Mr. McInnes?"

I opened the door, swung my backside onto the seat, and closed the metal door in his face. I admit that—in the absence of a likely stalker—it would have been a rude gesture. He tapped on the glass. "Mr. McInnes? Mr. McInnes, we've got a message from Judge Savin."

Judge Luther Savin was the senior jurist on the Alabama Court of Criminal Appeals. I cranked the engine and rolled down the window. "What's the message?"

A blond kid with a whitewall haircut and long, thin sideburns came over to stand beside the kid with the wimpy Roman do. "Would you mind stepping out so we can talk?"

I smiled a nice, friendly smile. "What are you, the golf cops?"

The two men laughed. The blond reached for the door release. "Give us a break. The judge asked us . . ."

"Get your hands off my door."

Blondie feigned shock, but he tried to open the locked door anyhow. "Sir." The tone was growing firmer. "Judge Savin has asked us to invite you to his home."

"Sorry. I'm busy."

The blond kid reached through the window and plucked at the door lock. He said, "This is ridiculous."

I propped my left elbow in the open window, where I pressed down hard on both the lock and the young man's fingers. He yelped a little and snatched his fingers away.

The Roman hairdo looked at his friend. "Billy, step back from Mr. McInnes's car."

Blond Billy was red-faced, but he stepped back. The kid who had spoken turned to me and smiled. "Billy's a little pushy. Look, my name's Chuck Bryony. I'm Judge Savin's law clerk. The judge asked us to come out here and invite you to lunch."

"What's he want?"

Chuck held up his palms. "He didn't tell us. Just that he'd like you to join him for lunch, if that's possible."

I examined both young faces. "How'd Judge Savin know I'd be here?"

"He didn't tell us that either. Look, this is getting silly. The judge called this morning and asked Billy and me to lunch. We're supposed to play golf this afternoon at Montgomery Country Club. He asked us to stop by here and bring you along. I assumed you were a friend of his. I don't know what's got you spooked, but all we're doing is passing along a lunch invitation."

"And I guess Billy tried to help me with my door 'cause he's got a crush on me."

Chuck shrugged. "We're pretty sure that Billy's forte as an attorney will *not* turn out to be client relations."

I smiled. "Where does the judge live?"

Billy spoke up. "Judge Savin said to have you ride with us."

I nodded. "But that's not really up to the judge, is it?"

Billy turned and walked away. Chuck smiled. "He lives over behind Huntingdon College. You know where that is?"

I nodded. "Sure. Just pull out and I'll follow you."

Chuck smiled again and told Billy to get in their car.

The two young men pulled out ahead of me in an indeterminate Japanese sports car that someone at a plant in Tokyo or Tennessee had had the bad taste to paint sunshine yellow. As we left campus, I began driving too fast. I accelerated to within two car lengths of the yellow car, and Billy, who was driving ahead of me, sped up. I pressed the accelerator harder still until I was within one car length of Billy's rear bumper, and Billy once again did what people do under those circumstances and sped up ahead of me.

As we approached the interstate, Billy switched on his right-turn signal; so I switched on mine. He then hung a right toward Montgomery and accelerated down the entrance ramp onto I-85—clearly with the intention of putting some distance between the front of Joey's giant Expedition and the tiny rear end of his toy car.

I, on the other hand, drove on past the ramp Billy had taken, crossed the overpass, and turned left toward Auburn.

Unless blond Billy got pissed off enough to drive a sports car with six inches of ground clearance across the median, he would have to go another three miles to the next exit to turn around. By the time he got back where he'd started, I would have a six- to seven-mile head start. I didn't think he could catch me. But, if he did, what could he do about it? I'd just wanted to get out of the parking lot without another arrest-worthy altercation.

If Judge Savin's clerks wanted to drive a hundred miles an hour to catch up and then tailgate me all the way to Auburn, they were welcome to it.

* * *

Fifteen minutes outside Auburn, I had seen nothing more of Billy and Chuck. I pulled out my cell phone and punched in Kai-Li Cantil's home number.

A small voice answered. "Hello?"

"Yes. I was trying to reach Dr. Kai-Li Cantil."

The tiny voice said, "Hang on," and I heard a clack as the phone was dropped on a hard surface.

Almost a full minute passed before Kai-Li's familiar accent crackled through the line. "Hello?"

"Hi. This is Tom."

"Tom, I'm sorry. I was just stepping out of the bath."

"Was that your daughter?"

"Yes. Was she polite? We're working on phone manners."

"She was fine. Look, I'm calling because I've got the disk. . . ."

Kai-Li interrupted. "Great. Tom, would you mind bringing it to my apartment? I don't have a sitter, and I can't leave Sunny here alone. And, believe me, we wouldn't get much work done shut up in my little office with a six-year-old."

I was curious about whether there was a husband around somewhere. And I wanted to ask about that very thing, but then that was none of my business. So all I said was, "I'm not sure that's a good idea. I wanted to tell you about something strange that happened in Montgomery. Two men were waiting for me in the parking lot at A.U.M. after I picked up the disk from Beth. They claimed to be law clerks for one of the judges on the Court of Criminal Appeals."

"Which one? I mean, which judge?"

"Luther Savin. They said he wanted to invite me to Sunday lunch at his house."

"Maybe he did." She paused. "But then, how did he know you would be there? Did you tell anyone?"

"Nope."

"You obviously didn't go with them."

"Nope."

"I hope there was no disturbing of the peace this time."

"No, no. I was a good boy."

She paused. "Sunny and I were planning a lunch of microwave lasagne in about thirty minutes. You're welcome to join us."

"Kai-Li, are you sure you want me coming to your home? Somebody's following me everywhere I go these days."

"Actually," she said, "someone seems to be way ahead of you. If anything, your movements seem to be following someone else's plan." And that was an infuriatingly accurate way to describe my progress on Sheri Baneberry's case. She said, "So, considering all that, you may as well come since *the Shadow* already knows you're thinking about it."

"I think you should take this more seriously, Kai-Li."

"Maybe. Come eat lunch anyway."

"I don't think so. On top of everything else, I've got a missing friend and a lot of unfinished business in Mobile. I'd like to get home this afternoon."

"I thought you were going to stick around and play Sherlock Holmes with me." Kai-Li's voice lost body and, surprisingly, sounded almost like her daughter's.

"I can't, and I'm not sure it'd be a good idea even if I had the time. Right now, I'm not that worried about your level of involvement. Whoever followed me to Auburn was busy stealing my film at Tiger Tooth Photo while I was driving to your office. Maybe they knew about my trip to Montgomery because Beth told them about you, or maybe somebody followed me from the hotel.

"But, even if someone knows I came to see you... hell, I'm a lawyer and you're a jury expert. I think the worst that could happen is someone might come see you and want to know what we talked about."

"My lips are sealed."

"Cute. But, Kai-Li, if a Cajun gentleman stops by and you feel the least bit threatened or even uncomfortable, just go ahead and tell him everything you know. Is that a deal?"

"I'm no hero."

"Good. Now as to this disk I got from Beth. Do you know the arboretum next to the university president's mansion?"

She said, "Sure."

"Okay, stop by there later this afternoon and look under a small bench about ten feet from the northeast end of the arched footbridge..."

Fourteen

IT WAS DINNERTIME and black dark when I rolled onto my driveway in Point Clear. Coming through Fairhope minutes before, the downtown streets had sparkled with tiny Christmas bulbs scattered over trees and shrubs along the sidewalks—all of which now made my own abode seem particularly dark and neglected. With Susan a thousand miles away and no one else to worry about, I had already decided it would be a little silly to put up a tree. Now, though, it suddenly seemed just a little too damn depressing not to.

Inside the house, I flipped on lights, mixed a large scotch and soda in a plastic cup with WAR EAGLE printed on the side, and strolled out onto the downstairs deck. Eight hours behind the wheel of Joey's Expedition had not improved the lingering effects of carbon-monoxide poisoning and crashing into a horse trough. Neither had the time allowed me to figure out what might have become of my investigator. Repeated cell-phone calls along the way—to my office and to Loutie Blue, even to a restaurant where Joey liked the crab cakes—had been useless. No one had heard from him. No one had seen him.

A drive-thru cheeseburger I'd snagged outside Mobile sat comfortably in my stomach next to a large fry and a fried apple pie—all good, solid, American cuisine. Otherwise, I felt like hell. A dull ache capped the back of my head. The bones in my legs felt thin and brittle. But the night air tasted cold and clean, and my neighbor's pontoon-supported Christmas tree—just visible out on the bay through a small stand of twisted pines—moved lazily on black water like a dream of childhood.

I stepped down off the deck and kept going until Mobile Bay lapped the sand at my feet. The Grand Hotel lay down the beach to my right. I turned left and started walking. My drink sloshed, and I drank in gulps between strides. Beach homes with tasteful sprinklings of pinpoint lights drifted by on the left, and a hidden moon cast a soft glow over sand and water.

The ache at the back of my head dissipated into a tingling skullcap and disappeared. The muscles in my legs warmed and lent strength to aching joints. I was bushed. I thought of nothing. Soon the houses grew less familiar, and I realized I had been walking for most of an hour.

I turned toward home.

Forty minutes later, as I stepped into my own back yard, I could see him sitting on the steps. He wasn't Joey or Jonathan Cort or even my Cajun stalker, but I did know the man from somewhere.

I stopped just inside the yard and called out. "Who's there?"

"Tom McInnes?"

"Yeah, I know who I am. Who are you?"

"Whatsa matter with you?"

Whoever he was, he was drunk—maybe a drunk former client, maybe a vengeful drunk I'd once irritated on the witness stand, or maybe just some friendly, I'm-too-drunk-to-drive-home drunk. There were several options, but they all involved an inebriated stranger waiting for me in the dark.

It had been a long, exhausting day. I began to back toward the beach.

He called out. "Whoa! Wait up. Don't you know me? We met before. Chris Galerina. I'm Chris Galerina. We need to talk, Tom."

I stopped. "You were the plaintiffs' lawyer on that fourteen-million-dollar Federal Life case."

I could see his pale face bobbing up and down in the night.

"That's the case where Kate Baneberry was a juror," I said.

Clouds shifted, and the moonlight highlighted Galerina's starched white shirt and loosened tie. He was bobbing his head again. "Yeah, that's me. We met before. I met you at a bar party or a seminar or something. You remember?"

I didn't answer.

"We need to talk, Tom. I'm telling you. We need to talk *tonight*."

I called out. "Are you alone?"

His pale face bobbed some more above the white collar. "Yeah, I'm alone. But at least you got enough sense to ask. That's what we need to talk over. You and me, we need to get some things straight. I'm here to help you, Tom. You may not believe it, but I drove out here tonight to save both of us a world of hurt."

I glanced around the yard, listening hard for footfalls on sand.

If it was a trap and someone else—someone who planned to do me damage—was with Chris Galerina, then he or she was probably crouched behind me in the dark already. If it was a trap and Galerina was alone, well, I'd met the man and he did not put me in fear of my life. But, if it wasn't a setup and a senior partner with Russell & Wagler wanted to talk about Kate and Jim Baneberry, then, hell, I had to hear this.

I started walking toward my drunken visitor. "Well then, Chris, I guess we better go inside and talk."

Galerina stood as I walked up the stairs. When we met, I passed through a bourbon-flavored haze. He still wore suit pants, a starched shirt, and a loosened, hundred-dollar tie from work, but the man reeked.

I unlocked the door and walked in ahead of him. He followed; then he closed and locked the door himself.

I turned to look at him. "Have a seat."

Galerina looked smaller inside. He stood about five-eight and looked soft around the middle and pretty much everywhere else. A black smudge of five-o'clock shadow glowed beneath nervous perspiration. It was forty degrees outside, and the man was sweating.

He walked to an upholstered chair and sat down, draping his suit coat over his lap. He caught my eye and nodded at the empty WAR EAGLE cup in my hand. "You going to have another drink?"

"Would you like one?"

"Yeah. Thank you. Bourbon on the rocks."

"It's in the kitchen. I'll be right back."

I walked into the kitchen and looked longingly at the telephone. I wanted to talk to someone about Jim Baneberry's lawyer sitting in my living room, but I didn't know who that someone might be. So, what I did was mix two drinks and rejoin my uninvited guest.

Galerina thanked me and took the bourbon in his left hand. His right was pushed deep inside the folds of the suit coat in his lap.

I sat down opposite him and sipped my scotch. "What have you got in your hand, Chris?"

He turned to look at the door leading out onto the deck, then gulped down half his drink before answering. "Nothing. Don't worry about it."

There was something odd about the way he was gripping whatever he had under the coat, like maybe his life depended on it. So it seemed to me that either he was inordinately fond of himself, or he had a gun. "Well then, why don't you take your hand out of there?" I smiled. "It looks like you're playing with yourself."

Galerina flushed red. "I don't think you know me well enough to talk to me like that."

I said, "Yeah. And you don't know me well enough to sit in my living room playing with yourself."

My sweat-shiny guest sat his bourbon on the rug next to the chair and swiveled his neck to crack the tension out of it. "Fine. You wanna see what I'm playing with?" He eased a snub-nosed revolver out from beneath the coat. "This is what I'm playing with, Tom. This is what I've been playing with ever since you got in my business."

"Did you come here to shoot me, Chris?"

"I came here to help you."

"And, by any chance, does that include sending me to heaven? Because—just so you'll know—I'm not real sure that's where you'd be sending me."

I was trying to break the tension. He didn't smile. "I look crazy to you, don't I, Tom? Crazy little wop lawyer come out here to shoot you and shoot myself. Is that what you think?"

I let some silence settle between us.

No, I didn't particularly think Chris Galerina had come to my house to blow my brains out. Maybe that's why I wasn't really scared. But that's not right. I was deeply frightened of what was about to happen. I just didn't think it would involve me getting shot. Of course, I'd been wrong before.

"What are you afraid of Chris?"

"Same thing you are."

"Okay. Then what am I afraid of?"

"I heard about your wreck."

I drank some scotch. "What do you know about my wreck?"

He shrugged.

I said, "I thought we were going to talk about the Baneberrys. So let's talk." I motioned at his revolver with my drink. "Put that thing away and let's talk like reasonable people."

Galerina pressed the release on the side of his revolver, swung the cylinder open, and dumped all six bullets on top of the coat in his lap. "See, no problem. Nothing to worry about. We're both lawyers here, Tom. We can work this out. That's what I'm here to do—you know, work it out. This is like any other case.

You and me, we're in settlement negotiations right now."

"You want to settle with my client?"

Galerina lifted the revolver and pointed it at me with the empty cylinder hanging open to one side.

I held up an open palm. "Point that somewhere else."

"It's empty. I'm just trying to make a point."

"Point it somewhere else, or I'm going to make a point of shoving it up your ass."

He put the gun in his lap. "Shit. I'm trying to show you something. I'm using the gun for a friggin' exhibit. I'm telling you that *right now* you got a gun pointed at your head. And I don't mean this one. I mean, you know, figuratively. I mean there're people who're waiting to see how close you get. And, Tom, you get close enough and they're gonna drop the hammer on you."

I said, "Figuratively speaking," but I don't think he was listening.

Galerina looked at the outside door again.

I looked too. "You expecting somebody?"

"No. But you should be." He shook his head in a kind of drunken shudder. "So, uh, how much? We're in negotiations right now. How much you *need* to go away?"

"How much do *I* need, or how much does Sheri Baneberry need?"

Galerina plucked his glass off the rug and killed the rest of the bourbon. "*I* write *you* a check. Split it up any way you want."

"Is this a settlement of the wrongful death suit Jim Baneberry's bringing against Dr. Laurel Adderson?"

He swung his five-o'clock shadow from side to side.

"Nope. We'll still represent Mr. Baneberry on that. This is just for you. And, you know, for the girl— for your client—if that's the way you wanna do it." Galerina turned once again to look at the door; then he picked up one bullet and stuck the business end of the thing in his mouth. He twirled the brass casing between his lips and pulled it out. "Tom? You ever see actors in the movies do that? It's when somebody's gonna shoot themselves. I think Mel Gibson did it in *Lethal Weapon.* He's got this special bullet he's been saving to kill himself..."

"Why don't you give me the gun, Chris?"

"He's got this bullet, and he puts it in his mouth and sucks on it before he loads it into the gun." As he spoke, Galerina dropped the moistened bullet into one of the six empty chambers and swung the cylinder into place.

"Give me the gun, Chris. We've gotten past this. We're in settlement negotiations, remember? Just like any other case. Come on. Put the gun down and give me an offer."

He swung the cylinder open again and gave it a spin before snapping it shut. "How about a million dollars, Tom? Would you go away and forget about us for a million bucks?" Galerina crossed his legs, lifted the pointed toe of his polished loafer into the air, and took aim.

"Chris!"

Clack! The firing pin snapped into an empty chamber.

"Goddamnit, Chris!"

He popped open the cylinder and gave it another spin before flicking his wrist and slamming it shut. "Whatcha gonna do, Tom? You gonna shove this little pistol up my ass? That's what you said. Come on, Tom, answer me. You gonna shove this gun up my ass, or you gonna take a million dollars?" He screamed, "Come on, goddamnit! Let's negotiate!"

I had already placed my drink on the end table. Now I eased forward in the chair, centering my feet under me, getting ready to move fast if the crazy bastard pointed his gun at me. "Fine. Okay, fine. We're negotiating, Chris. There's a million dollars on the table. I'll take your offer to my client tomorrow morning."

Galerina pointed the revolver at his toe and popped the hammer against another empty chamber. "Shit! Can you believe that? Man, I'd be the king of Russian roulette. Remember *The Deer Hunter*? Guy stayed over in 'Nam after the war just to play Russian roulette with the gooks? Remember that? Hell, I'd've been king of that shit. Watch this."

I saw him swing open the cylinder again, and I almost made a move. But I was torn between going for the gun and running the hell out of there. And, in that split second of indecision, Galerina had spun the cylinder and swung it shut again.

"It's funny." Tears pooled in his eyes. "I mean, you know. Shit. We were trying to do good, Tom. Can you understand that? We were trying to do good. Help the little guy. Make it come out right. That's what he tells you at first."

"That's what who tells you, Chris?"

He ignored me. Maybe didn't even hear me. "Comes to you and says, 'How'd you like to win more cases, help more of your clients.' Then you're in, and you wish you weren't. You wish you could go back. But you take one step and then another. It . . . it doesn't seem . . . shit." He shook his head. "You can get used to anything a little at a time, Tom. Did you know that?"

My eyes were on the gun. I didn't answer.

He wiped at tears with the palm of his free hand and repeated. "Get used to any fucking thing." His mind seemed to loop back on itself, and he smiled. "Watch this."

He jerked the trigger three times in quick succession. Two loud *clacks* were followed by an explosion and someone yelling. The yelling was me. I'm not sure what I said.

I *was* sure that my drunken idiot of a guest had fired the only bullet in the gun straight through the outside edge of his loafer. I sprang out of the chair, reached Galerina in three steps, and twisted the still-smoking pistol from his hand.

I stepped back. "You dumb sonofabitch."

Galerina dropped the back of his head against the chair and started to chuckle. "A million dollars is on the table, Tom. A million fucking dollars."

Fifteen

"IS THAT ALL he said?" Sheri Baneberry hunched forward in the client chair across the desk from me. She was completely focused. The mention of a million dollars has that effect.

"That's it. I've told you everything he said from the time he got there until he stumbled out and climbed into his car."

She nodded her head. "And you think he's serious?"

"Yeah, I do. At least, I think he was last night. The man's scared out of his mind that we're going to find out something about his firm's business. And, by the way, Chris Galerina could write you a personal check for a million bucks tomorrow."

"He's that rich?"

"Rich enough."

Sheri leaned back and studied Mobile Bay through the window over my shoulder. "Why'd you let him drive when he left? He could've hurt someone."

"I tried to call him a cab, but he wasn't having it. And, to tell you the truth, I wasn't much interested in being around him any longer. Drunk and suicidal is a lousy combination. I did take away his bullets, though, before I let him have his gun back."

Sheri let some time pass. "How much of the million do you get, you know, as my lawyer?"

"None of it."

She lowered her lids and tucked her chin. My client looked like a blonde, disbelieving lizard.

I said, "I told you at the outset I wouldn't take the case on contingency. You're paying me by the hour. I can't switch over to a percentage now just because there's money on the table."

She laughed. "How about that? An honest lawyer."

I shrugged. "I'm just not a crook. But what we're talking about isn't exactly on the up-and-up either. First of all, you didn't hire me to sue anybody. You hired me to find out the truth of what happened to your mother. So, what Galerina will be paying *you* for is to forget about the truth and keep your mouth shut. And since you haven't brought suit or even threatened suit, the whole thing is really more of a payoff than a settlement, which means we'll all have to do some fancy lawyering.

"Galerina and his cronies will have to invent some imaginary scenario that supports them giving you a million bucks, seeing how they aren't about to admit to having anything to do with your mother's death. And I'll have to come up with some way to keep the payment from looking like you blackmailed Russell and Wagler—which, just so there's no confusion here, is pretty much what you'd be doing."

Sheri's strained and angry smile appeared. "So if I take the money, I'm a blackmailer?"

I picked up a half-empty coffee cup and swirled the cold contents before placing it back on the desk. "Well, it's close, but no. Galerina *would* be paying for your silence. But *he* made the offer, not you. So you're not threatening exposure to make him pay."

She studied my face. "But you find the whole subject offensive."

And she was right. I did find it offensive to be bought off, to be offered money to forget about the likely murder of an innocent woman. But . . . "A million dollars is a lot of money, Sheri. And, whatever we find out, nothing's going to bring your mother back. So it's up to you. At base, it's not all that different from taking money to drop a wrongful-death action in court."

"Okay, okay, I don't like it either. But what if we take the money using some kind of 'fancy lawyering,' as you call it, and keep on looking for the truth? I mean, if Galerina or his firm *did* have something to do with Mom's death, then, you know, screw 'em."

"Nope."

"But if we . . ."

"Look, Sheri, I'm no Boy Scout. I'll bend the law as much as I need to to draft a settlement agreement that keeps you and Galerina out of court and out of jail. But what you're talking about is taking money—a lot of money—under false pretenses."

She shook her head. "And it's taking money to let my mother's murderer go free. That's what it boils down to, isn't it?"

"Well, we don't know that for sure, and I didn't

want to put it that way. But, yeah, that's basically what we're talking about."

She puffed up in her chair and raised one medium eyebrow. "Then the hell with them."

"Yeah," I said, "that's pretty much what I was thinking."

It was after lunch, and a dark little man named Vynuvese Rapazaar stood across the desk from me, showering the carpet and furniture with profuse thanks. He and I had spent most of the last hour on a conference call with the INS. We were making progress toward an extended work visa. Mr. Rapazaar was uncommonly pleased, which was nice. But I couldn't understand a word he was saying.

In the midst of the little man's smiling gesticulations, Kelly poked her head into the office. She was smiling too. "Joey's on line two."

"You're kidding."

She shook her head. "Nope."

I stood and held my hand out to Mr. Rapazaar. He clasped my hand in both of his, pumped all three hands eight or ten times, and followed Kelly out of the office.

I grabbed the phone. "Where the hell are you?"

Joey laughed. "I'm in Montgomery, and your client is going to owe me a wad of cash."

"Loutie's looking for you."

"I called her."

"You okay?"

"I'm fine." My giant friend laughed some more. "Shit, I just saw you Friday. Now it's Monday. That ain't a real long time to go missin'. Loutie got a little worried 'cause I didn't answer my cell phone. But you can't much answer one that's outta juice.'"

"You didn't have a charger with you?"

"You know, Tom, you're a friggin' genius. I wish I'd thought of that. Only you had my car, which, if you think about it, has my charger on the dashboard."

"And I thought I was glad to hear from you."

"You are glad. I've been tailing the Cajun. Picked him up when he came back for the cooler we thought might have his prints on it."

"You're kidding. It occurred to me *after* you disappeared that maybe the Cajun had the same idea about the cooler."

"He did. But at least you thought of it first. I parked down the road there and got to the alley about two seconds before he did. Didn't have time to get the cooler; so I just hung back. You know, in the diner there. I was standin' inside the screen door checkin' things out when he came prancin' over the back fence like a ballerina or somethin'."

"I don't think they call the men ballerinas, Joey."

"Whatever he was, I thought about shootin' him in the leg or somethin', but decided it'd be smarter to tail him a while and see where he went."

"And he went to Montgomery?"

"Yep. At least, that's what he did early Saturday night. Up till then, he was looking for you. Sonofabitch checked out your beach house, your office, Kelly's townhouse, even my place."

"But he's in Montgomery now?"

"Beats me. I lost him."

"That's good."

Joey made a sound like a verbal shrug. "Shit happens. What do you want me to do now?"

I took a few seconds, staring at the corner of the ceiling. "I'll check with Sheri Baneberry to see if she's willing to keep paying. In the meantime, check out Judge Luther Savin."

"Criminal Appeals?"

"That's him. Lives over behind Huntingdon College somewhere there in Montgomery. He had a couple of alleged law clerks try to strong-arm me into a meeting on Sunday. Who knows? With everybody showing up in Montgomery, maybe there's some connection between the judge and the Cajun."

"Okay. You got the clerks' names?"

I said, "Hang on," and punched up my notes on the laptop. "Here it is. The smarter one's named Chuck Bryony. The other one's a pushy little blond bastard named Billy. They both have really cute hairdos. The two of 'em look like Backstreet Boys in golf clothes."

"You didn't like 'em."

"Not much. Give me a buzz at home tonight and let me know if you're finding anything. I'll check with Sheri in the meantime."

"Got it."

"And, Joey? Buy a phone charger that fits the cigarette lighter on that damn Safari vehicle and send me the bill."

"Yeah, okay. Listen, there's something else you need to know. I called a buddy of mine this morning. Ben Stilham. He's a Mobile cop, and I wanted him to run the plates on the Cajun's car. The plates turned up stolen, so that was no use. But he told me somethin' about you."

"Did you tell him you were working a case for me?"

"Hell, no. But Ben's been around a while, and he knows I work for you some. Anyway, he tells me that there's been a statewide O and R out on you since Friday."

"A statewide what?"

"Oh. O and R. Observe and report. Just means somebody—usually state or federal—wants to know where you are but doesn't want you stopped or arrested. Goes out on the wires to cops all over the state."

"Could he tell you where it originated?"

"Nope. That was all he'd say. But hell, Tom, I was surprised he said that much. Doing a Big Brother on the citizenry ain't something cops usually talk about."

I asked Joey to keep his ear to the ground and dropped the receiver back in its cradle. Almost immediately, the door opened and Kelly's head popped through.

I smiled. "Joey's fine."

"Good." She widened her eyes. "Sully Walker's on line two. He says pick up fast."

I snatched up the receiver and punched a blinking button. "Sully? What's wrong?"

A good friend, an even better criminal attorney said, "A warrant was issued this morning for your arrest in the death of Chris Galerina."

"What? He was at my house last night."

"I'm not sure I'd share that with anyone else. And, listen Tom, I know you're gonna want to turn yourself in and clear this up. But, right now, if you think you should find another location—somewhere safe—and call me back, well, I suggest you haul ass. The police are on the way to your office to execute the warrant."

As I got to my feet, I asked, "How do you know about this?"

"Tom! Go!"

Sixteen

I WAS WALKING FAST. At five-foot-one, Kelly was trotting to keep up. She looked scared. "What is it, Tom? Is Sully okay?"

Kelly and Sully had dated for a while a year earlier. I said, "He's fine. The cops are coming here to arrest me."

"Wha . . ."

"Listen, please. Go back to your desk. When they get here, you don't know where I am. That's all you need to say. I'll call you as soon as I can."

As I stepped into the hallway, the elevator ding-donged. I cut straight across the marble floor and opened the door of the CPA across the way. Her receptionist, a frail, henna-haired woman named Lucille, said too loudly, "Well, good morning, Tom. Did y'all run out of coffee again?"

I held my finger in front of my lips. I winked. "I'm trying to avoid someone."

Lucille bobbed her bony head and gave me a wrinkly wink in return. "Crazy client?"

I nodded. "Something like that."

"I know whatcha mean. Patricia's got a few of those. Some people live in their own little purple world. You tell 'em to go away, and they stick to your foot like bubble gum."

Rubber soles squeaked against marble, and I heard the door to my office open and close. I needed to get to a window. "Mind if I help myself to a cup of coffee while I'm cowering in your office?"

She started to stand. "I'll get it."

I walked toward the short hallway to the CPA's office. "No, no. I know where it is. Patricia in yet? Thought I might say hello."

Lucille settled back into her chair. "Sorry, she's out on an audit." She picked up a bottle of blood-red nail polish. "Holler if you need anything."

The coffee machine sat in a shallow alcove off the hallway. I stepped up and sloshed brown liquid into a Styrofoam cup—just in case Lucille got curious or helpful and came back to check on me—before heading for Patricia's office. The window in my office faced the Bay. Hers looked out on Water Street, which fronted our building.

Her door was locked. I clamped the Styrofoam rim of my coffee between my front teeth and fished a credit card out of my wallet. The lock was a standard inside-the-office job built into a round, stainless-steel knob—a keyhole on one side, a push button, on the other. Even better, the door—like most office doors—opened in, which meant the rounded part of the lock faced out.

Seconds later, as the card slipped through and the

door clicked open, Lucille called out, "Find everything?"

"Yep. Sure did."

I reached around the open door to twist the inside knob, and the lock button popped out. Now, if Lucille came back, all I had to do was look wide eyed and say, "It was open, so I stepped inside to look out the window."

I left the door open—open is more innocent—and crossed to the window. A dark green Ford with a whip antenna sat in a no-parking zone in front of the building. Close behind that, a City of Mobile patrol car supported the rumps of two uniforms.

Lucille still hadn't made an appearance. I punched the lock button on the way out and pulled the door closed. When I walked back into Lucille's outer office, she smiled. "Hiding?"

I smiled and listened. "Heard anything?"

She shook her head without looking up from the long strokes of crimson she was applying to her nails.

I peeked out into the empty marbled hallway, parked my coffee cup on a bookshelf next to the door, and slipped out. I was inside the freight elevator and headed for the first floor and the parking deck when a thought hit.

I punched the 2 on the elevator control panel. By dead reckoning, I decided a door labeled TEMPURA WONG, LICENSED CHIROPRACTOR led to the best view of the entrance to the parking deck. I stepped inside.

"Well, hello. What can we do for you this morning?" *Weh, hewo. Wha cin we do fo you these moning?*

The diminutive, white-coated doctor was her own receptionist. She was smiling. It was a symbiotic relationship. She needed a patient and I needed to look out her window to see if I could get out of the parking deck.

I said, "Uh, well, I get this pinchy thing in my back when I dance."

After a period of twisting and popping and embarrassing closeness, Dr. Wong let me use her phone and her window. I called Kelly. The detectives were gone. I looked out the window. The uniformed cops were gone. I put my shirt on, handed the doc three twenties, and headed for the elevators.

Working on the assumption that the parking attendant had orders to call the cops if I showed, I exited through the parking deck stairwell, where a metal security door led straight out onto the sidewalk. Two blocks away, I hailed a cab. Ten minutes later, I called Sully Walker's office from a bar near the waterfront.

Sully was out, but my call was expected. His paralegal told me to wait. She promised to find Sully. Seventy-six minutes later, Sullivan Walker entered through the front door of Cocktails for Two.

I waved him over. He sat without shaking hands.

I asked, "How bad is it?"

Sully caught the waitress's eye, then turned to face me. "It *was* bad. I've been blasting Buddy Foxglove over at the DA's office for most of the last hour. Bottom line is we got the warrant lifted, but you're going to have to answer some questions."

An aging waitress in a puckered-tight outfit stopped by the table and looked at us. Sully ordered coffee. We sat quietly while she fetched it from a nearby stand. She filled a cup for Sully, warmed my cup, and took a seat at the bar. A soap opera played on a television bolted to the wall above the bartender's collection of shimmering bottles.

As Sully stirred cream and sugar into his coffee, I said, "Questions I could understand. I mean, hell, the guy was at my house last night. He had a gun, and I've got a bullet in my floor where he damn near shot his toe off. What I don't understand is . . . I can't see how anyone would know Chris Galerina stopped by to see me. And, hell, I'm pretty well known around the courthouse. Why didn't the DA just ask me to come in if he wanted to talk to me?"

"Tom." Sully drank some coffee. "First of all, I don't think anyone *does* know Galerina came to see you. But they don't have to know that if your fingerprints are all over the weapon."

"I took his gun away from him last night so he wouldn't shoot himself."

"Guess you gave it back."

"Yeah, after I took the bullets away from him."

Sully drained his cup and said, "Apparently, he had an extra in his pocket. Some guy out jogging on the beach this morning found him. Looks like Galerina drove his car out on the sand last night after he left your house, took a thirty-eight revolver and popped himself in the temple."

"Shit."

"Yeah. Anyway, that explains your first question. The cops didn't know Galerina was at your house, just that your prints were on the gun. But why the DA's office issued a warrant instead of just picking you up for questioning, that's where it gets a little scary. Buddy gave me a lot of BS reasons, but he finally admitted getting pressure from 'upstairs,' as he put it, to go ahead and arrest you."

"What's that mean?"

"Beats me. Could mean several things. None good." Sully stood. "It's not going to be a lot of fun, Tom, but come on. The sooner we get you to Buddy's office for questioning, the sooner we can start trying to figure this thing out."

I followed Sully through a jumble of dimly lit tables and out into the sharp December air.

Seventeen

A LONG DAY made for a longer night. Still, I dozed enough for the alarm to jolt me awake at 6:00.

The previous afternoon's questioning had lasted three hours, and I'd learned not all that much—just that my prints were on the gun Chris Galerina had used to shove a bullet into his brain, and my home address had been scribbled on a pink message slip found on the seat next to his corpse.

When the lab had matched the prints on the gun to the ones I had on file as a member of the bar, ADA Buddy Foxglove's admitted first impulse had been to pick up the phone and call me. But he'd also admitted getting pressure from an undisclosed superior to issue a warrant instead. He'd admitted all this because he was pissed. He figured somebody was playing politics with one of his cases. He didn't say it in so many words, but that's what he thought. And he had not been happy about it.

I lay in bed and thought about that for a while, took a shower, and was standing in front of the bathroom mirror in boxers, socks, and a shirt, knotting my tie, when the phone rang. I jogged out of the bathroom and picked it up on the second ring.

"Mr. McInnes?"

"Yes."

"Mr. Tom McInnes, the attorney?"

"Who is this?"

The man announced his name like it was a baseball score. He was a television reporter. "We wanted to give you the opportunity to comment on the warrant that was issued yesterday for your arrest in the murder of attorney Chris Galerina."

He caught me off guard. I said, "That warrant was withdrawn."

"Yes." He paused, and I knew he was taking notes. "Was that before or after you met with Assistant District Attorney Foxglove?"

Okay. Now I was awake. "That's all I can say right now."

"No one else can tell your side of the story, Mr. McInnes. If you'll just..."

"How do you know about this?"

"We have our own sources, but it's in this morning's *Journal.* Right there on the front page. So there's really no reason..."

I hung up and ran to the closet for pants.

The *Mobile Register* was on my front lawn. I grabbed it and quickly scanned the front page. I thumbed through the metro and state sections on the way to the car.

Nothing.

I do not take the *Mobile Journal*. It's a second-tier newspaper. It covers sports more than politics, gossip more than economics. Basically, it's a rag. And I found a machine full of them at the Piggly Wiggly on Highway 98.

I dropped a quarter and a dime in the slot, yanked open the fold-down door, and took the top paper. Back in Joey's Expedition, doors locked and motor running, I read about my life.

LOCAL ATTORNEY ARRESTED
ON CHARGE OF MURDER

Exclusive to the Mobile Journal

Early yesterday morning, the District Attorney for Mobile County issued an arrest warrant for local attorney Thomas McInnes, charging him with first-degree murder in the death of fellow attorney Christopher Galerina. The *Journal* has learned that Mr. Galerina, a successful litigator and civic leader, was found dead on the beach near Mr. McInnes's home in Point Clear just hours before the warrant was issued. Mr. Galerina reportedly had been shot through the temple.

Well-placed sources inside the Mobile Police Department confirmed that Mr. McInnes's fingerprints were found on a small pistol that forensic analysis has verified to be the murder weapon. Those same sources reported that Mr. McInnes was arrested in Auburn this past Saturday and charged with the assault and battery of an employee of Tiger Tooth Photo in that city.

Auburn police were summoned after Mr. McInnes allegedly threatened and physically attacked a photo shop clerk for mistakenly giving his photographs to another customer. According to police records, just minutes after the altercation in Tiger Tooth Photo, Mr. McInnes was arrested inside a nearby restaurant where he reportedly was engaged in threatening that establishment's employees. Mr. McInnes was arraigned later that evening and pled not guilty. He was subsequently convicted of disturbing the peace and released after paying a fine.

Mr. McInnes first gained notoriety last year in connection with the death of a woman who may have been instrumental in the murder of Mr. McInnes's younger brother, Hall McInnes. In that incident, it was determined that Mr. McInnes acted in self-defense when he drowned the woman in the surf outside his beach house in Point Clear.

Three months prior to the drowning, Hall McInnes had been shot to death with a high-powered rifle near the town of Coopers Bend in what authorities believe to have been a drug-related contract killing...

And so it went.

The article concluded by briefly outlining Galerina's civic and charitable activities in the Greater Mobile Area before finally, in the last sentence, noting that the previous day's warrant for my arrest had been "withdrawn pending further investigation."

It was a good job. Chris Galerina looked like the Pope. I looked like a serial killer.

I drove back home, went into the kitchen, and made coffee. The first time my phone rang, I picked it up. After that, I let the reporters leave messages. Five calls in, I heard Kelly's voice on the machine. She was telling me about the newspaper story.

"Kelly?"

"Oh. Hi. Did you hear my message?"

"Yeah. I've got the paper in front of me. Some schmuck with Channel Three called this morning while I was still in bed."

Kelly sounded scared. "What are you going to do?"

"Right now I'm drinking coffee."

A little time went by before she spoke again. "We got a fax this morning from the State Bar."

I waited.

"There's no good way to tell you this, Tom. The letter says you've been temporarily suspended from the practice of law until they can set up a hearing before the disciplinary committee." She paused. "You want me to fax over the letter?"

"Might as well. And you may as well cancel my appointments for today while you're at it."

"You've got a hearing Friday in the Meyer case."

"Right. Call Sully and see if he can come out here. I'll ask him to cover the hearing. I need to talk with him about the newspaper and the bar suspension anyhow."

"Will do." She paused again. "What's going on, Tom?"

"Somebody's trying to destroy my credibility."

"Why?"

"The Baneberry case."

"Do you have something on someone who's connected enough to do all this?"

"Beats me."

A light rain had begun to fall when Kai-Li parked her aging Volvo in my driveway and jogged through the mist to the front porch. I'd watched her coming from the entry hall, through a column of square panes lined up against the doorframe. It was past 5:00 and close to dark. Tom Brokaw's voice floated in from the living room.

Kai-Li had called Kelly from the Montgomery Airport around lunchtime. She had been waiting to meet a flight from Iowa, waiting to hand off Sunny to her ex for the holidays when she picked up the afternoon paper. My fame had spread. She'd told Kelly she wanted to talk with me in person. She'd said it was urgent. Kelly had called me on the other line to get an okay before giving Kai-Li directions to my house.

I'd spent the afternoon talking with Sully and trying without success to run down Sheri Baneberry. Around 3:00, I'd tried to get Dr. Laurel Adderson on the phone. I figured she was wondering what kind of nut she had confided in. I was right. After leaving me on hold for eight minutes, Dr. Adderson's office manager told me that my message had been conveyed to the doctor, and she couldn't promise that the doctor would call me back.

I opened the door as Kai-Li reached for the bell.

I smiled. "You here to fire me in person?"

Kai-Li stopped just outside the door. Her eyes, more

gray than green in the dusk, scanned my face. She smiled back. "You don't get depressed very easily, do you, Tom?"

I stepped aside. "Just mad. But I've had some time to get over it." Kai-Li passed me in the foyer and continued into the living room. I said, "I've already been fired by a couple of clients today, and Dr. Adderson—the physician who treated the dead juror—won't return my calls. So I was a little surprised you wanted to drive down."

She smiled again, and I noticed her eyes had grown bright green in the lighted room. "I can't fire you. I work for *you*. I guess I could quit." She walked over to the sofa. "Mind if I sit down?"

"Oh, yeah. Sorry. Can I get you a Coke or a drink or something?"

She shook her head and collapsed onto the sofa. I walked over and clicked off the evening news before sitting beside her. She turned sideways, tucked one leg under the other, and trained those eyes on my face. "Back to the point—I guess I could resign as your consultant. And I'm ashamed to say that I likely would have done just that if I hadn't already analyzed the data you gave me before I saw the newspaper."

"You've already run the analysis?"

"You were in trouble. And, anyway, once I had the disk from the State Bar, it was mostly a programming job. It took a couple of hours to decide how to best analyze the data and a few more hours to write a simple program. Nothing to it, really."

"And?"

"And Chris Galerina's firm, Russell and Wagler, is

definitely hazardous to your health if you're a juror on a big-money case."

Hazardous to your health. That was the joke at the courthouse, according to Curtis Krait. But I didn't think I'd shared that with my Chinese-Scottish-American consultant. I asked, "Have you talked with any lawyers or anybody else around the state about Russell and Wagler since we met in Auburn?"

She moistened her lips with the tip of her tongue and shook her head. "No. I've been putting all my time into running the analysis. Why?"

I studied her pretty face. "No reason. Tell me what you found. Please."

"Okay, how much do you know about statistical analysis?"

"I think I made a 'B' in sophomore business statistics."

"Did you like it?"

"No."

"Okay, we'll go with the layman's overview." She paused briefly before going on. "I was lucky starting out. The State Bar Legal Directory was already in ASCII format and it was clean—you know, not full of typos or formatting problems. So all I had to do was load it into my database program, assigning addresses to the pertinent data fields. I used a system of cataloging the data that reflected the sequence of data in my existing database, so if we need to make other, additional comparisons in the future . . ."

I interrupted. "This is what you call the layman's overview?"

A light blush crept up her cheeks. "Sorry. I get into this. Anyway, once I had the legal directory in my database, I wrote a simple comparison program to check the trial attorneys in my original sample with their firms in the legal directory. I pulled everyone who wasn't a sole practitioner and divided them into their respective firms so I'd have a large sample to compare with Russell and Wagler. Then it was a simple matter to pull juror illness rates for each firm in the directory. Now all I had to do was apply p-factor analysis . . ."

"Kai-Li?"

"What? Oh. That's probably the kind of thing you wanted me to skip."

I smiled and nodded. "You know you're way too good-looking to be this big a nerd."

She laughed. "And I guess you don't get excited by legal bits, like, what do they call it? The 'rule against perpetuities' or something?"

"Actually, no, I don't. But I know what you mean. Right now, though, I'd really appreciate your skipping to the end."

"Okay, but you're missing out."

I looked at the floor.

"Okay, okay. Here it is. The illness rates among jurors assigned to cases being tried by Russell and Wagler *cannot* be the result of naturally occurring factors."

"You can *really* tell that from a formula or two?"

"Yes. I really can."

A day's worth of tension flooded out of my neck and shoulders. I said, "I think you just saved my career."

"Does that mean you'll feed me? I'm starving."

Eighteen

DECEMBER IS A GRAY, wet month in the deep South. My memories of Christmas mornings are of speeding downhill on steel skates or a new bike from Sears with freezing raindrops cutting at my face like razor blades, which was more fun than it sounds.

Now, as I lay in bed ruminating on my ruined career, a tingle of nostalgia or maybe just remembered cold trickled down my spine as a steady drizzle patted the roof like watery fingertips. Down the hall, Kai-Li slept in a New Orleans Jazz Festival T-shirt I'd found for her. She'd put it on in the privacy of my guest room. I imagined how she looked swallowed up inside my old shirt, sleeping on her side, the covers pulled back just enough . . .

This was not getting me anywhere.

Weak light framed closed drapes. I clicked on the bedside lamp and got onto my feet. I found running shorts and a Birmingham City Stages T-shirt in my top drawer and pulled them on. My hooded sweatshirt and shoes were in the downstairs closet. I pushed bare feet into cold running shoes—I could never understand how anyone jogs in socks—and let myself out the back door.

It was time.

Feeling like I'd been beaten with sticks in my sleep, I leaned over and hugged my knees to stretch my back and hamstrings. I pulled each foot back against my butt, and then, falling forward against the house in a sort of vertical pushup, I touched both heels to the ground, one after the other, and turned toward the beach.

Sand sprayed against the backs of my legs with each kick. An orange glow framed houses and trees to the east and tipped the swells in Mobile Bay. My neighbor's floating Christmas tree bobbed on the water, its bulbs growing dim in the early-morning light.

And someone was following me.

Around the one-mile mark, I'd caught the barest glimpse of a figure running about two hundred yards back. I sped up. So did he or she. I never turned around and took a good look. I used the corner of my eye as I looked out over the Bay in one direction and watched the sun rise in the other.

I realized I wasn't the only person who runs on the beach before work. Being able to do that very thing is why many people live there. I also realized that Kai-Li could be back there, taking a morning run, watching me but keeping a distance, allowing me my privacy. But I didn't think so. The same primitive alarm I'd felt in Auburn before my film was stolen was blaring inside my skull.

My shadow had been drifting closer as I ran faster.

Now I slowed to bring him or her inside a hundred yards. Around a small curve in the beach, I planted my forward foot, spun, and tried my best to make a ten-second hundred out of it.

It was a man. He froze for two beats, which was what I was counting on. It's an old saying among cops—action is twice as fast as reaction. And, in the time it took his brain to process the change, I was twenty yards closer. I could see the Cajun.

He spun and started pumping, but I was going full speed and he was just out of the blocks. I closed to thirty yards, then the quick little bastard started pulling away fast. I'm middling fast. This guy could fly. There was no way to outrun him. I had to think fast, and what I came up with was more meat cleaver than scalpel.

I cupped my hands on either side of my mouth. "You better run, you fucking coonass coward."

He looked back.

I slowed to a walk. "I bet your two-dollar swamp whore of a mother was fast too."

He stopped.

I kept walking and talking. "Come on, asshole. You're good at sneaking around in the dark. You any good at acting like a man?" I was within fifteen yards now. The Cajun's nostrils flared with each breath. "I called your mother a two-dollar whore. That okay with you? Or maybe it's true. Is that it?" I stopped five feet from the Cajun. "Why don't you run away and put a dead bunny rabbit on my car? That'll show me."

He locked eyes with me, and a tiny shudder rippled across the skin on my back.

Long black hair swept back from a bony forehead. His sunken cheeks were marked with old scars, and the skin on his neck seemed to strain with the effort of containing thick, twisted cables of muscle and sinew.

I'd wanted him to stop. Be careful what you wish for.

Seconds passed as we stared at each other. Finally, he said, "You want me? Heah I stan'."

I caught a swift movement at his side and glanced down. He held a lockblade knife in his left hand, and I noticed a dagger tattoo on the thick pad of muscle between his thumb and index finger. I'm no rube. I've seen *Oz*, and I recognized the sign of a prison-yard assassin.

I nodded at the knife. "That your specialty in prison? Knifing unarmed men?"

He shrugged.

"But you're not supposed to kill me, are you?"

Surprise flickered across his features before he caught himself. He said, "Accidents dey do happen."

"I want to know who hired you."

He shrugged his shoulders again and held up the knife. "Steers want balls."

I decided that was just about enough talk. "Lose the knife."

"Fug you."

"Fuck me? Fuck you. You break into my house, poison me in my own car. You wanna act tough? Drop the knife. We'll find out."

He waved me off with feigned disgust and turned to walk away. The Cajun expected me to jump him when he turned his back. And I knew he expected it. But it was still the best shot I was going to get.

I was almost on him when he spun right, leading with his elbow. Stepping inside the arc, I ducked his elbow and grabbed a handful of Cajun testicles in my left hand and squeezed hard. The blade in his left fist slashed for my chest as he came full around. I threw up my right forearm to block his knife hand and felt the burn of his blade across the bridge of my nose. Still gripping his balls, I shifted weight to my right foot, dropped my elbow, and drove the best uppercut I had into his left armpit. A glint of morning sunlight caught my eye as the steel blade spun into the sand.

A solid right cross exploded into my temple. The beach faded to gray and came back. I clubbed wildly with my right fist, while clamping down and twisting his ball sack with my left. The Cajun squealed like a hog and pounded with both fists and kicked to get away from my hold on his nuts. Time got slow, like the dreamlike motion in an auto accident, and I could feel his breath on my face, burning the open cut across my nose. I tried to butt his pock-marked face and missed as he leaped into the air in some kind of Bruce Lee spinning thing. Out of nowhere, something, maybe a knee, slammed into my chest. I went down like I'd been shot—rolling, expecting him to come after me. But he went instead for the knife, his back turned slightly to reach for it.

Something like hot tar spread through my chest as I staggered to my feet. The Cajun didn't turn. He thought I was down, and he was counting on the knife to end it. Two quick steps, and I kicked him hard in the ribs. Nothing fancy. Just like punting a football, except I ended up on my back in the sand.

A sound like *whooah* gushed out of the Cajun in a wash of hot air, and my kick spun him away from the knife. Before he'd landed, I was scrambling across the sand on my stomach like a sick animal. My fingers found the blade. I rolled up onto one knee and saw the man who had been making my life a living hell stumble away.

First he staggered. Then he ran. He was bent over; he held his side; he limped badly and painfully each time his left foot struck earth. But he *was* running, which was a damn sight more than I could have done right then.

It was a stupid plan. It hadn't worked.

I pushed up onto my feet to try and follow. But, as the Cajun limped away from the water, he stopped short and tried to turn in his tracks. I could see his hard black eyes focus on mine just before a white-haired giant stepped into sight and smashed him across the base of his skull with the butt of a shotgun.

The Cajun spun into the sand face first and went limp. Joey reached down, flipped him over, and removed his belt. After using the belt to tie the Cajun's hands behind his back, Joey walked over to check on me. He was dragging the Cajun by one limp foot, like a toddler dragging a rag doll across the playground.

I could feel liquid heat flowing from the gash across my nose, coating my lips and chin with blood. I said, "Good timing."

"You did okay."

"If this is okay," I said, "I'd hate to get my ass kicked." I reached out and handed Joey the knife. It was taking too much strength to hold it. "What took you so long?"

Joey laughed. "It probably seemed like a hell of a long time to you, Tom. But that whole nut-snatchin' fight you just had probably lasted six or seven seconds."

My friend glanced down at the unconscious stranger. "Good thing he wasn't supposed to kill you. You'd've never seen him comin'."

"Yeah." I spit a mouthful of blood into the sand. "I feel lucky as hell."

Kai-Li's ashen face was close to mine. Her bright eyes jumped over the Cajun's handiwork. She guided a cotton swab over cuts and bruises. She'd dipped the cotton in something cool. Whatever it was stung and felt good.

She straightened to examine her work. "What's your friend going to do with the man who did this? Nothing stupid, I'm hoping."

I shook my head. "I'm sure Joey will wait till the guy wakes up and try to get some information, if he can. But then he'll call the cops."

"Shouldn't you have waited for the police? You were the one attacked."

"I couldn't wait. I was too traumatized by the vicious brutality of an unknown attacker."

Kai-Li gave me a look and turned to the first-aid kit she'd laid out on the kitchen table. She began tearing thin strips of adhesive tape and snipping them into one-inch lengths.

Her hair was clipped into a loopy thing on the back of her neck. I spoke to her back. "We don't expect him to tell us anything. We set this up to get the Cajun arrested, not to torture information out of him. Mostly we just want the guy ID'd."

She turned back and grimaced. "I'm going to have to pull that cut together."

I watched her fingers work.

"Twist the strips in the middle."

She nodded.

Kai-Li gently pressed one end of a bandage beneath the gash across the bridge of my nose. She put the index finger of her other hand above the cut and pushed. Firecrackers exploded inside my eyeballs, and a less-than-masculine yelp sounded deep in my throat.

She shook her head. "Sorry."

"It's okay. I knew the pain was coming sooner or later. It didn't really hurt when it happened."

"Adrenaline?"

"Sharp knife."

She stretched two more twisted strips of tape across the cut. "You said you set it up."

"What?"

"You said you set up your fight with the, uh, the Cajun man. Why would you do that? I mean, if you knew where he was . . ."

"We didn't know. Joey's tried tailing the guy twice. Both times the Cajun lost him. So, I was sitting around here after you called from Montgomery yesterday, and something occurred to me. I called Joey—he was in Montgomery too, checking out Judge Savin—and asked him to come down here and tail *me*."

Kai-Li smiled. "Instead of trying to track the lion. You decided to stake a lamb in the jungle."

"Baaa."

She smiled. "Did you ever stop to wonder why you *chose* a trap that would put you in physical danger?"

I shrugged. "It was all I could think of."

"You couldn't have taken a gun? You couldn't have led him to the police? Think about it."

I looked into her eyes. "You're not going to start telling me about how I'm three people again, are you?"

Kai-Li raised her eyebrows and sighed. "Anyway, I've done the best I can on these cuts, but you're going to need stitches on your nose. Who's your doctor? I should call ahead."

I thought about that. "Call Dr. Laurel Adderson. Her number should be on a pad by the living-room phone. Ask her to meet us at the emergency room in Daphne."

Kai-Li spun and hurried toward the door. Then she stopped short and turned back. "Isn't that the juror's doctor who won't take your phone calls?"

"That's her."

"Why would you think...?"

"She hears I've been attacked, I think curiosity will get the better of her."

Kai-Li raised an eyebrow. "And your natural charm will overwhelm her once you're face-to-face? Is that it?"

"I don't need charm." I tried to smile. "Look at me. I'm pitiful."

Nineteen

I LOCKED THE DOOR and turned to trot down the front steps and almost ran into Kai-Li. She was frozen at the edge of the porch.

"What's that?"

I looked. Joey had reclaimed his giant Expedition and left my *Hatari!* loaner in its place. "I think it's called a Land Rover Safari something-or-other."

Kai-Li looked at me, but I couldn't read her. All she said was, "Good name for it."

Small-town emergency rooms don't look like much. I shared space in a tired yellow cube with two other patients—one, a bald plumber with soiled overalls and a broken finger, and the other, a pretty, young housewife who complained of migraine and occasionally vomited into a trash can.

The volcanic housewife went back first. I went ahead of the plumber.

Triage.

Kai-Li went back with me. I wanted her to meet Dr. Adderson and explain that I wasn't crazy. A nurse in baby-blue scrubs told me to remove my clothes and put on a cheap apron that she called a robe. I sat on the examining table in my running clothes and waited.

Kai-Li asked, "Aren't you going to put on the robe?"

I shook my head. "They always say that."

"Do you want me to step outside?"

"Nope."

"Do you need me to help you?"

"Thanks. But I don't think getting naked's going to help her sew my nose up."

Kai-Li stepped in front of me and unzipped my sweatshirt. "Do you know the difference between men and boys, Tom?" She paused. "There isn't one."

She pulled the sleeves off by the cuffs and gently lifted the sweatshirt away and draped it over the back of a cheap plastic chair in one corner of the examination room. Next she slipped her fingers under my shirttail.

"Lift your arms."

When my hands reached shoulder height, I felt a hot coal fire up inside my chest, and I made a noise appropriate to the sensation.

Kai-Li shook her head again. All she said was, "See?"

"I don't think my arms are going much higher than that."

She worked the T-shirt up and over my head and arms and tossed it across the sweatshirt. When she turned back, Kai-Li made a little gasping sound and pointed a finger at my chest.

"My God, Tom. What'd he do to you?"

I looked down at a black, purple, and green bruise about the size of a softball. It was not unimpressive.

"I think he kneed me in the chest."

"And you didn't want to take your shirt off." She had her hands on her hips. I had the feeling I was getting a look usually reserved for her daughter. "I'll step outside if you need to remove the shorts. I mean, be a grown-up about this. You aren't hiding something under there too, are you?"

I could have said something sophomoric, but that's when Dr. Adderson walked into the room. She didn't look happy to see me.

"I am *not* your doctor, Tom."

"You treated me after the wreck. You were close by, and I needed help."

Dr. Adderson held a manila folder in one hand. It had a row of colored squares along the edge with numbers on them. My name and social security number were typed across a label stuck on the top corner. She stepped in front of me and tossed the folder on the examining table.

Placing the tips of her fingers on my cheeks and tilting my face toward the light, Laurel Adderson nodded toward Kai-Li and asked, "Did you do the butterfly bandages?"

"Yes."

"Good job. I need a plastic surgeon to look at this." She stepped outside the room and spoke with a nurse. When she came back, she said, "We're seeing who's here."

Seconds later, the baby-blue nurse came in with a stainless steel bowl full of chipped ice. As the nurse began filling a clear plastic bag from the bowl, Adderson asked, "How long ago did this happen?"

I said, "A couple of hours."

"How'd you do this, Tom?"

I told her I had been attacked on the beach by a man who had been shadowing me since I started work on the Baneberry case.

She asked if I'd be willing to consult with a staff psychiatrist.

I said, "I'll make you a deal. I'll talk to your shrink if you'll sit down with Dr. Kai-Li Cantil here..."

Kai-Li said, "I'm not a medical doctor. Professor of psychology."

Laurel Adderson nodded.

I went on. "If you'll sit down with Dr. Cantil for ten minutes and hear her out, I'll talk to anybody you want me to."

Dr. Adderson's eyebrows arched. "I'm not in the habit..."

"I'm not talking about habits. I'm talking about ten minutes of your time to get me to do something that you, as a physician, believe is necessary to my health. Are you too proud to swap ten minutes for a patient's health?"

"Don't try to manipulate me, Tom."

"I'm trying to help you. You don't believe it yet. But I'm trying to help both of us."

Sunshine had melted December drab into bright, cloudless skies. Sitting in my living room, chewing a mouthful of pepperoni-and-banana-pepper pizza, it looked almost like early spring through the windows.

The noonday news played beneath squares of bright sunlight that faded the screen. The pretty blonde was anchoring—Gina something. Apparently, there were only fifteen shopping days till Christmas. Another pulp mill was closing. Pollution in Mobile Bay would be reduced. Two hundred thirty-three people would lose their jobs the week before Christmas. The high temperature was going to be thirty-eight degrees.

And I couldn't find my client.

Sheri Baneberry was not at work. *She's out of the office on business. Try back next week.* Her home number yielded an answering machine. I tried a listing for Bobbi Mactans and got a series of unanswered rings.

Rather than waste time trying to get information out of Jim Baneberry, I called Joey's cell phone, then his house. When he answered his home phone, I said, "We've got a missing client."

"That's not good."

"Yeah, that's what I was thinking. What are you doing today?"

"Nothin' really. Just hangin' around here, you know, waitin' to hear if the cops have ID'd the Cajun."

"The country cops have him?"

"Yeah," Joey said, "Baldwin County sheriff's Department. The Mobile cops would be movin' faster, but you're in the sheriff's jurisdiction out there."

Kai-Li and my lawyer, Sully Walker, walked into the living room from my study. They'd been huddled in there getting ready for an upcoming hearing on my fitness to practice law—what with my being a ruffian and a possible murderer and so on.

Sully wanted to submit Kai-Li's research at the hearing in Montgomery to show that Chris Galerina had been fixing jury trials before he caught a bullet in the temple near my beach house. But, I thought, even if the State Bar Disciplinary Committee accepted Kai-Li's data, I wouldn't necessarily be in the clear. I would, however, be taking a lot of powerful people down with me.

Sully had argued that the political types at the Bar would choose to leave my license to practice alone—until I was actually convicted of something—over stirring up a hornets' nest at Russell & Wagler. I figured he was right. Probably right.

Joey said, "Tom? You there?"

"Oh, yeah. Sorry. I was thinking about something."

"That Cajun boy scramble your brains?"

He didn't expect an answer. "Think you can find Sheri Baneberry?"

"It's what I do."

"Call me when you know something...about Sheri or the Cajun."

Joey said, "You got it," and hung up.

Sully, Kai-Li, and I talked. She'd hurried down yesterday after dropping off her daughter at the Montgomery Airport, which meant she'd arrived at my doorstep without a change of clothes or a bottle of shampoo. Fortunately, though, Kai-Li had a habit of carrying work projects around in an ancient satchel that moved with her from home to office to wherever. She had her jury-fixing data on disk and in her satchel. Now Sully had it too. And he had more faith than I did that he could make use of it.

He and I argued about that some, and he left.

Kai-Li needed clothes. She left to buy some.

I settled my head against the sofa's back cushions. Dr. Adderson had prescribed something for the ache in my chest, and, as the painkiller kicked in, the television began to fuzz around the edges. I focused on blue sky through the window to clear my eyes. When I looked back down, the screen wobbled like the view through a handheld video camera. An unnecessarily happy guy in a beard and a chef's hat prattled about "holiday treats." I could have sworn he said the words, "Bake the cookies or die," just before I fell asleep.

The news anchor had changed, and the window over the television had gone black. One lighted lamp cast long shadows across the room. I sat up and looked around.

"Welcome back."

I turned and saw Kai-Li sitting in an easy chair. She had my Beretta over-and-under laid across her lap.

I smiled. "Expecting trouble?"

"The Cajun made bail."

"What?"

"The Cajun..."

"I heard you. Why didn't you wake me up?"

She shook her head. "I tried, Tom. Whatever Dr. Adderson gave you really knocked you out. It's probably an overreaction, but Joey said to 'take measures' so I called your secretary, Kelly, and she told me about the gun closet."

"Where'd you get...?"

"A key? Your pants pocket. As I said, that stuff really

knocked you out. I could've stripped you naked and painted you blue if I'd wanted."

I reached over and clicked on the lamp next to the sofa. I glanced down at my forearms. They weren't blue. "Where's Joey?"

"Looking for your client, the Baneberry woman."

Kai-Li stood and walked over in front of me and held out the shotgun. "You take this, okay?"

I took the gun. "Do we at least have a name on the Cajun? I assume the sheriff found out that much before he let him go."

Kai-Li turned and picked up a curled sheet of fax paper from the coffee table. She read out loud. "Zion Thibbodeaux."

"You're kidding."

She smiled. "Nope. That's his given name. Zion Thibbodeaux. Let's see. I saw something." Kai-Li sat down on the sofa next to me and held the paper toward the lamp. I could smell the scent of shampoo in her hair. She'd had a shower while I slept—I guessed before she heard about Mr. Thibbodeaux. "Here it is. Under 'aliases,' it says 'Zybo.'" And she spelled it.

I held out my hand. "Can I look at that?"

She handed it to me, but then scooted over and leaned against my shoulder so she could continue to read. I glanced over at her emerald eyes as they scanned the sheet.

She pointed. "Look. Here's what I wanted you to see. Four years and, what is it, about eight months in maximum security at Louisiana State Penitentiary in Angola?"

"Yeah." I skimmed down the page. "He went up for manslaughter."

Kai-Li nodded. "That's why I got the gun from your closet."

I stood and walked to the window. The sun had set while I slept and, out past the yard, the beach floated like a strip of golden haze between dark borders of grass and saltwater.

I asked, "Has Joey made any headway finding Sheri?"

"Haven't heard anything." Kai-Li stood and walked over to stand beside me just as a wash of headlights swept a sliver of beach. "What's that?" She sounded alarmed.

"Somebody just pulled into my driveway." I broke open the Beretta, checked to make sure it was loaded, and snapped it closed. "Let's go see who it is."

Twenty

"IS SHE DRUGGED?"

Joey shook his head. "Just drunk, I think."

Sheri Baneberry lay unconscious on top of the covers of the four-poster in one of the guest rooms. Joey turned and walked out. I stood there alone and watched my client sleep.

Her hair looked as though she had run a comb through it after a shower and let it dry, and she wore no makeup. Her eyelashes, which had been touched with mascara before, now were as pale as her hair. Her lips were parted, just barely, to reveal a slice of those big white teeth.

Sheri Baneberry looked about sixteen years old. I left the room, killing the light and closing the door on the way out.

Downstairs, I found Joey and Kai-Li in the kitchen. The better-looking of the two stood by the stove, shaking dried spices into a boiler of beef stew. Kai-Li returned the spice jar to the cabinet and asked if Sheri was all right.

"Seems to be," I said. "Joey thinks she's just had too much to drink." Kai-Li looked doubtful, so I added, "I've seen her drunk before. Not like this, but pretty bad. Sheri said at the time she was grieving for her mother. But people who grieve with a bottle . . . well, I think any excuse'll do if you want the stuff."

Joey spoke up. "Dead mother's a pretty good excuse, Tom."

He was right. I could have tried to explain what I'd meant, but I didn't.

Joey popped the cap off a bottle of Foster's and took a long swig before saying, "You haven't asked me where I found her."

"I assumed she was holed up at home on a binge."

Joey shook his head. "Nope. Not at home."

"Bobbi Mactans's?"

Joey nodded. "Second place I thought of too. Took a while 'cause I didn't wanna have to beat up a woman to get her out of there."

"I think you'd have had to kill Bobbi to get Sheri out."

"Yeah. Could be. So, I hung around until Bobbi went out for groceries or more liquor or an extra dildo or somethin' and went in and got Sheri off the sofa."

Kai-Li looked mildly shocked and asked, "Who's Bobbi Mactans and why does she need an *extra* dildo?"

Joey grinned. "She's a friend, more or less, of Sheri's. Bobbi Mactans's father—a prick named Jonathan Cort—and Sheri's father, Jim, are business partners. Both Bobbi and her father been trying to get Sheri away from Tom since she hired him."

Kai-Li asked the obvious question. "Why?"

Joey glanced at me. When I didn't answer, he said, "We don't know. Could be the father's business is crooked, and he doesn't want Tom screwing around in his operation, kickin' over rocks to see what crawls out. Could be Bobbi—who's your basic man-hatin' bull dyke—is a control freak and doesn't want anybody getting between her and her little blonde poontang."

Kai-Li said, "You're not a democrat, are you, Joey?"

Joey chuckled and turned to me. "Am I wrong?"

"No. No, you're not wrong. You explained it a little more colorfully than I would have." I turned to Kai-Li. "Joey values clarity over diplomacy."

"Yeah," Joey said, "that's me."

Dinner was Irish stew, French bread, and Australian beer. Kai-Li, Joey, and I watched some TV, talked a little, and sat in silent thought a little. I took another painkiller for my chest. By nine, I was nearly gone. I went to my room. Kai-Li went to hers. Joey carried a club chair upstairs and wedged it in front of Sheri's door, where he would sleep the rest of the night.

The house grew quiet. But then, as I lay there beneath cool sheets and warm covers in the seconds before exhaustion pushed me under, I could have sworn that I heard the soft murmur of Kai-Li talking quietly on the phone in her room.

It was around 7:00 A.M. when Kai-Li and I arrived at the little landing strip in Fairhope. A lavender haze filled the east, providing the only relief from gray fields, gray cloudcover, and, it seemed, gray air.

We climbed aboard Sully Walker's little Cessna twin engine. I'd had a painkiller hangover when I awoke at five. The lingering cottonmouth, vague nausea, and mild headache had lingered and grown less vague and mild. Now Sully wanted me in front so we could talk about the hearing that morning before the State Bar Disciplinary Committee in Montgomery.

After some sphincter-tightening bumping, rolling, and weaving, we were airborne and headed north to Montgomery. Between mumbling nonsense into a gray, handheld microphone, Sully yelled at me over the roar of his engines, telling me his strategy for the hearing, filling me in on what documents he had filed with the committee and why.

I took sips from a warm bottle of Coke and tried to listen, tried to become engaged in defending my license to practice law. But the truth was that I just wanted to go home. I could never remember being so relatively safe and yet still wanting so badly to be somewhere else. I hadn't thought the disciplinary hearing would bother me so much. I'd been wrong.

I felt a hand close on my shoulder, and I turned around. Kai-Li was leaning forward from the back seat. "Are you okay?" She had to yell over the engines, and the private question felt rough and intrusive.

I thought about lying, but just looked at her.

She yelled, "You thinking about the hearing?"

"Kind of woozy from the painkillers, I think."

"Worried too, I suppose."

I shrugged.

"Is it that you aren't in control of what's going to happen to you? Is that what's bothering you?"

Kai-Li was being a psychologist again. And she was probably right. But I didn't want to talk about it, so I just looked at her some more. She kept looking back, so I gave her my best thanks-but-leave-me-the-hell-alone look.

She smiled a smile meant to pacify. "Okay. But if that

is it, just go ahead and recognize that it's a control issue. Sheri's safe with Joey, and you're safe here. *And*, you said yourself, Sully's a great lawyer. This is going to work out." She gave me her reassuring analyst's smile again. "It's just a control thing, Tom. Think about it. You'll feel better."

I turned back toward a windshield full of gray sky and drank some warm Coke.

The night held Sully's twin-engine Cessna in a black-velvet glove. There was no moon. No light of any kind. There wasn't even a sense of forward movement toward home—just vibration mixed with the stomach-tingling dips and sways of a private plane.

Sully was yelling again, but not this time because of the engines' roar. "Goddamnit! I've never seen anything like it. In all the years I've practiced law . . ." He couldn't finish his sentence. Sully sputtered and shouted again. "Goddamnit!"

I felt Kai-Li's fingers squeeze my shoulder. I shook my head, and she withdrew her hand.

It had been a red-letter day for the forces of good.

The Auburn clerk from Tiger Tooth Photo had appeared in all his pious, injured glory. The police detective assigned to Chris Galerina's homicide investigation had driven up from Mobile to introduce evidence that my fingerprints were on the murder/suicide weapon. The three dour members of the disciplinary committee had accepted into evidence the highway patrol's pictures of my wrecked Jeep—whatever the hell that had to do with anything. They had accepted articles from four newspapers outlining my alleged involvement in Galerina's death; they had accepted twice that many news clippings reciting the facts surrounding the unsolved murder of my drug-dealing younger brother a year earlier; and they had readily accepted into evidence news stories and court records reciting my admitted guilt in the self-defense killing of someone who may or may not—according to the record—have been instrumental in my brother's murder. The committee had even accepted as relevant evidence an affidavit from my former law firm stating that I had been "a gifted attorney whose poor impulse control and capricious temper had stalled an otherwise promising career."

The only thing the committee had excluded from evidence as "wholly irrelevant" was Dr. Kai-Li Cantil's research, which meant her testimony also was irrelevant to the proceedings and was not heard.

The hearing had lasted just over two hours. And, by the end of it, even I was beginning to agree with one committee member's statement that I was "perhaps too volatile and unpredictable for the solemn and demanding life of a counselor at law."

Sully shattered my thoughts. "You know, we've got fourteen days before the committee publishes its decision. And we can appeal to the courts after that. But I don't wanna have to appeal a bullshit lynching like the one we saw this afternoon." He paused and said, "We can do a hell of a lot in fourteen days, Tom."

I nodded.

Sully cut his eyes at me. Pale light from the control panel deepened twin furrows above his nose. "You *are* going to keep fighting this, aren't you?"

I nodded again.

"We cannot let them get away with this, Tom."

"We won't," I said. "It's a control issue."

Twenty-one

WHEN KAI-LI AND I pulled onto my driveway a little before eight that evening, I thought I'd taken a wrong turn. A small spotlight—which was something I didn't know I had—highlighted a holly-encircled front door, which, in its center, held a fat wreath covered with nuts, pine cones, ribbons, and other seasonal knick-nacks.

Kai-Li smiled. "Did you have this done?"

I said, "Nope," and stepped down out of the Safari.

By the time we mounted the steps, Joey opened the front door. "How'd it go?"

I shook my head. "Not good."

Joey stood blocking the door. He was thinking. "We'll just come at 'em a different way."

"Tomorrow morning," I said. "I've got an idea."

Joey made a noise, getting ready to speak, and was interrupted by a seemingly sober Sheri Baneberry, popping her head around his shoulder. "Come around to the beach." Sheri squeezed by Joey and trotted down the front steps, where she paused on the walkway. "Come on."

Kai-Li caught my eye and gave me a look I didn't quite understand; then she turned and followed Sheri. Joey and I waited a few beats before bringing up the rear.

Joey whispered when he spoke. "We've been decorating." He didn't sound happy about it.

"Your idea?"

"Yeah, you know me—Martha Stewart with a dick."

"I'm guessing you were keeping her busy."

"Yeah, well. It started out like that and ended up the other way around."

Sheri led us around the house and to a point about twenty feet behind the lower deck, where she held out an upturned palm and gestured toward the house. I turned. A towering, Christmas-tree–shaped mass of tiny white lights twinkled at us through the beach-side windows.

Kai-Li said, "Wow. That really is beautiful." Then she gently poked me in the ribs.

"Yeah, it's great, Sheri. Thank you."

Sheri nodded. "It's not much in return for screwing up your life. But, for whatever it's worth . . ."

The next morning, December 10, the temperature in Point Clear was twenty-two degrees and snow flurries rolled across Mobile Bay—surely both signs of impending Armageddon. Eastern Shore residents enjoy the appearance of snow swirling over salt water perhaps two or three times a decade—and even then it's usually late in February when a warm front rolls headlong into a sudden freeze. I'd hardly ever seen the white stuff stick for more than a few hours, and I'd never seen it happen during the holidays. Perhaps pigs would fly later in the afternoon.

The day before, while I was being shamed in Montgomery, Joey had intercepted Sheri's friend, Bobbi Mactans, at my front door. Joey told me that Bobbi had screamed and spit and threatened him some—to which he had responded by explaining that he had absolutely no qualms about throwing a woman down my front steps. Bobbi had decided to leave.

Now, over breakfast, I tried to convince Sheri to take some personal days away from work. I wanted to keep her away from her friend until I had a better handle on the Cort clan.

"I can't."

"Why not?"

She looked at me as if I'd just asked why the sun comes up each morning. "Because I have responsibilities, Tom. You should understand that."

"Do you have any vacation days coming?"

"Well, yes. But that's not . . ."

"How many?"

Sheri's skin flushed at the base of her neck, just above the indentation between her collarbones. She reached up and patted at the hot skin without thinking. "We've been busy on an expansion. Not everyone . . ."

"How many *weeks* of vacation do you have saved up, Sheri?"

Her eyes flashed something like pride. "Five or six."

"You're kidding. How long have you worked there?"

"A little over three years. And during that time I've had three promotions. You don't move up like that lying on a beach, Tom."

"And you don't live very long with nothing in your life but work. Damn, Sheri. It sounds like you've taken less than a week's vacation in three years."

My client wouldn't meet my eyes.

I thought about telling her that no one employee is that important to a large corporation, that life is about balance, that no one ever lay on her death bed wishing she'd spent more time at work. Instead, I said, "What's more important right now, Sheri? Crunching numbers for an insurance company or finding your mother's killer?"

It was a lousy, manipulative thing to say—especially since I wanted her to take time off more so I could keep an eye on her than because her presence might be a boon to the investigation. But the comment worked, the way lousy, manipulative behavior often does. Sheri agreed to take some time off and help.

My young client was a personality type I'd seen too many times in my own profession—a perfectionist and workaholic with absolutely no clue of how to handle life and relationships outside the office.

After breakfast, Sheri insisted on cleaning up the dishes. She felt she had ruined my career. I, on the other hand, felt that I had turned a simple wrongful death investigation into a major cluster-fuck. Between the two of us, the kitchen fairly oozed with guilt.

Later, Sheri and Kai-Li retired to the living room where they swapped sections of the *Mobile Register*. Joey left to gather more information on Zion Thibbodeaux.

I sat in my study wondering if it was time to call Judge Luther Savin.

My plan was to get the judge on the phone and throw around the Cajun's name, maybe make up some lies about how closely the judge had been tied to Chris Galerina, and see if anything stuck to the wall.

Then the phone rang.

"Tom?"

I said I was.

"This is Luther Savin, with the . . ."

"Court of Criminal Appeals."

He paused. "Uh, yes. That's right. Have I caught you at a bad time?"

"Yes," I said, "but not the way you mean it. I was sitting here thinking about calling you."

The judge paused again. "Are things beginning to add up for you, Tom?"

Now I paused.

Judge Savin laughed. "You think you're the only smart lawyer in the state?" He paused only for effect. "I tried to get you early on in this thing, Tom. Are you ready now to sit down and have a little talk?"

I noticed that, like the politician he was, the judge managed to use my first name in every other sentence. I said, "I just came from Montgomery last night . . ."

"I know."

"And I'm not much in the mood to go back." I glanced over at the recorder Joey had hooked up to my phone after my brother was killed. I punched the red record button. "Can't we just talk about this now and save me a trip?"

"You should learn to switch that thing on without

stopping to think about it. It makes for a telling and pregnant pause the way you do it."

I found myself stopping once again to digest what he'd said.

Judge Savin seemed to know too much and I too little. I needed Joey to finish his investigation and bring me up to speed on both Zion Thibbodeaux and the Russell & Wagler law firm before I stepped into a pissing contest with the judge.

Finally, I said, "I'm not coming back up there today. I need a day or two to make arrangements."

The judge chuckled, and the phrase, *a right jolly old elf*, flashed across my thoughts the way silly things do.

He said, "You don't *need* a couple of days, Tom. You just want 'em. Anyway, you don't have to ask Mister Walker to fly you up to the capital again. I came to you. I'm just up the road from you right now. I believe you know how to find the Mandrake Club."

A light snow swirled in the air like lint around a cotton gin, clinging to my clothes and dusting the dark needles of longleaf pines along the walkway to the clubhouse. The prancing copper horse at the roof's apex swivelled in abrupt quarter-arcs as if unsure of where to go. I ducked under the covered veranda and made my way to the front door, where my old friend, Harvey, tipped his hat and opened the door.

It was 2:00 on a weekday afternoon. It was freezing outside. The place was empty. I said, "Hello," to the nothingness, and a young woman appeared.

"Guess that's the password."

She wrinkled her forehead. "I'm sorry?"

"I'm here to see Judge Savin."

"Oh. Yes. Straight back and down the corridor to your left. The men's locker room will be the second door on your right."

I thanked her and went straight back to the corridor on *my* left. Inside the locker room—perched on a wooden bench that ran the length of parallel rows of lockers—was the Honorable Luther Savin, Chief Judge of the Alabama Court of Criminal Appeals. He wore nothing but a white terrycloth towel around his waist, and he looked, for all the world, like a pink, bearded Buddha. On either side of him stood his Backstreet Boys rejects, Chuck and Billy—the same two who had "insisted" I join the judge for lunch when I'd picked up the bar association disk for Kai-Li.

The judge beamed. "Hello there. Good to see you, Tom."

Something white and hot flickered at the back of my mind. I know myself enough to know there's something about old rich guys that triggers animosity in me. I even know myself well enough to have a pretty good idea why that is.

I just looked at Judge Savin. He smiled. Then he stood and walked out of the room.

I looked at Frick and Frack, Donnie and Marie, Chuck and Billy. "That was interesting."

Billy, the angry blond, squared off in front of me. "Take your clothes off."

I felt my sphincter tighten. Not much. Just a little. "I've gotta tell you, I'm more of a dinner-and-a-movie-first kind of guy."

Billy flushed. "Do it."

"I don't think so."

"I can make you."

I looked at his partner. "I thought you were the smart one, Chuck. Can you do something about this?"

Chuckie shrugged. "I think I'll let you and Billy work it out."

Billy grinned; then he stepped forward and threw a long, looping right at my jaw. I brought up my left fist next to my ear and took a decent blow on my shoulder. Pivoting while he was still off balance, I shot my right hand up between his cocked fists and grabbed him by the throat. Planting my foot and driving with my leg, back, and arm, I slammed Billy's gelled blond head into the steel door of a locker.

He collapsed. He wasn't unconscious. But he wasn't exactly conscious either.

I looked up at Chuck. "You want me to undress too?"

He nodded. "Yeah. As a matter of fact, I do. We," and he pointed over his shoulder in the direction the judge had gone, "would like you to join us in the steam room."

"Very Sam Giancana." I motioned at Billy with my chin. "That didn't have to happen. All you had to do was explain."

"Billy takes some handling. Ever since you embarrassed us by heading back to Auburn instead of coming along to the judge's house, he's been talking about 'straightening your shit out,' as he puts it. You were gonna have to deal with him sooner or later. I thought you might as well get it over with."

"So, slamming him unconscious is going to make him *less* angry? Is that your story?"

"Mr. McInnes, Billy's pure trash. The judge wouldn't

like me saying it. But that's just the way it is." He nod-ded at the crumpled form of his unconscious cohort. "And I learned a long time ago that little Billy here doesn't respect anyone who isn't as violent as he is."

"Does he respect you and the judge?"

Chuck smiled. "Please, remove your clothes. The, um, the meeting is waiting."

I reached under my shirt and peeled loose the minia-ture tape recorder that Kai-Li had helped tape to my chest. Chuck held out his palm. I handed the tiny ma-chine over. He popped the tape out and dropped it into his shirt pocket.

"Okay," I said, "where's my locker?"

Twenty-two

JUDGE LUTHER SAVIN'S rotundity shrank the steam room. He looked past me at the mostly naked young man who had followed me in. "Chuck. Step outside. Make sure we're not interrupted."

I kept my eyes trained on my host. A puff of cool air washed over my bare back when Chuck exited the room. I heard the *thud* of the door and crossed to the far wall, where I planted my towel-wrapped butt on redwood planks and leaned my head and naked shoulders against a checkerboard of white tiles. I wanted a place where no one could get behind me—like Doc Holiday in a Tombstone saloon.

Judge Savin asked, "Nervous?"

"Careful."

The chief judge was covered from the neck down with a fine spray of white hair, as if he had shaved a white cat and rolled in the clippings. A spiky Vandyke covered his chin and pointed neat white arrows along his jaw. The close fringe of hair above his ears looked starched. Thick, snowy eyebrows curved upward into peaks near his temples.

I tried to be friendly. "Billy's an idiot."

Savin nodded.

"Why do you keep someone like that around?"

Savin hunched forward and looked at the floor. "He's my son." There was no apology or excuse in his tone, just a statement. Some time passed. I tried to imagine the trouble the kid must have given the old man, then realized I didn't care.

The benches were tiered where the judge sat, and he leaned back against the next bench up. Hot steam swirled around his head like heavy smoke when he moved. "How much do you know?"

"How much do I know about what?"

He thought about that, looking down at swirls of white fur on his hard round belly. "Chris Galerina offered you some money. I don't know how much, but I'm guessing it was a pretty good chunk of change."

He stopped for me to say something. I just looked at him.

"At any rate, he made an offer that you either turned down *or* he thought you were going to turn down. Either way, the poor jerk figured his life was shot and put a bullet in his brain."

He paused again, and I nodded.

The judge wiped drops of sweat from his bright pink face with thick palms. An ornate gold ring bearing a two-carat blood ruby cut into the pudgy little finger of his left hand. "Let me tell you a story, Tom. And to understand this story, you need to forget about being Law Review at Duke, which is what you were, and think about being another kind of lawyer. Can you do that, Tom?"

I shrugged. "I don't see why not."

"Good. Good. In this story, Tom, you're a young guy working as a bank teller or an insurance salesman or maybe even a common laborer by day—every day of your life, if you get my point. And you want something better. You see all these lawyers driving around town in Mercedeses and BMWs, spending money, getting the good-looking tail, you know, the well-kept women with StairMaster asses and silicone tits.

"So you apply to one of the unaccredited night schools. And you work your butt off. You study hard. Give your life up for three or four years to get a law degree. And guess what?"

He stopped and looked at me, so I said, "What?"

"Nobody'll hire you. You beat the pavement, mail out résumés, and still no one cares. So you find a plaintiff's lawyer who'll give you a few loser cases to hustle. And, guess what? You find out you're good at it. You know how to talk to common folk because you are one. So you push and push and push some more until you make it to a bigger, more lucrative firm, and on to another one after that. Years pass and you're doing fine. But you're never doing as fine as you want to be."

I decided to join in the conversation. "Who is?"

The judge nodded. Sweat pellets flipped off his nose. "Who indeed, Tom? But, in this story I'm telling, you *find* the answer. You stumble onto the golden ring. All you gotta do is pull it, and out's going to fall all the Kraut cars and silicone knockers you ever dreamed of.

"You see, Tom, what you did was figure out that a hell of a lot of cases are lost—that poor, injured plaintiffs

are forever denied justice—because *only* one or two obstinate, misguided jurors hold out for the defendant.

"At first, you're tempted to try a bribe or two. After
all, what's a bribe when you're fighting to keep a wrong-
fully injured client off welfare. Like everything in the
law, it's really more an issue of balancing wrongs than it
is balancing competing rights." He paused—but just for
a second as his eyes searched my face. "But, Tom,
bribery's not only wrong, it's also dangerous. You've got
to worry about wires and undercover stings and all sorts
of nasty interferences. And the last thing you want is to
get busted and—if you're lucky enough to stay out of
prison—go back to working at the bank or the insurance agency or maybe loading spools at the textile mill.

"But here comes the good part. Someone—someone who comes *quietly* recommended by one or two of
the richest lawyers in the state—comes to you and says:
'Look, Tommy, how'd you like it if your win ratio improved by twenty or thirty points? You won't win 'em
all, but you'll win more than you ever dreamed of.'

"You'd listen to something like that, wouldn't you,
Tom?"

I shifted my weight—the hot planks were making an
impression—and wiped sweat out of my eyes. "I'd be
curious."

Through the white haze of manufactured steam, I
could see the judge bobbing his round head up and
down. "Damn right you would! And here's the
kicker—nobody gets hurt."

The judge's skin had grown progressively redder in
the searing heat, and his white beard and horned eyebrows stood out in stark contrast to the shiny flush that
enveloped him.

Now, his voice rose and took on a slight echo in the tiny room. "*You* win. Your poor, injured schmuck of a *client* wins. And the corporate bad guys get what they have coming. And you get all this because one or two obstinate jurors get nothing more dangerous than a well-timed stomach bug or a case of the trots." He held his palms in the air. An overhead bulb caught the ruby and momentarily threw crimson patterns on the tiled floor between us. "That's it. The juror standing between you and the truth gets excused from jury duty due to illness, and someone—an alternate with better sense—takes her place."

I leaned forward and propped my elbows on my knees. "But who makes them sick? Is it this Zybo, this Zion Thibbodeaux, from Louisiana?"

When I mentioned the Cajun's name, Judge Savin wrinkled his forehead in puzzlement and swayed his whiskered jowls from side to side as if trying to make sense of nonsense.

I marched ahead. You never know if someone will answer a question until you ask it. "And, obviously, jury deliberations are private. How would you know whose soup to cough in?"

The judge leaned forward again, mirroring my posture, and rubbed his meaty palms together. "Hard to say, Tom. I'm really talking about a hypothetical situation here. Heck, Tom, this isn't even my area. I'm a criminal judge."

Judge Savin paused.

I wondered if he'd caught the double meaning in his words and stumbled. But his round, flushed, politician's face revealed nothing but total concentration on his subject.

He went on. "*All* I'm doing here, Tom, is proposing an *idea*—a, ah, *fiction*—to get you to examine your actions from a different perspective."

"Well, you're definitely getting me thinking, judge."

"Good. Good. While you're at it, consider this: With this alternate, hypothetical path to justice, if you will, no one *ever* dies. Not by design. Not by error. It *cannot* happen."

And that, I realized, was the crux of it. *That* was the central message of Judge Savin's sermon. *No one dies. Not by our hand.* We both sat still. Soft lines of perspiration traced fine lines across the bare skin of my chest and legs—tickling like the touch of an insect's legs.

I decided to ask a practical question. "By any chance, is part of this thinking I'm doing going to help me keep my license to practice law?"

The judge hoisted his girth off the bench and flashed a practiced smile. "You never can tell, Tom. You never can tell. Could do that *and more.* You try cases before juries, don't you, Tom?" Then he opened the door and walked out, trailing a swirling train of steam in his wake.

And now I'd said the magic words: *Will this help me keep my license?* My host's work was done. He'd made his point about Kate Baneberry's death. I'd gotten the hint about how to hang on to my law practice and maybe even join the poison-a-juror club to boot.

He was gone; so I sat and thought. It's what he wanted me to do. Some things were making sense. Some weren't. Just like real life.

I breathed in thick lungfuls of heat, and the dark bruise Zybo had punched into my chest pinched and throbbed with each expansion. I held up my palm and blew steam at it to feel the burn.

When I finally stood and crossed the tiled floor, young Billy Savin's face greeted me through the tiny, double-glass window in the insulated door. He was wearing a demonic grin and holding the door closed. Billy had watched too much bad TV. I reached over to the left and pushed the round red *help* button. The club had followed the common practice of installing one—like the ones you see in garage elevators—to assist older members who sometimes have a tendency to stroke out in the sauna.

Then, resting on the assumption that I had summoned someone from somewhere, I sat back down to sweat some more. Maybe thirty seconds passed before the deep voice of Harvey, the doorman, echoed through the locker room. He was yelling at Billy.

"Heah, now! Young man! What you think you're doin' there?"

"I'm Judge Savin's guest."

The waiter didn't look as though he believed me. "Judge Savin has left the club, *sir*."

"Thanks." I tried smiling. "But I'm still here, and I'd like some coffee, please."

The waiter smiled, but he didn't mean it. He went to get coffee.

I was alone.

The judge had disappeared immediately after our semi-naked conversation, taking Chuck with him. Then, when Harvey freed me from steamy incarceration, Billy Savin had run like a kid caught smoking in the boys' room.

Now the waiter appeared and placed a cup and

saucer on my table. He added my own little stainless steel coffee pot. I had planned to order a late lunch—something expensive—and charge it to the judge, but just then Dr. Laurel Adderson walked in and sat down across the table from me.

She smiled. "What can I do for you?"

I tried to read her. "What do you mean?"

"Luther Savin told me you were looking for me."

A faint bulb warmed a corner of my brain. "That's interesting. Is *Luther* a friend of yours?"

A light blush crept up the powdered cheeks of fifty-ish, unflappable Dr. Adderson. "Why, yes. I...I've known Luther Savin for years."

"Is he staying with you while he's down here?"

Now her eyebrows arched, and the old Dr. Adderson reappeared. "I can't see where that's any of your business. Luther said you wanted to see me. Please get to the point, Tom."

"We're at the point, Laurel. We were at the point as soon as you walked in."

"You may still need to see that psychiatrist, Tom." Laurel Adderson pushed back from the table, but as she stood, curiosity got the better of her. "So, what *is* the point I made by walking into my own club's dining room?"

I was growing angry, and I wasn't precisely sure why. "He's everywhere. That's the point, Laurel. Your friend, Judge Luther Savin, is everywhere. And there's nowhere for me to turn that he hasn't gotten to ahead of me. That's what your friend *used* you to convey."

Dr. Adderson's cheeks blushed a deeper red. "I think you may be crazy, Tom. I really do."

"Yeah," I said, "it's sure starting to look that way."

Twenty-three

CLOSE NOW TO the shortest day of the year, I drove through a deepening lavender dusk from Daphne to Point Clear. Inside the beach house, Sheri had lit the tree and lit herself a little with a "holiday cocktail"—something in a mug with steam that smelled of rum and cloves. Kai-Li was holed up in my study, staring intently into some corner of the Internet.

Being the host, I wandered into the kitchen with the vague idea of whipping up something for dinner. I opened the refrigerator. Nothing volunteered to be eaten. I closed it again, found a mug, and poured myself a little holiday cocktail of my own from a boiler on the stovetop where Sheri had concocted the stuff. The first two sips were good—the heat helped, and the spices screwed up the muscles at the points of my jaw—but that was enough. The drain got a holiday cocktail. I poured some scotch over ice and ordered a pizza.

As I wandered through the living room, Sheri looked up from a Stephen King novel to say hello.

"I ordered pizza."

She smiled. "Sounds good."

I was almost out of the room when I decided to open my mouth. "Sheri?"

She looked up, her eyebrows raised in an open and helpful way.

The club chair next to the sofa was empty. I sat in it. "Mind if I ask you a few questions. Some . . . some personal information?"

Sheri marked her page with the dust cover and dropped the book on the cushion next to her hip. "Shoot."

"Did you get along with your mother and father?"

Her medium brown eyes scanned the room and came to rest on a charcoal seascape over the fireplace. "As well as most people get along with their parents, I guess. When I was little, I thought they were the most perfect people on earth. When I was a teenager, I decided they were idiots. Starting in college, I concluded they were probably somewhere in the middle with the rest of us."

"Nice noncommittal answer."

She shrugged.

I took in a mouthful of scotch and swallowed hard. "What'd they think of your relationship with Bobbi?"

Sheri's cheeks and forehead, even her neck, blushed red. "What's that supposed to mean? What'd Mom and Dad think of their lesbo daughter? Is that what you're asking me?"

The question was on the table. Nothing to be gained by taking it back now. "I guess it is."

My client turned on the hateful smile I'd seen in my office. "Are you telling me that's relevant to the case?"

My fingers were numb from the ice. I switched the tumbler to my left hand and swirled the whiskey so I'd have something to look at besides an angry houseguest. "Could be."

"Look at me, Tom."

I met her eyes.

"I am *not* sleeping with Bobbi."

I nodded. I didn't believe her, and I was pretty sure it showed.

Sheri's angry grin faded. She picked up the luke-warm remnants of her own drink, killed it, and cleared her throat before speaking. "I've known Bobbi all my life. Her father wasn't there much when she was growing up, and he tended to be a bastard when he was. My father wasn't like that. Bobbi figures all men are evil. I don't." She tried to take another pull on her toddy and found it empty. "I really don't know if Bobbi likes women so much as she hates men. Maybe she's in love with me. I don't know about that either. But it's not like that, and she knows it's not ever *going* to be like that."

I nodded and got to my feet. All I could think to say was, "Sorry. I'm trying to figure some things out."

She pushed forward onto the edge of the sofa. "You do believe me, don't you, Tom?"

And I realized that I did. "You haven't lied to me yet."

My bland young client smiled wanly, picked up her mug, and went in search of alcohol. I went in search of Kai-Li.

* * *

Across the room, the study door was open. And, through the doorway, Kai-Li looked much like she had the first time I'd seen her. She wasn't sitting on the floor, but she did have her head bowed over the laptop on my desk, holding her head in her hands and gently massaging her temples.

I interrupted. "What are you working on?"

She glanced up with an expression devoid of comprehension. Kai-Li rubbed at her eyes and stretched her arms over her head, cocking her jaw to the side and shuddering a little. I was beginning to believe the professor's depth of concentration approached another state of consciousness.

"Thomas."

That, I thought, *is new.*

She smiled. "How was your meeting with Judge Savin?"

"Threatening, informative, vague. Pick one."

"I need details."

I gave her the three-minute version. She asked some questions I didn't have answers to.

I asked, "Are you doing anything that can't be interrupted?"

"No." She pushed away from my desk and stretched again. "Just running searches on Judge Savin and Zion Thibbodeaux."

"Find anything?"

She shrugged. "Everything and nothing. Like most public officials, the judge's name brought up reams of news articles, campaign stuff, important legal decisions he'd penned. Mr. Thibbodeaux's activities, on the other hand, have not penetrated the World Wide Web."

I walked around the desk. "Let me try something."

Kai-Li got out of the desk chair and propped her right buttock on the edge of the desk as I took her place. All she said was, "What?"

"Tummy bugs and backdoor trots."

She laughed. "Sounds like cockney."

I clicked on favorites and went to Yahoo! In the search box, I typed *Black Angel of Death* and hit enter. Kai-Li scanned the screen over my shoulder. She didn't ask questions or wonder out loud or even fidget. She sat and concentrated on the listings.

A small, unpolished nail bumped the screen. "Try that one."

I clicked on *serialkiller.com*. As the site opened, the pumping rhythm of a heartbeat pulsed through the speaker. Black-and-white mug shots filled the screen. The rush of labored, obscene-caller breathing and the muffled footfalls of someone running on pavement mixed with the thumping heartbeat. I turned off the speaker.

A graphic designed to look like blood on concrete spelled out: WELCOME TO SERIALKILLER.COM—HOME OF THE WORLD'S BEST.

As the page loaded, Kai-Li pointed again. "Oh, my Lord. Look at that. There's a place to order mug shot trading cards. Who would want..." Her voice trailed off.

"I don't think I want to know. Look." I pointed to a link at the bottom of the page: EXTREME TORTURE AND SADISM—ADULTS ONLY. In the search box at the top of the page, I repeated my query. Seconds passed. "Slow," I said.

"Must have lots of traffic." Kai-Li shuddered and walked around the desk to sit on the tufted leather sofa. "I've seen enough of that."

The page popped up. This time, the same finger-dipped-in-blood font spelled out the title on a black background: BLACK ANGEL OF DEATH.

I started reading. Seconds passed.

Kai-Li broke the silence. "What's it say? I mean," she hesitated, "does it say anything useful?"

"Maybe."

"Is it about Zion Thibbodeaux?"

"Oh." I realized Kai-Li had the wrong idea. "No, no. This is something Dr. Adderson mentioned early on when she was, I think, just kind of grasping at straws to explain what had happened to Kate Baneberry. When I asked how Mrs. Baneberry could have died without anyone knowing it was murder, she said to read up on the Black Angel of Death."

"So." She sat up straight and searched my eyes. "What's it say?"

"You want the details?"

"Absolutely not."

"Okay, then. What it says it that some limp-dick nurse in New York murdered at least ten hospital patients by injecting something called Pavulon—whatever the hell that is—into their IVs."

Kai-Li stood. "It's a paralytic agent."

"Yeah, it says here they found one of his victims gasping for breath."

She grimaced. "Paralyze the muscles, and the patient suffocates. The really hideous thing about that particular drug is that the patient remains mentally alert and fully aware of what's happening."

"Oh."

"Yes. Oh," she said. "And there's a variation on the theme. Sometimes the killer gives a paralytic agent to the victim and then administers a potassium push so the death looks more natural."

"What's a potassium push?"

"A syringe of concentrated potassium solution. The idea is that the paralytic agent—some of which are absorbed by the body with no trace—keeps the victim from convulsing when the potassium is administered."

"But the potassium..."

"Is a naturally occurring substance within the body and would not set off alarms during the autopsy."

I logged off the Internet, shut down the laptop, and closed the cover. As I shoved the laptop away from me, Kai-Li motioned at the computer with her chin. "Are you going to burn it, too?"

I hadn't thought about what I was doing. "Maybe just hose it off." I stood up. "Look, you seem to know about this stuff."

"Just what I've read."

"Well, tell me this, what does this potassium push—which I guess is what actually kills the person—what does it do? I mean, I understand the killer is giving the victim too much of the stuff. But what is the actual cause of death?"

"Oh. I thought you got that from the web page." Kai-Li turned toward the living room. Over her shoulder, she said, "The flood of potassium causes cardiac arrest. You know, a heart attack."

★ ★ ★

Endless dreams of floating, serial-killer trading cards had filled the night, leaving me feeling a little grumpy—and a little ridiculous. You never know what's going to get to you.

"I want someone inside Russell and Wagler."

Joey had come over with a handful of paperwork on a Mr. Zion Thibbodeaux and ended up joining Kai-Li and me for breakfast. Sheri was still sleeping off her holiday cocktails. When the food was gone, the three of us had wandered into the living room to talk things over.

Kai-Li said, "I could do it. Law firms have a huge turnover in secretaries. I could just walk in . . ."

I interrupted. "And say, 'Hello. I have a Ph.D. in behavioral psychology and can type eighty words a minute.'"

Kai-Li sat up a little straighter. "Well, as a matter of fact, I can. And I wouldn't have to give them the right name."

Joey sat his mug of morning coffee on the end table and leaned forward. "Wouldn't work. If we're right about what they're doin', these folks are breakin' the law seven ways to Sunday. They'd be bein' careful, and they'd check you out and find out you volunteered evidence at Tom's hearing that they been buyin' juries."

Kai-li said, "I wouldn't have to give them my real name, I could . . ."

Joey was shaking his head.

"Who then?" A note of aggression had crept into Kai-Li's voice. She wanted to play undercover cop and wasn't happy about Joey's attitude.

Joey answered her with two words. "Loutie Blue."

Kai-Li asked, "Who is Loutie Blue?"

Joey was on to something. I said, "Can she type?"

Kai-Li asked again, "Who are we talking about?"

Joey looked at me. "Yeah, she can type. Used to work some as a temp after she stopped stripping."

Kai-Li stood up and raised her voice. "Who the hell is Loutie Blue and why was she stripping?"

Joey looked amused. "You don't know Tom that well, but he dates a lot of strippers. Poor bastard proposes marriage to one about once a month."

I told Joey to shut up and then explained that Loutie Blue was Joey's best operative, *his* girlfriend, and someone who once took her clothes off for a living.

Kai-Li crossed her arms. "And I guess it doesn't matter if she can type because she's such an unbelievable babe that they'll hire her just for office decoration."

I looked at Joey, and he nodded. "That's about the size of it."

Kai-Li turned to leave the room. On the way out, I'm pretty sure I heard her utter the word "neanderthals."

A few minutes later, Joey left to make arrangements for Loutie Blue to wear something short and tight to the offices of Russell & Wagler Monday morning. Knowing Kai-Li was smart as hell and wanted to be useful, I handed over Joey's research on Zybo and asked her to take another whack at the Internet.

An hour later, when my sleepy and slightly hungover guest, Sheri Baneberry, stumbled into the kitchen and poured a cup of coffee, I carefully explained to her exactly why she was going to fire me. To her credit, she thought it was a hell of an idea.

Twenty-four

FREEZING RAIN HAD fallen the night before. Now, as Sheri Baneberry bid us farewell, a light snow blew in from the bay, spreading a perfect white sheet across slick roads and crystalized winter grass.

Back inside, Sheri's lighted tree filled the house with some kind of hope. Logs crackled in the fireplace. I walked into the study, unlocked the gun closet, and pulled out insulated boots and a heavy Marmot ski coat with fleece lining. I grabbed a hunting cap off the top shelf.

Kai-Li stuck her head into the room as I was dressing to go out. "You look like Elmer Fudd."

"I was thinking more Jeremiah Johnson."

She propped her hip against the door frame, crossed her arms, and smiled. "I'm sticking with Elmer."

"I'm going to check outside."

She didn't ask a lot of questions. And she didn't lecture when I pulled my Browning nine-millimeter out of a drawer, loaded the clip, and seated it in the gun. She simply nodded.

As I walked through the living room to the front door, I spied my twenty-gauge over-and-under leaning in one corner. It was stupid, really. I'd relied on the bird gun for protection—carrying it from downstairs to upstairs at night, keeping it empty, carrying shells in my hip pocket—instead of arming myself properly.

My father told me as a kid, "If you've got a handgun, you'll be tempted to use it when you could better talk your way out of trouble. Or when a bigger guy takes a swing at you, it's easier to reach for a gun than take a beating. But," he said, "the prisons are full of people who would rather've had a hundred ass whippings than to've pulled a trigger and ruined their lives."

Sam was never a font of fatherly advice, but I'd always remembered that one. And, truth be told, up until now I hadn't worried about getting shot by the Cajun. He could have done that any time he wanted. Instead, the man had locked into my fears with waking nightmares—what my mother used to call "daymares"—of vile poisons and blind-alley attacks and, worst of all, horrible mental pictures of my disabled form lying in a hospital bed at the mercy of shadowy strangers.

But now, things were beginning to come together. Loutie Blue would, with any luck, be in one camp with Russell & Wagler and their ties to Judge Savin; Sheri would be in another, sitting by her father's side where she could keep an eye on Jonathan Cort and company; and it would be up to Joey to find out enough about the final point of the triangle, Zion Thibbodeaux, to give us the edge and the opportunity to fold one of the triangle's points in on itself.

I pulled open the front door and stepped back out into the frigid December air. Tiny, drip-shaped icicles lined bannisters and hung from the front edges of snow-powdered steps. Stepping carefully down the steps and out to the driveway, I paused and looked for tracks. I could see Sheri's small footprints leading up to the tire treads of the taxi that took her away. Nothing else.

The plan was to make a straight-line walk of my property's perimeter—not to wander around leaving a confusion of footprints. Nature, or maybe Santa Claus, had been nice enough—finally—to powder the ground so that anyone approaching my house would leave tell-tale prints. The least I could do was not screw it up.

Frozen turf snapped and squeaked beneath rubber soles, bouncing small echoes into the empty afternoon air. Pausing every twenty yards or so, I swept my eyes over the yard and then the beach. I stared down the shoreline, looking for nothing in particular, and watched my breath fog against the charcoal water of Mobile Bay. My neighbor's floating Christmas tree bobbed out on the bay, and I wondered how in the hell they lit something like that. Finally, after trudging through snow-covered brush along the far side of the house, I found what I hadn't wanted to find. And I found it in the place where I had started my armed search.

Just inside the driveway, maybe a hundred feet from where I stood, sat a generic, black automobile. And leaning against the center of the hood was Mr. Zion Thibbodeaux. Zybo to his friends.

Fingering the nine-millimeter in my pocket with freezing fingers, I walked across the front of the house and stopped at the walkway. Thibbodeaux had a long, heavy revolver in one gloved hand. The gun pointed at the ground. Inside my pocket, I eased the safety off the nine-millimeter.

He raised his empty hand and, with his palm facing the sky, made a cupping motion like he was squeezing a ball.

I raised my voice. "You want me to come there?"

He nodded.

I shook my head and pointed at a place midway between us.

He nodded again and began walking. His gun still hung loosely from his fingers, pointed at the ground but swinging in an arc as he walked.

I walked forward, feeling at once ridiculous and deadly—like a grown man playing at being a gunslinger.

Maybe he wanted to talk. Or maybe he just wanted me inside the killing range of his handgun. I had, after all, tried to pull his nuts off. But I didn't think he wanted me dead. If he had, as Joey said, I never would have seen him coming. Just in case, though, as we came within *my* killing range, I raised the barrel inside my pocket and aimed it at his chest.

When we were six or seven feet apart, he stopped. "Lower your muzzle." Puffs of fog followed each syllable into the winter air.

I never took my eyes from the oversized revolver hung casually from his gloved hand. "No." I breathed deeply and caught the barest whiff of something like the scent of smoke or soot coming off the man's dark clothing.

"Okay, Tommy. What you say I point mine at you to make it be fair?"

I moved my jaw from side to side without taking my eyes from his revolver. "That gun moves, even a little, and I'll empty my clip into your chest."

His free hand moved slowly to his crotch, and he gingerly gripped his package like a teenage rapper. "I owe you one."

"And I owe you about six."

He said, "Could be," and slowly moved the gun behind his back, where he tucked it into his waistband. "You met with Judge Savin."

"How would you know?"

"Don' waste time, Tommy. You and him had a sit down at de Mandrake Club. His two gofers dey were there. Yeah, I hear tell you taught dat Billy some manners."

I studied Thibbodeaux's dark eyes. "What's it to you, Zybo?"

Something small and serpentine flickered behind the Cajun's black irises when I said his name. "I wanna know what de old man he had to say."

"Ask him."

"I'm askin' you."

I was locked into his eyes, but tried to keep his black-gloved hands inside my peripheral vision. "You're asking me to screw my career."

Thibbodeaux smiled. "Screwed career. Fuggin dead. Up to you, Tommy."

I pulled the Browning out into plain view and pointed the muzzle at his nose. "Get off my property."

"I gotcha now." He nodded. "You don't tink I'm bein' serious, or you more nuts than I tought. Either way..." He stopped to think. "I believe I'm gonna nose 'round some. You get a call from somebody sayin' dey... what? Lookin' for a good university psychologist? Somethin' like dat. You know I wanna meet up."

I thought of Kai-Li inside the house. "You start threatening my friends and I'd just as soon shoot you right now."

Zybo grinned and held up gloved palms. "No threat, Tommy. Jus lettin' you know dat there's *nothin'* you do I don' know 'bout." He turned his back and walked away—slowly, deliberately. When Zybo reached the car, he turned to find my gun still trained on his head.

His coat and hair, even his gloves, were black. Standing there framed by ice and snow, the man looked uncannily like a raven in a winter field, like some physical manifestation of death. All he said was, "We be talkin', Tommy Boy."

His voice echoed across the frozen landscape. He climbed into his idling car and turned left toward Fairhope and Mobile or, just possibly, toward the Mandrake Club.

Zion Thibbodeaux was leaving. That was enough.

I waited to make sure he was really gone before turning toward the house. When I did, I found Kai-Li standing on the front porch, staring at me and shivering in jeans and a blue cotton turtleneck.

I walked up the steps. "Let's go inside."

She turned and went in ahead of me without speaking. When we were in the living room, warming ourselves by the fireplace, Kai-Li said, "That was the first time I've seen him."

I poked at embers from the fire I'd built that morning. "You okay?"

"Not really."

I placed the poker back in the wrought-iron rack. "Mr. Thibbodeaux's a scary guy."

She turned her bottom to the fire and looked out at the room. "It's not just that. Seeing him standing in the driveway brought home how real this is. I should've known after he gave you that beating on the beach. But, somehow, seeing him . . ."

I said her name, and she turned and looked into my face with those deep green eyes. "Would you like to go home?"

"There's nothing there." She was, I thought, talking about her daughter's holiday absence.

"There's safety."

Before I could expand on that bit of nonsense, she said, "I don't think that's true, Thomas."

I thought about arguing with her, but anything I said would've been a lie. And Kai-Li was plenty smart enough to have known it.

Some time passed. I moved the fire screen and put another log on the fire. Kai-li put the screen back. Then she reached out and touched my cheek. "How's your nose?"

"Fine."

"And your chest?"

"It's fine too."

She tilted her head. "What would happen if I thumped you in the middle of your chest right now?"

"Pain. Maybe some weeping on my part." I smiled. "It hurts, okay?"

"Okay." She kept her fingers on my cheek. "You're

a frightening person to spend time with, Thomas McInnes."

"I've heard that before."

She let her hand trail down to my shoulder. "I don't doubt that. It's your fatal flaw."

I started to speak. She put a finger against my lips and shook her head. Then Kai-Li turned and walked across the room, where she disappeared into my study. Seconds later, I heard her speaking quietly to someone on the phone.

Some time later, the phone rang and I came back from some faraway place. I'd been standing by the fire, thinking. I didn't know how long, but my pant legs burned my skin when I walked over to pick up the receiver.

"Hello?"

"It's me, Joey. Loutie got the job at Russell and Wagler. She's gonna be a receptionist."

"Good." I rubbed the stubble along my jaw with my free hand and tried to think. "Tell her to see if she can steal some stationery. We're also going to need some firm memo paper, a few old memos for forms, and some signature samples, especially Chris Galerina's. And see if she can lay her hands on one of those manila routing envelopes with the to-and-from lines on it. Every law firm I've ever seen uses them. I want one that's been circulated among some of the top partners. You know, with old names scratched out and new ones added."

"Got it. Anything else?"

I didn't answer. Memories of Kai-Li's frightened green eyes filled my thoughts, mixing with images of Zion Thibbodeaux swinging a knife on the beach, hiding along some imaginary dark path, and walking up my gravel drive as though it belonged to him.

Joey spoke. "What's wrong?"

"Other than the lost-my-license, accused-of-murder stuff? Zion Thibbodeaux was just here."

"You're shittin' me."

"No." I found myself scanning the beach through frosted windows. "I went out to check around the house. Make sure everything was okay. When I came back around from the beach, he was standing next to a car at the end of my driveway."

"You shoulda shot him."

"Thought about it."

Joey let a few seconds pass. "What'd he want?"

"He wanted to know what Judge Savin had to say when we met at the Mandrake Club."

"Think he got there followin' you or followin' the judge?"

I thought about that. "Probably me."

"Probably." More time passed while I let Joey work it out for himself. "The Cajun don't trust the judge. You think we can do somethin' with that?"

"Yeah," I said, "that's exactly what I think."

Twenty-five

GHOSTLY PATCHES OF white spun by in the night. Most of the snow and ice had turned to water in the late-afternoon sun, but there remained just enough white, scattered under evergreens and along the eastern side of hills and houses, to lend the night a feeling of magic, a feeling that, "If I reached my hands down, near the earth, I could take handfuls of darkness."

I glanced over to see Kai-Li watching the night, her profile barely visible inside the car. Then I turned back to watch the road. I needed to think.

Dr. Laurel Adderson lived in one of the too-perfect farmhouses I'd noticed outside Daphne on my first trip to the Mandrake Club. She'd said there would be a silhouette of a long-haired pointer mounted on the mailbox. She'd been right. I turned in and followed the red dirt-and-gravel road about two hundred yards, through a thinned pecan grove, before reaching the clapboard house.

I parked next to an ancient Jeep Wagoneer—the kind with wood grain along the sides—and cut the engine.

Kai-Li reached over and grasped my knee. I looked straight ahead and nodded at the house. "You sure you want to do this?"

"Why don't you look at me?" I turned to face her. She smiled, but it looked forced. "They already know about me. You said this Zybo character talked about a 'university psychologist' yesterday afternoon."

I nodded.

She asked, "And you think this is a good idea?"

"Well." I shrugged. "Let's just say it's *an* idea."

Kai-Li's smile seemed more genuine. "Well, so long as you've thought it out," and popped open her door.

Before we reached the threshold, Dr. Adderson's paneled front door swung open to reveal the doctor and Judge Luther Savin standing arm in arm like an old married couple, framed by the warm light behind them.

Judge Savin beamed. "Right on time. Wouldn't have expected anything less. Come on in."

At his side, Dr. Adderson looked disturbed or confused. I couldn't read her look. But, as we covered the last few steps of the walkway, Kai-Li leaned over and whispered in my ear. "Dr. Adderson looks pissed." And she had put her finger on it. Dr. Adderson seemed to understand that there was gamesmanship all around her, but I would have been willing to bet just then that she was clueless about the evil that shared her life and her bed. The doctor, it seemed to me, had the innocence of one who spends her days helping others.

The odd couple backed up so Kai-Li and I could step inside. But I paused in the doorway and held out my hand to the judge. He had to step forward to shake it. It made for an awkward moment, but it also made for a highly visible moment for anyone who might be watching us from the dark shadows of the pecan grove.

As the judge stepped back, I handed a bottle of my best cabernet—a 1996 Silver Oak—to the doctor. "You said venison?" I think I startled her.

"Ah, yes. That's right." She looked at the bottle. "Come on in."

Dr. Adderson handed off the wine bottle to Judge Savin, and he disappeared into some other part of the house. The doctor looked at Kai-Li. "Would you two like the grand tour?"

Now Kai-Li looked a bit startled. "Yes. Sure." She glanced at me. "We'd love to look around your home, Dr. Adderson."

"Please, call me Laurel. Why don't we start with the living room. I have some interesting glass pieces salvaged from a home in Savannah." And so it went. Everything in Laurel's house seemed to have a story behind it. And it was beautiful. At one point, Kai-Li leaned over to me and whispered, "This is depressing the hell out of me."

I smiled. "You should've gone to medical school."

She pursed her lips and turned to listen to the history of something called a breakfront. It was a piece of furniture I'd heard of but had never really known what it was. And when Laurel had finished her description and moved on to the next room, I still didn't. I was thinking.

* * *

Dinner was great—if, that is, your tastes run to foods that once had a heartbeat. In addition to the main course of grilled venison, there were bacon-wrapped quail breasts for appetizers, a seafood gumbo with andouille and a deep-fried, whole turkey on the table just in case someone didn't like deer meat.

I admit it. I ate a lot.

After a dessert of bananas foster, which I also ate, Judge Savin said the words I'd been waiting to hear. "Tom, you mentioned that you have some business you'd like to discuss."

As we stood up from the table, I asked, "Is there somewhere we can talk?"

The doctor volunteered her study, and Judge Savin led the way.

When we stepped inside, he turned to me and winked. "Was this on the tour?"

"No. We missed this one somehow."

"Too private." He nodded in the direction of the dining room. "I was surprised when she said we could use it."

I walked around the room. At least a dozen shotguns were hung from brass mounts on the walls. On an antique sideboard, Laurel had arranged a display of seven shooting trophies, which were mixed in with black-and-white photos of her hunting doves, quail, pheasants, and ducks in different locales. I said, "She likes her guns."

From behind me, he said, "She's good at it."

"I know. She took me shooting just after I first met her."

The judge chuckled. "I heard."

I pointed at a faded photo on the wall above the sideboard. The picture, which was about a foot square, was of a downed elephant. A man with a brush mustache and Hemingwayesque safari clothes sat atop the giant beast's rib cage, holding the rifle that was presumably the proximate cause of the great animal's demise. "Is this Laurel's father?"

"That's him. She thinks he hung the frigging moon." He stepped up to stand shoulder to shoulder with me and lowered his voice to a conspiratorial whisper. "Just between you and me, I hear he was the biggest sonofabitch ever to set foot on Southern soil."

I motioned at the picture again. "I guess he liked killing things."

"That bother you, Tom?"

I shook my head. "Not really. I don't think I'd get any pleasure out of killing something as majestic as that. But I've shot my share of ducks and quail. So I don't have any business lecturing anyone else."

The judge stepped away. When I turned, he was standing beside a tea cart and filling two snifters with cognac. He held one out. "I'm always amused by folks who bitch about hunting while they've got a stomach full of McDonald's, part of a cow's hide on their feet, and their money inside a piece of an alligator's underbelly."

I took in a healthy swallow of the cognac. "Moral consistency is not a characteristic of our species."

"Damn right." Judge Savin laughed. "Where's that come from?"

"I think I just made it up."

He laughed some more and then suddenly changed

demeanor the way someone can whose expressions of emotion aren't real. "Let me ask you this, Tom. Are you characteristic of the species?"

"I *try* to be moral, if that's what you're asking."

The judge plopped down in a tufted club chair. "Well, shit, Tom. We all fucking *try*. It's a more complicated question I'm asking."

"I've thought a lot about what you said the other day at the club." I reached inside my coat pocket and pulled out a manila, interoffice routing envelope with a half-dozen scratched out names on the routing list. I held it out to the judge, with the list of names turned away from him.

"You wouldn't be trying to bribe a state appellate judge."

"Of course not. Just look at it."

Judge Savin unwound a string on the back of the envelope and pulled out a folded sheath of papers.

I looked over his shoulder. "Sorry. I think they're in reverse order."

The judge snorted disgust, showing a bit of his true personality, and began thumbing through the papers—placing the top document on his knee and stacking each successive page on top to fix the order. As he proceeded, the judge worked slower rather than faster. Some of the forms and reports in the packet were ringing bells, and he was trying to think. I stood and watched him do it.

When he finished, Judge Savin was looking at the prison and arrest records of one Zion Thibbodeaux, a.k.a. Zybo. "What's this?"

"A background report on a Cajun hit man with a biochemistry degree from Southwest Louisiana State and one year of med school at Tulane. He spent a few years locked up in Angola for killing a man."

Judge Savin sat perfectly still. I could hear his breathing and mine. I could hear the ticking of the antique wall clock above Laurel Adderson's desk. Half a minute passed before he said, "I don't know why you're showing me this. I see too much of it. A young man with brains and a future gets drunk in the wrong place at the wrong time." He looked up with hooded eyes and handed me the papers. He almost whispered, "It's tragic, really."

I held the judge's eyes. "And it's a tragedy that could spread, judge."

He nodded. I placed the papers back in the envelope, slid the package inside my coat pocket, and sat down on a short sofa opposite the judge. I waited.

Finally, Judge Savin asked, "Is that yours, Tom? Did you have that report done?"

I moved my head from side to side. I lied.

"Then, just out of curiosity, how'd you come by it?"

"A dead lawyer gave it to me."

Judge Savin nodded. "That was nice of him."

The engine had cooled while we were inside. Joey's drug-dealing client had equipped his Safari-toy with heated seats. I flipped them on.

Less than twenty feet down the driveway, Kai-Li asked, "Did it work?"

"Who knows? His fingerprints are on every page. He knows Zybo's identity is out, and I as much as told him that I got the report from Chris Galerina. Doesn't mean he believed me, though."

"Still. You did what you came to do. And nothing went wrong." Kai-Li hugged her coat tight around her. "We smiled. We made nice. We gorged on inferior life forms. I'd say it was a successful night."

I turned onto the blacktop and pointed the grille toward home. "We'll see."

Kai-Li insisted she wanted coffee on the deck when we got home. It was thirty-four degrees outside, but I found myself pulling over in Fairhope to buy fresh beans.

Back in Joey's Safari-mobile, I could feel Kai-Li's eyes on me as I pulled out of the parking lot and turned toward home. Being the subject of so steady a gaze was both uncomfortable and comforting. I thought about that and about Susan Fitzsimmons in Chicago and about what happens when you find yourself working closely with someone who's sexually attractive to you.

And those thoughts were enough to keep me from picking up on a strange sight off the road to our right. I was nearing my driveway and had just clicked on the turn signal when Kai-Li spoke in a tone that communicated alarm without raising her voice. "Look! Look, quick! Is that your house?"

Twenty-six

YELLOW LIGHT FLASHED through rows of narrow evergreens along the roadside, like blinding headlights cutting between the cars of a moving train. I stepped on the accelerator, jammed the brakes at the turn, and skidded sideways onto gravel, where I punched the accelerator again. Two seconds later, I slammed on brakes and skidded to a stop fifty feet from my front door. I didn't say anything. Kai-Li saw everything I did.

She'd thought my house was on fire. I'd thought the same. It wasn't.

The front door stood wide open. The same was true for every window in the place, and all the blinds and drapes had been pulled aside. Bright light from inside, outside, and around the beach house threw a jumbled pattern of rectangles and trapezoids across grass and sand. Irregular patches of snow and ice shone like polished steel in the night.

I reached for the door handle. "Stay here, okay?"

Kai-Li's door popped open before mine. "No."

She was right. I had the gun. Why sit alone in an idling car? I pushed open my door and stepped out in one movement. I heard the sound even before my foot hit the ground.

Kai-Li stepped forward and spoke across the hood. "What's that?"

"Music."

She looked at me.

"It's . . . it's called Zydeco." I explained over the din. "It's Cajun music."

She listened. "It's recorded."

I nodded. I hadn't really thought there was a band in my living room, but people say funny things when they're scared.

Kai-Li walked around the front of the truck and stood beside me. "Thomas, this is where a smart person would leave and come back with the police."

I nodded again. I was studying the house through open windows and scanning the lighted yard.

Kai-Li put her hand on my arm. "This is what your friend in Birmingham was talking about, Thomas. You need to learn to back off sometimes." A few seconds passed as a falsetto yelp—backed by accordion, guitar, a scrub board, and a wailing harmonica—echoed across the yard. She turned to face the house. "You're going to go in there, aren't you?"

"I guess so."

"I changed my mind. I'm not going."

"Don't blame you." I waited for her to get into the driver's seat. I tapped on the window, and she rolled it down. "If something goes wrong or if it feels like I've been in there too long, head back to town. Find a place with lots of people—the grocery store where we stopped—and call the sheriff's office." I glanced up at the house. "Be careful."

Kai-Li shook her head. "I will never understand this American male thing."

"Yeah," I said, "me either."

I circled the house, staying to shadows when I could, then checked the Browning's safety and rushed in through the back door. The lamps were lit, the overhead lights were on, and my stereo speakers were pounding the glaringly bright house with Louisiana swamp music.

Zybo would expect me to go first to the stereo to get relief from the crashing cacophony, but I did it anyhow. The din was swirling my thoughts, and the too-bright house was more disconcerting than it would have been in darkness. I crossed the room and hit the power button on my receiver. Silence filled the room with the intensity of the music.

Now he knew for sure that I was there. I called out his name. "Zybo!"

A door closed upstairs. I moved to the stairwell and looked up to the second floor—to the place where I slept and bathed and occasionally made love—and thought about what a good place it would be for a killer to corner someone. Then I thought how much easier it would've been for Zybo to have plugged me stepping out of my car onto a dark driveway. I stopped to breathe and to think.

The lights. The music. This was something different. I started up the steps, slowly. A car horn blared, rippling nerve endings and scattering my thoughts—every thought but the image of Kai-Li sitting outside in Joey's Safari vehicle. Alone.

I was down the stairs in one stride, then through the house and out onto the porch too fast for someone expecting trouble. Glancing quickly at the driveway and scanning the yard like a running back clearing the line, I glimpsed of jumble of pictures—Kai-Li's form inside the Land Rover; gravel, sleet, and snow gleaming in the moonlight; dark grass edged with pale sand.

I caught the middle step with my toe as I leaped into the yard and sprinted fifty feet to the car. Kai-Li was inside. She stared at me through frosted glass. I looked at her. I straightened up to look once again at the empty yard. I heard the buzz of an electric motor. Kai-Li was rolling down the driver's side window.

Before she could speak, I said, "You scared the hell out of me." Then I stopped short. She was no longer looking at me. Her eyes moved in spastic rhythms, scanning the ground behind me. The fingers of her left hand moved against her temple the way they did when she focused on work, only now I could see the pale tips of her fingers trembling in the moonlight.

I looked around the yard again and then back down at her. This time I whispered. "What?"

Kai-Li didn't meet my eyes. She couldn't stop hers from roaming the yard. "He was here."

"Zybo?"

She nodded. "I think so. I didn't really see him. Just..." She started, and her breath caught up short. She pointed toward the beach and then shook her head. "I'm sorry. I thought I saw..."

I passed the Browning to my left hand and reached

through the window with my right to touch her arm. "Kai-Li? Look at me, Kai-Li."

She turned and held on to me with those amazing green eyes.

"I need to know what happened."

"He attacked the car. Maybe he was trying to get in. I'm not sure." She pointed back over her shoulder. "Look."

Frost clung to the side windows, blurring my view of whatever she was pointing at. I stepped back and walked to the rear bumper.

Just left of center, the back window had taken a blow from a heavy object—something like a pipe or a jack handle. A spider web of razor-sharp breaks radiated out from a six-inch circle of glass that looked now like crushed ice.

A line of light caught my eye, and I looked down at a thread of bare metal. I reached out to touch what I feared was a wire. Instead, my fingers ran across fresh scratches in the Land Rover's paint.

I asked Kai-Li to step on the brake pedal, and a red glow lighted large, misshapen letters gouged into the tailgate. Someone had scratched the word *IOWA* into the vehicle while Kai-Li sat inside deafened by swamp music.

I straightened up and, once again, scanned the yard, examining shadows, looking even harder for something out of place. There was nothing. There was, however, someone inside my house. Or, at least, there had been. Someone had closed a door.

I walked back around to Kai-Li's window. "Are you okay? Did any of the glass hit you?"

She took in a chest full of air and dropped her head

back against the headrest. "I felt some glass hit up here, but I don't think I have any cuts."

"There's someone inside the house. I heard a door close after I turned off the music."

This time Kai-Li reached through the window for my hand. "Can we please not be brave anymore? I'm scared, and you *should* be."

I tried to smile. "I am."

"Good." The strength was coming back into her voice. "I'm leaving. Are you coming?"

I pointed at the cell phone dangling from the dashboard. "How about if we call 911 and then just sit here and wait on the sheriff?"

Kai-Li said, "I'd rather leave," but she handed me the phone.

The deputy seemed like a nice guy. He went into the house alone, holding an oversized revolver in both hands. He came out shaking his head. Later, he even helped me close windows and turn off lights while Kai-Li called her ex in Iowa to make sure Sunny was okay. I could hear the tone and cadence of Kai-Li's voice change when she spoke with her daughter.

As Kai-Li spoke into the phone in hushed tones, the deputy spoke to me about whether I had a licensed firearm. He wanted to know if I had an alarm. He spent a lot of time looking at Kai-Li while he was supposed to be talking to me. He promised to drive by a couple of times during the night to keep an eye on the place. He left.

I walked out to the Land Rover to collect the coffee beans we'd stopped for in Fairhope. When I stepped back into the house, I dead-bolted the door and set the alarm before taking off my coat. I found Kai-Li standing by a window in the living room, looking out at the bay. I said, "It's pretty at night, isn't it?"

She looked over her shoulder and then turned back to the window before speaking. "I imagine, living here, it's pretty all the time."

"It is. How's Sunny? Everything okay there?"

She nodded. "Fine. They're spending Christmas at the farm of a woman Stephen is seeing. He says his parents and I are the only ones who know where he is."

"Does he live in Iowa? I mean, is he just spending the holidays there or does he live there all the time? Because if he's just there for the holidays . . ."

She ended my sentence, "That means whoever was here may know where my daughter is. But, no, I don't think that's it. Stephen teaches computer science at the University of Iowa. He's ninety miles away from the campus right now."

"So you're okay?"

She looked out over the bay and nodded.

"Do you still want coffee? I got the beans out of the car."

Kai-Li turned and stepped away from the window. "Do you have any cognac?"

"Sure. You want some in your coffee?"

She smiled. "I want some in a glass."

"Good idea."

She turned back toward the beach. "Best one tonight."

I was being reprimanded by the professor, which was fine. She'd earned the right. I walked into the kitchen and came back with two snifters of cognac.

"What about dinner with Judge Savin and Dr. Adderson?"

Kai-Li walked across the rug to meet me. "I'm sorry. What?"

"Oh. You were saying a drink is the best idea of the night. I was trying to surreptitiously redeem myself by mentioning it was my idea to meet with Judge Savin and let him know that we know about Zybo."

"This is you being surreptitious, huh?" She smiled. "Needs work. And, anyway, how do we know that meeting with Savin tonight isn't why this happened? Maybe this Zybo character wanted to teach..."

And something clicked into place.

She was right. It couldn't have been a coincidence. Zybo had already sent his nighttime messages, and, earlier that day, he had delivered his message in person. There really was no reason to pay another spooky visit to the McInnes home *unless* it was tied to our meeting with Judge Savin and/or Dr. Adderson. And tonight the intruder's message had been much less subtle than before. This time, there had been no quiet trespassing, no living-room sculptures, no dead squirrels. This time the warning had been almost overdone. Plus, the zydeco music seemed wrong; it was too obvious. *And*, I thought, *what about the busted window on the Land Rover and the implied threat scratched into the paint job?* That was evidence of a crime, evidence of an attack on property and of an assault on Kai-Li inside the vehicle...

"Thomas? Hello, *Tom!* Are you in there?" Apparently, Kai-Li had been talking, and I guess it had been just as apparent that I wasn't listening.

"Sorry." I took a sip of cognac and paused to feel the

burn in my throat, to let the scent pass up the back of my throat and into my nose. "I was thinking."

"Yes. I was able to determine that much." She sipped her drink and said, "It's a gift."

"What? Rudeness or the inability to focus?"

"You're not unable to focus. You do it too well. I do too."

"I've seen you work."

She nodded. "Like I said, it's a gift. Like perfect pitch or a good eye for art. You thought of something, didn't you? You think you've figured something out."

"Maybe." I sloshed the copper liquor around in my glass. "I'm not sure. Let me ask you this. How sure are you that it was Zybo who bashed in the window on the Land Rover?"

Kai-Li walked to the sofa and sat down. "Not sure at all. I just caught a glimpse of movement." She had a strange look. "Why? What are you thinking?"

"I'm not sure it makes sense."

Kai-Li patted the cushion next to her hip. She smiled a little, and her eyes were dilated.

She said, "Tell me."

Twenty-seven

THE RAIN WAS BACK. A thousand rivulets on the beachside windows dissected and warped the lead-gray expanse of Mobile Bay. Diffused lightning touched one corner of the smudged-charcoal sky and then another. Inside, the fire cast twisting gold reflections across the hearth and floor.

Joey stretched his legs out from the chair, crossed his ankles, and laced his fingers behind his neck. He started to speak, and a yawn caught him before he started. The giant man's eyes watered as he tried to hold back.

I asked, "You comfortable?"

"Tired."

"I just wanted to make sure the conversation's not growing tedious for you. That you're engaged and, you know, *comfy*."

"Bite me." He repeated, "I'm tired. Been running around checkin' on our boy Zybo. What's he's been up to since he got outta the pen. And he ain't exactly been droppin' bread crumbs." Joey gathered in his legs, sat up straight, and cracked his neck by rotating his jaw first to one side and then the other. "Truth is, though, this whole friggin' case is gettin' tedious. The way I see it, it's pretty simple."

I knew Joey was getting ready to make a list. I've always admired the way he does it. Joey could break down the invasion of Europe into three or four basic ideas.

"Number one, Zybo's playing head games with you 'cause either Judge Savin or Russell and Wagler, or maybe both, told him to. Number two, Judge Savin—let's say it was him—told Zybo to screw with *you* 'cause *you* wanna screw his money pooch."

"Screw his money pooch?"

Joey smiled. "Like that one?"

I held up a hand, palm down, and wiggled it.

"Anyway," he went on, "number three is we don't know what's goin' on with Jim Baneberry. But you're more or less covering that by havin' Sheri playin' spy," he paused, "for whatever that's worth." He stood and walked to the window. "That about it, or am I missin' somethin'?"

Kai-Li strolled in during Joey's analysis. She said, "Yes."

Joey drew in his chin and moved his eyes over the floor. "Yes, what?"

"Yes, you're missing something."

Joey pushed his hands down deep inside the hip pockets of his khakis. He had been studying Mobile Bay through the window, and it seemed he was fighting off cold absorbed by just looking out at the weather. "You gonna tell me what it is?"

Kai-Li looked over to check my reaction before answering. "You're failing to consider the progression of events...the various levels of harassment, if you will."

"And what would that tell me, you know, *if I will*?"

I cut in. "Zybo's careful, *and* he's smart."

Joey nodded. "Boy had a year of medical school at Tulane before messin' up and killin' somebody."

Kai-Li had been crossing the room to one of my club chairs. She stopped short. "Yes. That struck me when we first heard it. Do you know what happened?"

"I haven't gotten the trial transcripts yet," Joey said, "but the story goes that he and some buddies from school were out celebrating after first-year exams, and some kind of fight broke out. Two of his med-school buddies hauled ass and left him in an alley with three oil-rig workers who decided it'd be fun to mess up a college boy."

"Bad idea, I guess."

"Yeah. Again, the story goes—and I don't know how accurate this is—the story goes that Zybo took a carpet knife away from one of 'em, killed him with it, and was in the process of skinning a second one when the cops showed up."

Kai-Li walked over and sat beside me. "But isn't that self-defense?"

I said, "Maybe. But the courts do not look favorably on claims of self-defense in a drunken bar fight. They cut him some kind of slack, though. He's out."

Kai-Li looked incensed. "With a ruined life."

Joey laughed. "Let's don't get to feeling too sorry for somebody who strapped a carbon monoxide canister to the heater in Tom's Jeep."

Kai-Li was unfazed. "Nothing's simple."

I turned and smiled at her. "Is Zybo three people too?"

She gave me a look. "At least." She turned back to Joey. "How'd some med student take on three rough-necks?"

"Well, first of all, he grew up down in a Louisiana swamp where he'd probably been fighting since he could walk, *and* he was some kind of jock at Southwest Louisiana. I'm guessing gymnastics or maybe wrestling from the way he moves. So, looking at all that, these oil-rig tough guys just chose the wrong boy."

Joey stood there, his forehead wrinkled, thinking about Zybo's life. Finally, he said, "We got off the subject here. Y'all were sayin' that I'm missin' somethin' about the 'sequence of events.'" He pointed his nose at Kai-Li but held my eyes. "Something about," Joey switched into a bad English accent, "'the levels of *harassment.*'" Like a Brit, he emphasized the first syllable of "harassment," rather than the second.

Kai-Li asked, "Am I being made sport of?"

"Just yankin' your chain a little," Joey said. "You gonna answer my question?"

I broke in. "I started out by saying this Zybo is smart."

Joey nodded.

"Think about what he's done. Carbon monoxide poisoning that would be almost impossible to trace. Piling furniture in my living room with me asleep and the alarm set, making it so it'd look like a joke if I called the cops. Then he just put a dead squirrel on my hood."

Joey got it. "The lighted house with music playin' and the busted window on the Land Rover. That was too much."

I agreed. "Way too much. Almost as if someone else did it. Someone who wanted us to stay focused on Zybo and not look elsewhere for answers." I glanced over at Kai-Li. "Bottom line is, we think Judge Savin's jury-rigging club is getting ready to bust apart from more pressure than we're putting on it."

Joey wrinkled his head again and turned back toward the window. "Something else's goin' on that we don't know about."

"Something else is going on."

Joey turned and propped his butt against the window frame. "Is that gonna affect what we're doing?"

"Seems like it should, doesn't it?"

Joey nodded and the phone rang.

Kai-Li picked up the receiver and said, "Hello... Thank you again for last night. We... I'm sorry, what? Hang on." She held the receiver out to me with her palm placed over the mouthpiece. She whispered. "It's Laurel Adderson. She's not happy."

Now I said hello, and that was pretty much the last complete thought I managed to work into the conversation. I listened. I tried a couple of excuses and said goodbye.

Joey was grinning, enjoying my obvious discomfort. When I hung up, he asked, "What's goin' on?"

I sighed and sat back against the sofa. "Basically, the doctor wanted to ask *how dare I* advise Sheri to join the lawsuit against her. *How dare I* come to her house and eat her food after doing such an underhanded thing. Pretty much, *how dare I* go on living and breathing on the planet."

Joey smiled. "She let you answer?"

"Hell no." I stood and walked over to stand between

Joey and Kai-Li. "I've been thinking. Sounds like we know about as much about Zion Thibbodeaux as we're ever going to." I nodded at Joey. "I'd like for you to switch over and see what you and Loutie can find out about Jim Baneberry's suit against Dr. Adderson. Check out the parties. Check out Baneberry's finances, his company, that kind of thing." I paused. "And check out that sonofabitch Jonathan Cort while you're at it."

Joey smiled. "You got it." Then he walked out, leaving Kai-Li and me standing by the window, staring off into the overcast sky.

Kai-Li and I drove into Fairhope for lunch. Inside a quaint café with twenty-foot ceilings, I ate half a dozen dry shrimp arranged on a bed of pasta. It was a "heart-healthy" menu item. Must have been. It tasted like hell.

Thirty minutes later, we were in Dr. Adderson's waiting room.

"The doctor can't see you today." The nurse wore white scrubs. She looked like a refrigerator with shoes.

I tried to look friendly. "It'll just take a minute."

She shook her head. "Sorry." And she disappeared through one of those swinging doors that mark the boundary of every doctor's inviolate territory.

I decided to violate it.

No one stopped me. The scrub-suited fridge had disappeared, and I wandered the hallways unmolested, finally locating Dr. Adderson's small, neat office in the back right corner of the building. I sat in the client chair—or maybe the patient chair—and waited. Nothing happened. I got bored and walked over to sit in Dr. Adderson's tufted leather chair. I looked at the phone.

Someone—maybe the fridge—had typed a little note and taped it to the doctor's phone: "To page, dial 6, wait for a dial tone, then dial 999."

Sounded good to me. I punched in the numbers. "Paging Dr. Laurel Adderson. Paging Dr. Laurel Adderson. You're late for a meeting in your office. Thank you."

Pretty professional, I thought.

A blanket of white uniform filled the doorway. "Get out of here this minute! Who do you think you are? Get out of the *doctor's* chair!"

Nurses tend to think of doctors as little gods. Doctors like it that way.

I stood to plead my case, but, before I could speak, Dr. Adderson's calm voice sounded behind the mainsail in the doorway. "It's okay, Millie. Go call the police."

"Yes, *doctor.*" She virtually spit the last word at me. She had me now. I was screwing around with the *doctor.*

Laurel Adderson entered the room. "Would you like to say anything before the police get here?"

"That's why I came." I moved around to the visitor's side of her desk.

"So," she said, "speak. Whatever it is must be very important for you to make this big an ass of yourself over it."

"Actually, this is about average on the ass meter for me."

She sat down and crossed her arms.

I sat in the patient's chair so I could look directly into her face. I placed my elbows on my knees and leaned forward—earnestly, imploringly, I hoped. "I did not advise Sheri to sue you. She fired me. Any actions she and her father take against you are outside my control."

"Is that it?"

"That's it. Except that she left owing me fees, which I can't collect now because I managed to get my license suspended trying to represent her."

Now Dr. Adderson leaned forward. She propped her elbows on her desk. "I do not feel sorry for you, Tom. You pursued Sheri's case in a way...well, let's just say that the judge believes you could have handled it better."

"Probably true." I tried to look ashamed. "But my reputation can't take much more right now. I wanted you to know I didn't release any information you gave me to Jim Baneberry's lawyers." And that much *was* true.

"Fine. You've told me. If you leave now, you may manage to avoid meeting the police on the way out."

I stood. "One more thing. I need a favor."

She sat back in her chair. "You're kidding."

"No. I'm not. I want you to explain all this to Judge Savin. Tell him about our conversation. And, if you would, tell him this. Tell him that I want to keep my law license. I'm prepared to do whatever it takes to hold on to my practice and to collect my fees from Sheri Baneberry." I walked to the door and turned back. "You weren't the only one who got screwed when Sheri joined the opposition, Dr. Adderson."

I walked quickly away. In the waiting room, I edged past a white refrigerator with a bright red face and crooked a finger at Kai-Li. She was on her feet and matching my pace as we hit the door and hurried through the foyer and out into the parking lot.

As we reached the Safari, a black-and-white pulled up alongside and rolled down a window. A lone, uniformed cop leaned out. "What's happening here? Did you come from inside the doctor's office?"

Kai-Li stepped into the passenger seat and closed her door.

I said, "Yeah. There's this big, red-faced nurse in there. Size of a Buick. She's in the waiting room, yelling something about the doctor's office and threatening to smother anyone who comes near her." I pointed over my shoulder at Kai-Li. "Had to get my wife out of there. Woman was scaring her to death."

The cop stepped out of his patrol car, told me to "wait right there," and ran inside the building.

I nodded. Then I stepped into the Safari and drove out of the parking lot.

Twenty-eight

THE SIGN READ, *Sunset Villas, Baneberry-Cort Construction, General Contractor.*

I raised my paper cup in the direction of a skeleton of rust-colored steel that slashed the evening sky into irregular, unnatural shapes. "Ugly, isn't it?"

Joey sat in the passenger seat of the Safari, eating his second Quarter Pounder with Cheese. "I think all these damn things are ugly. I like Saint George and Dog Island. Grayton Beach is okay. Hurricanes keep blowing Gulf Shores off the map, and contractors keep coming back and fuckin' it up. Beach always seemed to me like the wrong place for a ten-story condo." He took another huge bite of burger. "That's what I think, but nobody asked my ass about it."

"My condolences to your ass."

Joey grunted.

"Is this all you wanted me to see?"

My giant friend polished off his sandwich, popped

the plastic cover off a large Coke, and took a long swallow before answering. "Look at the completion date on the sign."

"Where?"

He placed his drink in a cup holder and opened his door. "Come on."

I followed him to the sign—a painted four-by-eight sheet of exterior plywood. In smaller print, in one corner, the sign read: AVAILABLE FOR OCCUPANCY, but the date had been painted over.

Joey flipped on a flashlight. "Look. You can just see it."

The date was almost a year past.

"Is that it? That's why I had to come way out here in rush-hour traffic? Hell, Joey. You know as well as I do, construction gets stalled for all kinds of reasons— zoning, owner financing problems, lousy advance sales."

Joey just listened. That's how I knew he had the answer. "But this one was financed, designed, and *almost* built by one company."

"Baneberry-Cort Construction."

Joey turned to walk back to the vehicle. "Amazing. Hit you over the head a few times, and you pick right up on it." He stopped to lean against the hood and look out over the Gulf of Mexico. "And guess who was the third partner in the firm of Baneberry-Cort Construction."

I stopped to think. "Kate Baneberry."

Joey turned and opened the passenger door. "About time."

I looked at him.

"I thought you were supposed to be the smart one." He grabbed his Coke from inside the truck and leaned back out. "Time to quit fuckin' around with these folks, Tom."

He killed his drink and threw the ice across the construction site before stepping inside the vehicle.

The skies over Gulf Shores were still tinged with the last bright smudges of daylight when we pulled off the construction site and headed home. I drove, and I took it easy, which is unusual. I needed to think.

Twenty minutes into the ride, Joey pointed at a Jr. Food Store coming up on the right, and I pulled over. I pumped gas while Joey went inside and came out with two six-packs of Heineken.

I asked, "You pay for the gas?"

He nodded.

That was it. Neither Joey nor I spoke for the next hour. He was thinking. So was I.

As we passed through Fairhope, I recalled that Joey had once worked for the investigative arm of the state troopers, and I broke the silence.

"You used to be with Alabama Bureau of Investigation, didn't you?"

Joey grunted an affirmative noise.

"You got any ABI friends left up in Montgomery?"

Joey was slow answering. "Yeah. I guess. A couple, maybe."

"Good."

Joey turned in his seat to look at me. And, for the rest of the drive into Point Clear, we discussed how we could best exploit his friends' loyalty to our advantage.

* * *

Kai-Li had enjoyed enough surprises during our brief time together. I honked the horn as we pulled up next to the house, and, seconds later, Loutie's face appeared in the column of windows next to my front door. Joey and I walked in. We were out of beer.

Loutie asked, "You two drunk?"

Joey reached over and absentmindedly patted her hip. "Just a few beers."

As Joey passed through to the living room, Loutie hung back. "Tom?" Her hard, clear eyes searched my face. "Kai-Li seems like a nice girl. Smart."

Something was wrong. "Yeah, I think so."

She nodded. "Susan called from Chicago."

My heart missed a beat, and I asked without thinking, "She okay?"

Loutie understood. I'd nearly gotten Susan killed once upon a time, and I felt more than a little protective of her. "She's fine. She wants you to call her."

I nodded.

"Go ahead and do it now."

I looked hard into her eyes. "And she's fine?"

"She's fine. Go call."

I said hello to Kai-Li on the way through the living room, and got a sympathetic smile in return. Both women knew I was about to get the there's-someone-else news. Now I knew it too.

I sat at my desk and dialed the number in Illinois. Susan sounded relaxed, happy, and concerned. *He* was an assistant conductor of the Chicago Symphony. I made a feeble joke about how I'd never believed the conventional wisdom that *all* symphony conductors are gay. She laughed. I wished her the best. She wished the same for me. I went back into my own living room to be pitied and treated with kid gloves by an ex-stripper and an Asian shrink.

Sometimes life sucks.

As I came into the living room, Joey said, "So. I hear she dumped your ass."

Loutie balled her fist, and Joey moved quickly out of reach. She was not a woman given to playful punches. Loutie was getting ready to pop Joey one, and he knew it. But the pity, the serious demeanor of the women, and Joey running from Loutie—it was all too much, and I started laughing.

Joey grinned. "Poor little fella. He's in shock." He winked at me. "Come on, Tom. Let's go get us a beer before Loutie kicks my ass in front of this distinguished professor you got stayin' with you."

I followed Joey into the kitchen, where we opened the first of an unknown number of beers that would be consumed that night.

I honestly didn't feel as bad about being dumped as I probably should have—Susan and I had split up weeks before—but, as Joey was sensitive enough to point out, "Not datin' a woman anymore and knowin' some other guy is bonin' her are two different things."

On top of that, it had been a hell of a week on a lot of levels. So, Joey and I conducted an inebriated tour of the beers of the world—as least as represented by the contents of my refrigerator. It is not an exaggeration to say we covered at least two beer-producing countries on each of the major continents.

By the time he and Loutie said good night some time around midnight, I was lit. Glowing. Basically drunk as Cooter Brown, as my mother used to say. And, as Joey's Expedition disappeared into the night,

I'm almost certain I tried to engage Kai-Li in a discussion of just exactly who Cooder Brown might have been.

As I recall, she had very few thoughts on the subject.

A door opened. I rolled over onto my back and opened my eyes. Bad idea. Bright sunshine stabbed through my pupils like steel needles. A bundle of nerves just behind my eyes seemed to explode before I could screw my eyes shut again.

Kai-Li's voice said, "Headache?"

I think I said, "Umm."

"I made some coffee. Would you like some?"

I repeated my all-purpose syllable.

By the time she walked back into the room, wearing the New Orleans Jazz Festival T-shirt I'd given her to use as a nightgown and carrying two stoneware mugs of steaming coffee, I'd managed to prop two pillows against the headboard and achieve a more-or-less upright position.

She carefully placed a hot mug in my hands and I said, "Thank you."

"Actual words." Kai-Li smiled and sat cross-legged on the bed facing me. "Impressive."

I looked down and felt a glandular jolt. "Umm."

"Words, Thomas."

"I can see your underwear."

She rolled her eyes and punched the long T-shirt down between her legs. "You happy now?"

"I was happy before." I tried to smile. It hurt.

Kai-Li returned my smile. "Then you should have kept your mouth shut. In any event, sexy small talk—

which is not something I'm completely adverse to engaging in with you at some future date—should probably be left to a time when you look less like a drunken toad."

I sipped some coffee. "Toad, huh?"

She pressed her lips together, raised her eyebrows, and nodded.

"Afraid so. Anyway, time to get up and hit the showers. You've had a call this morning from your colleagues at Russell and Wagler."

"You're kidding."

"No. I'm not. You said that's what you expected after your meeting yesterday with Dr. Adderson."

"Yeah," I said. "But I wasn't sure it was going to work."

"Well, it did. Get up. You've got a meeting at their offices at two this afternoon." As she talked, Kai-Li uncrossed her legs, rolled onto one hip, and bounced off the bed. When she did, I glanced down again at her cream-colored panties. I really meant not to, but that's what happened.

Kai-Li said, "I saw that."

"What do you expect from a drunken toad?"

Twenty-nine

THE GLASS AND steel of Mobile Convention Center interrupted the waterfront, and I hung a left on Government Street. The wide pavement made a "V" around the entrance to Bankhead Tunnel and passed by the old Admiral Sims Hotel, a television station, and a couple of municipal buildings before gaining some dignity beneath twin rows of live oaks, the tips of whose limbs touched and moved against one another over five lanes of traffic.

In summer, the oaks cast a cool, civilizing shade over the busy street. Now, a few days before Christmas, harsh light cut through a stark, black crisscross of limbs. Up ahead, at the apex of the park on Old Government, a cannon seated in white concrete at just about windshield height pointed straight at me.

"Look for the cannon. You'll see it, but we're a couple of blocks before the road splits. On the right." The directions had been friendly, professional, and impersonal, and they'd been delivered by Russell & Wagler's newest receptionist.

I slowed the Safari, then turned right and left again to ease into the paved lot behind the antebellum mansion that housed the law firm. It was not an unusual setup for successful plaintiffs' lawyers.

Corporate firms—lawyers who draft contracts and argue over tax issues and securities fraud—are, almost invariably, on the highest possible floor of some bank building. There are two reasons for this: Corporate clients feel more comfortable in corporate buildings, and banks generally insist that their own firms rent space in their newest overpriced building.

Plaintiff firms, by contrast, are trying to impress blue-collar workers, for the most part, so those workers will hire the firm to sue the kind of corporation that builds overpriced office buildings. Using an old mansion is a way of separating a "blue-collar" firm from the corporation the plaintiff hates, and it's a pretty good way of making your firm look like a winner. Nothing says success to an assembly-line worker like a mansion—and, of course, a receptionist in a miniskirt.

I stepped out into a hard winter day, swung the door shut, and shot the Safari with the remote. The alarm responded with that double beep that makes parking decks at 8:00 A.M. sound like they're full of bobwhites.

A concrete path beside the building and around the front led to tall steps. Up on the columned porch, green double doors held twin wreaths. A brass sign instructed me to COME IN.

The entry hall was twenty feet wide, almost as tall, and ran the depth of the house, ending at a wall of sheer curtains and floor-to-ceiling windows that framed the receptionist's desk. Loutie sat in front of those windows, where harsh December light silhouetted every curve of the curviest woman I've ever known.

I walked across marble and slate and handmade rugs, passed between staircases that curved onto the floor like twin parentheses, and stopped in front of a small desk designed to let clients check out the receptionist's legs.

Loutie flashed a beautiful smile. "Yes sir? May I help you?" No wink. No sidelong glance. She was playing her part to the hilt.

I told one of my best friends my name. "I'm here to see Mr. Wagler."

"Just a moment." Loutie punched a button on an electronic console and spoke quietly into a tiny microphone suspended from a single earpiece that seemed to bloom naturally from her ear. She punched another button. "His assistant is on her way down."

"Thank you."

"You're welcome."

"No," I said, "I really appreciate your help."

"It's no problem, sir."

"Seriously, you're great at this. Do they send you to school for this or what? I don't mind telling you. I've had some complaints about my secretary's greeting skills. And I'm thinking..."

Loutie looked hard into my eyes, and my stomach tightened a little. She whispered, "Get away from me."

I tried to smile. It wasn't easy. I'm a little afraid of Loutie Blue.

High heels echoed on marble, and I looked up to see an attractive, middle-aged woman descending the left staircase. As I met her eyes, she said, "Good afternoon Mr. McInnes. Mr. Wagler will meet you in his conference room." She reached the foot of the stairs and held out her hand. I shook it. The woman had a nice handshake. She told me her name was Cruella.

"I'm sorry?"

She smiled. "Sue Ella. Named for my grandmothers."

I apologized.

She smiled again. "Happens all the time. This way, please."

Upstairs, the ceilings fell to ten feet, and the flooring changed from marble and slate to heart pine. Cruella Sue Ella paused outside a paneled door and tapped with one knuckle.

A male voice said, "Come in."

My escort opened the door, stepped aside while I walked through, and remained in the hallway when she closed it.

Inside, Bill Wagler sat at one end of the conference table and Judge Luther Savin—chief judge of the Alabama Court of Criminal Appeals and Dr. Laurel Adderson's love machine—sat at the other.

Wagler rose out of his seat and took my hand. "Good of you to come, Tom. I've been looking forward to this." He motioned at Judge Savin, who sat watching me with a smile on his lips. "You know the judge, I believe."

"Yes. He and I had dinner together at the home of a mutual friend just two nights ago." I flashed my best fake smile. "Good to see you again, judge."

Judge Savin didn't respond. He just sat there—round, furry, and satisfied—like a tomcat who'd just batted around and then devoured the last rat in the barn.

He was starting to piss me off.

Wagler motioned toward an empty chair. "Sit down. Please. Judge Savin and I had finished up and were just catching up on Montgomery politics. He was getting up to leave when you came in."

And with that, Judge Savin pushed back from the table, lifted his girth out of the chair, and gave me a wink before exiting through Wagler's private office.

Wagler paused until he heard the outside door of his office close behind the judge. "Tom, would you like some coffee or maybe a Coke? I think we have Frog water too, if you like that kind of thing."

"No, thank you. I'm anxious to find out why you wanted to meet today."

A big man, Wagler leaned forward and propped his elbows on the table. He had the thickly veined hands of a manual laborer, and he used them in a way that suggested he knew the strength in his hands was obvious to other men.

"Well the truth is, Tom, I need your help. Up until a few days ago, you were representing Sheri Baneberry in the wrongful death of her mother."

I nodded.

"Well, Sheri thinks you're a fine lawyer, Tom. And I sure as hell agree with her. From talking with Sheri, my partners and I feel like you've got a handle on the case, and we could use your help getting ready for trial. So, what we'd like is to bring you in as associate counsel."

The man's handsome face bore a light, artificial tan. And I noticed that the delineation between the white at his temples and his black mane of loose curls seemed a little too precise. Everything around me just then seemed too precise.

I leaned back in my seat, moving away from the mannered aggressor across the table. He wanted to dominate me. I decided it'd be smart to let him.

"Bill, my license to practice has been suspended by the bar. I don't see how I can come in as any kind of counsel on this thing."

Wagler pursed his lips and bobbed his head. "I understand that. But—and don't quote me on this, Tom—I hear from some pretty good sources that your problems with the bar may go away."

"Who says . . ."

He threw up his hands. "Don't ask me, 'cause I can't say. But I will tell you that I think we can work around the licensing problem until it's resolved. How about if we say it's worth, oh, ten percent of any eventual verdict to bring you in as something like an *adviser* on the case? Would that work for you?"

And there was the payoff.

I tried not to react. "I appreciate the offer, Bill. I really do. But I've had just about enough of the Baneberrys. So what I'd rather do is waive any interest in a potential judgment in return for a check for the fees and expenses I've got sunk in this case right now." I leaned up to close the distance between us. "Is that anything you'd be willing to consider?"

Wagler actually reached up and stroked his chin like a bad actor who has been told to look like he's thinking about something. "What'd you be looking for here? Say twenty thousand?"

I smiled. "Say twenty-five."

"Done."

Wagler reached across the table to shake hands. I'd been officially bought off.

★　★　★

The firm's back office cut the check in five minutes flat, after which Wagler's efficient assistant escorted me downstairs. I was three or four steps from the bottom when Loutie called out to me. "Sir? Mr. McInnes?"

"Yes?" I answered as I hooked my fingers around the finial at the end of the banister and pivoted toward Loutie's desk.

She held up a pink message slip. "A call came in while you were with Mr. Wagler. I asked if it was an emergency, and the party said not to disturb you."

I reached out and took the paper. On the top two lines, Loutie had simply written *Call home* on one line and my home number on the next. I assumed that was what would show up on the carbon in the message pad. But underneath, in the lined, "message" section of the slip, Loutie had written:

1. *J. Cort arrived noon. Still here.*
2. *Judge S. arrived 1:00—Left building just after you went up.*
3. *Kai-Li called. Z left message: "Looking for good university psychologist."*

I looked up. "Thank you, Ms. . . ."

"Blue."

"Thank you, Ms. Blue."

She flashed a plastic smile and said, "Certainly." Then she dropped her eyes and focused her attention on an article in the December *Cosmopolitan*, which she had spread out behind her telephone panel.

Turning to leave, I nearly plowed into Wagler's assistant, who had been quietly hovering. Twin furrows had formed between Cruella's eyebrows.

"Is everything all right, Mr. McInnes?"

"To tell you the truth," I said, "I'm not sure yet."

Jumping inside the Safari, I fumbled for my cell phone and had tapped in six digits before intelligence overtook emotion. I scanned the parking lot and side street for Zybo, for anyone who might be equipped to listen in on a cell phone. There was no one who seemed remotely interested.

The key clashed with the ignition. The steering felt clumsy. Bumping out over a curb in reverse, I cut off a guy in a pickup and he flipped me the bird. I waved and dropped the gearshift into drive.

Quaint homes streamed by as cobblestones mixed with buckling pavement rumbled beneath my tires. Two rights and a left and I passed Loutie's place. No one followed. I punched in my home number. Kai-Li answered.

I asked, "You okay?"

"I'm fine. I was afraid the message from Zybo would make you freak. I think it just means . . ."

I interrupted. Too much adrenaline pumping not to. "It means he wants to meet."

"Yes, Thomas." Kai-Li's voice came out smooth and lilting, like a mother calming a child. "Are you ready?"

I sat at a red light, waiting. "I'm not sure. Let's talk when I get there. I'm on the way."

I think I hung up without saying goodbye. The light turned green, and I gunned the Safari back onto Government Street.

Zybo was rushing me.

I forced myself to wait an interminable ten minutes, to get calm and think. I was on I-10 and speeding across a thin strip of pavement stretched across saltwater flats when my self-imposed purgatory ended. I punched in Joey's cell number.

"Tom." He had Caller ID.

"Make the call."

"What call? What are you talking about? Is this one of those 'The cock crows at midnight' things?"

Off the causeway to the right, two old men hunkered in a flat-bottom boat. One of them cast a spinner out next to a likely looking swirl of water. As the lure hit, I came even with them and they passed out of sight behind me.

I said, "Make the call to your friend at the ABI in Montgomery. The one we talked about. Zybo's pushing for a meeting."

"Oh, yeah. That call."

"We up to speed now?"

Joey said, "Up to speed," and hung up.

Twelve minutes later, as I exited the interstate, my phone beeped. I flipped it open and said hello.

Joey's unmistakable voice, a comfortable mix of Southern and military accents, said, "The cock crows at four this afternoon."

"Cute." I glanced at my watch. "You sure?"

"Yeah. He'll do it. Whether it'll be enough to get the Mobile cops interested is up in the air, though."

"So he's calling thirty minutes from now."

"You got it. Anything else?"

I said no, and he ended the connection.

Thirty

THAT NIGHT AND most of the next day passed without incident or interruption. In the early evening, I drove to the diner and parked on a graded lot paved with oyster shells and mixed gravel.

The front door hung from spring hinges and slammed shut too fast behind me, nipping the heel of my shoe. A couple of sixty-watt bulbs spread dingy light across the diner. Heated air blew gently from some unseen vent, carrying the heavy scents of burned tallow and Pine-Sol. The same waitress with the same dyed hair and dry cleavage looked up and then down again at what looked like the classified section draped over the counter.

Four small tables fronted the place. Each one rested beside a screened window with plastic sheeting duct-taped over the glass to keep out winter. Zybo sat at the back corner table. He met my eyes across the top of a clothbound book.

As I walked toward the table, he glanced at the page he'd been reading, memorizing the page number, and placed the closed volume on the yellow plastic table-cloth. In gold block printing, the cover read,

THE CITADEL

BY

ARCHIBALD JOSEPH CRONIN

I remembered writing a book report on it in high school. Pointing, I said, "Good book."

Zybo motioned for me to sit. "Yeah. Nice diner, too."

I sat across from him with my back to the door. "Better than the barbecue pit in the alley."

He leaned back, rolled his shoulders, and looked at a spot over my right ear. It's an old trick that supposed to disconcert your listener. "Dis supposed to be an intim-idatin' place for me?"

"Nope. Just knew you'd know where it was. And I didn't want to meet where we'd be seen."

He nodded at the tip of my ear.

I leaned to the right to intercept his line of sight. "You afraid to look at me?"

Zybo met my eyes. Then he leaned forward until his nose was a foot from mine. His pupils dilated. "How's dat?"

"Fine, if you're planning to kiss me."

He grinned and eased back a bit in his chair.

I asked, "Why'd you call?"

"You met Judge Savin again. Dis time at de woman doctor's house."

"That's true."

"Yesterday afternoon, you drove to de judge's pet law firm for a meeting."

"Also true. So far, so good, Zybo. What's your question?"

"I wanna know what's goin' on."

"If wishes were horses."

"I could *make* you tell me."

"That's pretty much the same thing Billy Savin said at the Mandrake Club." I tried to keep the nauseating fear that roiled inside from registering on my face. "Billy ended up on the floor."

My Cajun tormentor broke eye contact. He leaned back in his chair and paused a few seconds before saying, "Not to be too confrontational, Tommy Boy. But actually *I* could." His accent was slipping. He paused again. "But what good would it do?"

I thought about that. "Some."

"Yeah," he said. "Some. But some ain't good enough. I tink I'm bein' set up."

"I know the feeling."

Zion Thibbodeaux, ex-con and psychological warrior, smiled. "Yeah, Tommy Boy. I guess you do." He held his hands in the air. "Question is, what is it we gonna do 'bout dat?"

"You've been cut off, haven't you? Nobody's returning your phone calls. Nobody's asking about trials that need fixing. No people who need poisoning."

His eyes narrowed, but he didn't speak.

"Everybody's hunkering down, Zybo. And you're the only one left standing out there like a Day-Glo® golf ball—all teed up and ready for somebody to take a whack at."

His eyes wandered the diner wall over my shoulder.

"Speaking of which, I need to know something." I asked, "Did you pay a visit to my house the night I had dinner with Judge Savin and Dr. Adderson?"

"No way."

"Would you tell me if you did?"

"Prob'ly not."

"Windows open, lights on, Cajun music blasting on the stereo?"

Zybo's color darkened, and thin cords of muscle worked against the skin at the hollows of his temples.

"I filed a police report this time. You can't take a whack at the back window of my Land Rover with a woman inside, Zybo. That's too much."

He leaned in, his fingers laced together on the table-top. Dark skin around his nails turned white from the pressure of his grip. "You tink I did dat?"

"Be kind of stupid, wouldn't it?"

He nodded. "Anyting else?"

"Hearing some rumors out of Montgomery about a Louisiana hit man hired by Chris Galerina."

He nodded.

I said, "You heard the same thing, didn't you?"

He shrugged his shoulders forward a little. "Dead men dey don' testify."

"That's right. Neither one of you."

He paused and rolled his shoulders in full circles. Then he leaned forward again. "Your investigator, he de one been messin' in my business."

I reached inside my coat pocket and took out two envelopes. One was a manila routing envelope with a series of scratched-out names on one side. "Take a look."

Zybo picked up the envelope and tilted the names toward the light. When he had examined each name in turn, he unwound the string holding the envelope closed and pulled out his arrest and prison records. This time, they were in the right order. He leafed through the records, holding them lightly by the edges, just as I'd hoped he would.

When he was done, he said, "Your investigator, he come up with dis?"

I shook my head.

He nodded. "I tink I'm gonna keep it."

"Keep the report. Not the envelope. They'll know it came from me."

He shook his head. "Nobody's gonna see it. And I ain't askin' for it. I'm takin' it."

Now I leaned forward. "You try to hold on to that"— I pointed at the envelope in his hand—"and you and I are going to go at it again right now. And I'm done telling you anything."

He shrugged. "So why you showin' dis stuff, anyhow? I figure you hate my fuggin gut by now."

"You figure right. But I want my life *and* my law practice back. And I don't want to have to be Judge Savin's punk to get them."

Zybo just sat there, thinking. Finally, he asked, "How do I know you not workin' with dem to set me up for de Baneberry woman's death?"

"Did you kill her?"

"No way."

"Would you have murdered that woman if they'd paid you enough?"

He shrugged. "Dat ain't what happened."

I leaned back. "Why should I believe you?"

"Why should I be believin' you're not already Judge Savin's punk?"

I lifted the flap on the second envelope I'd taken out of my coat pocket and placed a check for $25,000 on the table.

Zybo stared, but didn't touch. "I guess dey bought you, Tommy."

"They tried."

"You gonna cash it?"

"No. I'm not."

"Den why'd you take it?"

"So I could show later they *tried* to buy me." I held up my hands. "Look, I pretty much stumbled onto their operation. I didn't land hard enough to send everybody to jail, but just hard enough to make them stop what they were doing for a while. Maybe enough to kick off some kind of ethics investigation. I don't know. But the judge's got a good thing going. So he makes plans to cut my legs out from under me before I can get started."

Zybo sat quietly. Listening. This is why he had come.

"Basically," I said, "the judge has got three ways he can handle damage control.

"First, he could ruin my life and my reputation so nobody'll believe me—which is what they started out to do. But the problem there is that I still know what I know. And he can never be sure that some reporter or prosecutor isn't going to take my story seriously. Particularly since his people've still got a dead juror on their hands.

"So, he goes to the second option. The judge meets me at the Mandrake Club and invites me to join his little jury-rigging group and get rich along with the rest of them. I tell him I'll do whatever's necessary to keep my license. And he has his boys at Russell and Wagler cut me a check, which is intended to both shut me up and tie me to them with a paper trail."

Zybo nodded almost imperceptibly and said, "Right, but de woman she still dead."

I repeated. "The woman's still dead. The husband's still suing Judge Savin's girlfriend. And somebody's trying to tie you to Chris Galerina."

"You say *tree ways* dey could handle dis."

"Oh, yeah. They could kill every one of us."

He leaned forward again, but this time it was a natural movement—not something designed to intimidate. "Me, you, de psychologist, maybe your investigator *and* your lawyer? Prob'ly have to trow in your client to be sure." He shook his head. "I don' tink so. Dat ain't their style."

"I'll have to take your word for that."

"Yeah." He paused. "Okay." He slid the routing envelope across the table. "Keep it. I be talkin' to you." He gathered the loose pages of his criminal record and stood. "But listen up, Tommy Boy. I find out you tryin' to fug me over, I'll end all your worries in a heartbeat. Dat's *my* fuggin style."

He crossed the diner. As he pulled open the front door, I picked up both envelopes and my check and walked to the counter. I was curious about something. When the waitress glanced up, I asked, "Why didn't you wait on us?"

She nodded at the door, "That good-lookin' boy there. He give me a twenty to leave you be."

I nodded and walked out into the cold wet night. Zybo had disappeared.

Thirty-one

OVER A BREAKFAST of bagels and cream cheese, Kai-Li and I had discussed my meeting with Zybo. As we talked, I'd eaten my bagel and half of hers: She was still working on half of her half when she asked, "How did it feel?"

"What?"

"Sitting across from this Cajun who's attacked you and made your life miserable. How did it feel to sit across from him, making polite conversation? Trying to manipulate him?"

"It felt," I said, "like teasing a cottonmouth with a stick—which is something I tried once when I was a kid."

She smiled. "Think you'll get bitten?"

"I sure as hell hope not."

Kai-Li scraped a tenth of an ounce of cream cheese onto a piece of toasted bagel. "Well, did the snake bite you the first time? When you were a boy?"

I held out my right forearm and rotated it to display the faint scars from two puncture wounds near my elbow.

She paused with the bagel raised halfway to her mouth. "You're kidding."

"I wish."

"So you've always been like this?"

"Boyishly charming, isn't it?"

All she said was "no."

I went for a shower.

Upstairs, the tiled bathroom floor felt cold under bare feet. I switched on the overhead heater, left the ventilator off, and cranked on the hot water. By the time I'd grabbed a clean towel and stripped down, steam had filled the room. I adjusted the water temperature and stepped into the spray.

The muffled ring of the phone sounded twice. Minutes passed. A fist bumped at the door, and a faint puff of cool air touched my shoulders as the bathroom door opened and closed.

"Thomas?"

An opaque glass door was all that separated me from my houseguest. I turned my back. "Yes?"

"Mind if I come in?"

What was I going to say? "Of course not."

"The phone."

"Yeah, I heard it."

She spoke louder than usual to be heard over the shower. "It was Judge Savin's secretary. He wants you and me . . . he wants both of us to come to some affair tonight at the Mandrake Club." She hesitated. "You sure I'm not making you uncomfortable? You're sort of hiding in the corner there."

I turned to face the door. "Want me to step out there so we can talk face-to-face?"

"Maybe. I really can't see anything through the door, you know."

"What kind of 'affair' did he invite us to?"

"Oh. It's something called the Hunter's Ball, whatever that is."

"Formal?"

"Unh-huh. That's what the woman said. And the *way* she invited us, by the way, made it seem more like an order than an invitation."

"Probably was an order. The judge figures he owns me now."

I could see Kai-Li's form through the frosted glass. She was leaning with her bottom against the edge of the sink. I turned to rinse conditioner out of my hair.

I turned back. She was still there. "Worried?"

"Maybe a bit," she said.

More time passed. "Is there anything else? We can talk when I get out."

"Thomas?" She paused. "Am I reading you wrong? You seem to like me, but . . . I don't know how much longer I can bear to be ignored while walking around your house in a T-shirt and panties."

"Oh." It was all I could think to say.

"I'm not asking to jump in the shower with you or anything. And please don't come popping out of there in all your glory. But . . . I was wondering. So I thought, what the heck, may as well ask."

I turned off the shower. "Mind if I discuss this with my pants on? It'll make the answer less obvious."

She laughed. "See you downstairs."

I heard the door close behind her.

* * *

That evening, the drive into Daphne little resembled our earlier trip to Dr. Adderson's farmhouse for dinner with the judge. Now, the last remnants of snow and ice had melted, soaking the roadsides and turning frozen strips of tire-churned soil as black as chimney soot. The Gulf Coast had settled into the seasonal sameness of wet, gray, penetrating cold that moves through clothes and skin and bone as if they were made of gauze.

Kai-Li shifted in her seat. Again. She'd passed the afternoon shopping in Fairhope. Now she seemed uncomfortable inside the new silk wrap that circled her shoulders and the pale folds of evening dress surrounding her legs and ankles.

I could sympathize. In most places, "formal" means black tie. In Mobile and along the Eastern Shore, it means white tie and tails. My coat lay on the back seat, but I had on the tie and vest, the satin-striped trousers and thinly pleated shirt.

It wasn't comfortable, but I thought I looked pretty good.

Kai-Li pointed at the brick monument marking the turnoff into the club. "Is that it?"

I nodded. "Just up around the curve there. It's a nice place. Very horsey. You'll like it."

"No," she said, "I won't."

Around the curve, there was a line. Just to park.

When we finally approached the dropoff area, a young guy dressed like a waiter opened Kai-Li's door and then came around for mine. No parking under the hill tonight. All valet. All free. What the hell.

At the door, my old friend Harvey had traded his

usual getup for tails and spotless white gloves. He opened the door, and I noticed that his was a more expensive outfit than mine, but then he probably wore his more than once a year.

Inside the entry hall, Kai-Li leaned in close and whispered, "We could have crashed, Thomas. No one bothered to check an invitation."

I shook my head. "They never do. That would be tacky."

"Heaven forbid," she said. "What now?"

"I'm thinking we hit the bar, then snoop around a little."

"Is that it?"

I put my hand on the small of Kai-Li's back and guided her toward the bar where I'd first seen Zybo. "No, no. Later, after I've plied you with champagne, we'll wander into the garden where I'll pull you under a canopy of Confederate jasmine and do unspeakable things to you."

Kai-Li showed me her profile, and I caught a hint of perfume. She said, "It's about time."

Inside the paneled barroom, other perfumes mixed in the air with cigar smoke and cocktail chatter. I ordered scotch. Kai-Li asked, "Do I *have* to drink champagne to do things unspeakable in the garden?"

I laughed. "Whatever you want."

She ordered Stoli on the rocks. The bartender grinned at my beautiful date and winked at me. Kai-Li threw a green-eyed, flirtatious glance at the poor guy just to torture him and walked away. I rushed to catch up and almost bumped into Kai-Li when she stopped short. "Look who's here."

I glanced around the room and was about to ask

who she meant when I saw Sheri Baneberry. She stood ten feet away, laughing. Jonathan Cort and her father stood on either side of her as she talked with our host, Judge Luther Savin. And I was struck by the feeling that I'd never seen my young client looking quite so comfortable in her skin.

Sheri felt my gaze and turned. She held out her hand. "Tom!"

I walked into the group and took her hand. "Good to see you, Sheri. You look wonderful."

She laughed. She turned her back to Jonathan Cort and motioned at her father. "Do you know my father, Jim Baneberry?"

I offered my hand. He shook it, but he didn't look happy about it.

Judge Savin spoke up. "Tom? May I speak to you and Dr. Cantil, please?"

We excused ourselves and followed the judge through the bar and the entry hall to a glassed-in area overlooking lighted oak trees outside. The three of us were alone.

He began. "Bill Wagler told me about your meeting."

I looked at him.

"I understand you don't want to work with them on the Baneberry case."

"I've had enough of this one."

His eyes narrowed. His lips stretched tight as if grimacing from a bad taste. "I was sorry to hear that. Have you cashed the check, Tom?"

Something was wrong. "No offense. But I don't see where that's any business of yours, judge. I thought we'd worked this out. Are you planning to be in my business from now on?"

The taste in Judge Savin's mouth seemed to turn rancid. "You said you were interested in what we discussed here in the club."

"I am interested." I glanced at Kai-Li and turned back to Savin. "Did you invite us out here tonight to insult us? What the hell's going on here, judge?"

"You were invited to a celebration. Then, this afternoon, I heard about you turning down Wagler on the Baneberry case." I started to interrupt, and he held up a pudgy hand with the blood ruby on its stubby pinky. "Just hold on. After I talked to Wagler, I did a little checking. Looks like somebody at the Alabama Bureau of Investigation called down to the Mobile police asking about a Cajun hit man with a year of medical school."

I tried to look shocked. "You're kidding."

He glared into my eyes. "Fuck you, McInnes."

"What . . . ?"

"Who do you think you're dealing with? You think you can fuck me over? Blowing off Wagler, planting information about the Cajun. Shit. The man's disappeared."

"Who?"

"I'm warning you, McInnes. Quit playing the dumbass. Zybo's missing, and you know it." He turned and nodded at Kai-Li. "And this little bitch is still sitting on all that so-called research about jury fixing."

I raised my hand and poked the air. Before I could speak, Kai-Li broke in. "Who are you calling a bitch? You creepy little troll." I grinned, and she turned to me. "Is this funny to you?"

"Sort of."

Kai-Li's cheeks burned red. Fireworks exploded inside her emerald irises. "I'm leaving." She spun toward the doorway behind me, took one step, and stopped.

I turned. Billy Savin and Chuck Bryony stood shoulder-to-shoulder inside the closed door. Both wore tails, which is an outfit that was never intended to be coupled with jelled hair and hip-hop attitude. They looked ridiculous.

I said, "Kind of a bad place for a mugging. Isn't it, judge?"

"Nobody's getting mugged. These boys are going to take you and the chink professor home. We get her notes. We get your notes. Just so we understand each other and we won't have any more miscommunications, the professor's going to give Billy the address where her daughter is spending Christmas."

Kai-Li blurted out. "I won't do it."

Under his breath, Billy said, "Good."

The judge reached out and, almost gently, used one finger to turn Kai-Li's face to his. "Billy's in charge tonight. You hand over everything we want, he's *supposed* to leave you alone. You hold back on the research notes or anything else . . . well, Billy's looking forward to getting to know all about you." Judge Savin grinned into Kai-Li's face.

His fat, whiskered cheek was turned toward me; so that's where I hit him.

He dropped like a brick.

I grabbed Kai-Li's arm, pushed her toward the outside door, and said, "Run!"

As I turned back to the young men by the door, the

silenced muzzle of an automatic pistol appeared an inch from my nose. Chuck said, "Stop right there, ma'am."

Kai-Li froze.

The muzzle of Chuck's pistol bounced in front of my face as Billy lunged and hit and clawed against Chuck's other hand. Billy wanted to kill me. Chuck talked to him in a quiet voice. "Calm down, Billy. Somebody needs to check on the judge. Calm down and check on your daddy. I got these two. We'll take 'em home, just like the judge said. We'll take 'em to this guy's beach house and deal with this there."

Billy stopped struggling, and Chuck released the front of his pleated shirt.

Judge Savin spoke. "Motherfucker." *Moherfoher.* "Goddamnit." *Godum-if.* "Help me up." *Heh meh uh.*

Billy rushed around and grabbed the old man under his armpits. When he was vertical, Savin shoved off Billy and glared at me. "Tough guy. Hit an old man." His words had mushed together and lost the hard consonants.

"You're not that old."

"Fuck you."

"And you asked for it."

Savin shuddered a little, worked his jaw up and down, and spat a mouthful of blood and saliva onto the Oriental carpet at our feet. When he did, a broken tooth shot out in the thick red spray. "Get 'em outta here."

Kai-Li pointed at the door we had come through. "There are two or three hundred people out there. There's nothing you can do here. We're not leaving."

Savin moved faster than I thought he could. His hand shot out to backhand Kai-Li across the mouth.

She also moved faster than anyone thought. Savin missed, lost balance, and I kicked a knee out from under him.

My nose and cheekbones exploded in pain. Some sort of caveman noise tumbled out of my mouth, and I reached up to catch the blood flowing from the half-healed cut across my nose. Chuck had administered a pinpoint pistol-whipping with the silencer.

"Billy! Take care of the judge." Chuck shoved me stumbling toward the outside door. He glanced back at Kai-Li. "You want me to, I can beat this dickhead to death right here in front of you." I glanced at Kai-Li, and Chuck slashed me hard across the eyebrow with the barrel of his gun. I stumbled again and felt viscous heat running into my eye.

Then I felt Kai-Li's hands on me. "No."

She said, "Go, Thomas. We have to go."

Kai-Li twisted the doorknob, and we stepped out into bitter cold. As she and I reached the bottom of the flagstone steps, I heard Chuck step outside and close the door behind us.

Thirty-two

GETTING SLAPPED IN the skull with two pounds of steel pistol messes with your equilibrium. Dark ground bumped and swayed and moved like a treadmill beneath me. My feet moved, but the earth moved faster. I stumbled. Kai-Li's strong hands held my right arm. I concentrated on breathing. The cold helped. The world slowed.

"Up ahead, turn left at the path." Chuck's voice came from just behind us. "Move, goddamnit! Move!" He seemed to whisper and yell at once.

A huge vehicle rose out of the darkness. It had wood grain along the side. It was Dr. Adderson's Grand Wagoneer.

"Up by the hood."

We moved. I leaned on the cold metal. Kai-Li stood next to me, watching Chuck's every move, tensed and ready to run. I could feel the energy in her muscles when she brushed against me.

Chuck switched the gun to his left hand, reached into the hip pocket of his formal trousers, and pulled out a set of keys.

He glanced up at us, and something moved over his shoulder. I felt Kai-Li startle. I bent forward and let her catch me. As she did, I wrapped my arms around her. I whispered. "Keep your eyes on Chuck."

She nodded as I straightened up.

Chuck grinned. "Ain't that cute." Then he stopped as still as death.

"Jus let dat gun fall." Zion Thibbodeaux's bony features appeared over our captor's left shoulder. Chuck arched his back, jutting his chest forward. Zybo had something uncomfortable stuck in the man's back. "Now!"

Chuck dropped his handgun in the soft dead leaves beside the Jeep.

Zybo nodded at Kai-Li. "Tommy Boy, he look like shit. You go watch de way you came. De other one'll be comin'."

Kai-Li asked if I'd be okay. I nodded, and she trotted down the pathway.

Zybo lifted a short shotgun in the air and gently thunked Chuck on the head with it. "Take tree steps over to de left." The young man did as instructed. "Okay, now you take off your clothes."

Chuck objected without explanation. He said only two words.

From my position by the hood, I saw Zybo lean down behind Chuck. Zybo's hand shot up between Chuck's legs from the rear; he grabbed a handful of breeding equipment and twisted.

Chuck yelped, and Zybo bumped him on the head again with his shotgun. "You gonna get naked, boy?"

Chuck nodded. Zybo released his grip, and the young legal clerk fell to his knees and mumbled, "I'm doing it. You're crazy sonofabitch. I'm doing it, okay?" And he did. The young man pulled off his white tie and his tails, and began pawing at the studs on his shirt.

"Jus somethin' I learn on de beach one day." Zybo looked up at me and winked. "You in shape to go check on your lady?"

I nodded and went in search of Kai-Li. I found her twenty-five or thirty yards down the path, hiding behind an ancient magnolia with a three-foot trunk. "Heard anything?"

She whispered. "No. Are you all right?"

I nodded. "I'll live."

Kai-Li's eyes flashed back and forth from the direction of the Mandrake Club to the direction of Zion Thibbodeaux and his naked captive. "What should we do? Run? Go for help?"

"I don't know." I stopped to listen, then went on. "The guy just saved our lives."

Kai-Li ran her hands along my shoulders and looked hard into my eyes. "I'm scared."

"So am I." I searched her face. "Do you have any feel for where you are?"

"I think so. We made one turn." She pointed with her open hand, like a karate chop in *The Avengers*. "So I guess the club is that way."

"That's right. On further off to the right are the stables. Go to the left of the club and you're going to hit the shooting range."

The whites of her eyes expanded. "I can't leave you here with these people. You're hurt."

"It's okay. Somebody's got to stay. Zybo just saved our lives. We can't both run off and leave him after that. But," I said, "no one wants to rape *me*. You need to get out of here. I can do more . . . do better if I don't have to worry about Billy Savin drooling over you."

Kai-Li's head snapped around. The muted crunch of shoes on dry leaves floated on the night air. I lowered my voice again. "I'll warn Zybo. Wait here until Billy passes. When you hear me whistle, take off." I reached into my coat pocket and handed her a white parking stub. "Get to the club. Get in a group of people. Get the Safari out of valet parking, and get the hell out of here." I handed her my cell phone. "I'll call you."

The footfalls on leaves grew louder. I slipped away to join Zybo at the Jeep.

He would drive Dr. Adderson's Jeep. I was instructed to follow in his rental.

"Where are we going?"

Zion Thibbodeaux shrugged. "Don' worry 'bout it." He hadn't mentioned Kai-Li's absence. It was as if he had expected me to get her away from the violence.

Inside the Jeep, both Chuck and Billy lay naked in the backseat, their formal clothes wadded on the floorboards beside them. Zybo had used the pair's undershirts to tie their hands. "Soft cotton. Don' leave marks." I just nodded.

The Cajun produced a black sports bag, from which he pulled two clear-plastic face masks with attached canisters. He pulled the straps of the masks over the heads of his naked prisoners, leaving each man with a canister dangling like a metal dong between his eyes.

Zybo told me to get ready. He stepped into the Wagoneer and started out slowly, without headlights. Soon we hit blacktop, where he switched on high beams. A few miles, and he led me onto a red gravel logging road where he parked and, once again, cut the headlights.

Up ahead, through the Wagoneer's back window, I could see Zybo reach into the backseat and do something to Chuck and Billy. He moved back and forth several times, leaning first over the passenger seat and then twisting to lean into the back. His movements weren't violent. They were precise.

Minutes passed.

The Cajun stepped out onto the shoulder of the road and walked back to my window. I rolled it down. He said, "Just a couple more minutes."

"What are we waiting on?"

He looked up through a crisscross of limbs at the moon. "Don' worry 'bout it."

"Well, I am worried about it. What's going on?"

Zybo turned and walked away. He stood beside the Wagoneer and waited. Too noisy, I guessed, back standing with me.

Very little time passed before he opened the back passenger-side door and pulled out the two masks he had strapped onto Chuck's and Billy's heads. He closed that door, walked around and opened the other back door. After reaching inside his pocket, he tore something with his teeth and once again bent over the men in the backseat. Finally, Zybo opened the driver's door, cranked the engine, and pushed the door shut.

He walked back and climbed into the passenger seat of his rental. "Let's go."

I was getting angry. "What happened?"

"Tommy Boy? Believe me. You don' wanna be hangin' round this fuggin place." He paused and then added, "Stay off de shoulder."

I drove forward fifty yards before finding a side road and turning around. Back out on the blacktop, I asked, "Now what?"

"Go home, if dat where your lady supposed to be waitin'."

I tried to think it through. "I hit Judge Savin. Knocked out a tooth. He's not going to let that go."

Zybo laughed. "Fug 'im. I got your back."

I motioned over my shoulder with my chin. "What happened back there?"

"You don' wanna know."

"Yeah, I do."

He turned in the seat to look at me. "De boys, dey dead."

"What?"

"What de fug you tink I was doin'?"

"I thought you were leaving them tied up naked in an embarrassing position to teach them a lesson. I *thought* your damn specialty was *not* killing people."

"Fug it. Dey were gonna kill you, prob'ly rape your lady, and den kill her too." He reached into the glove box and pulled out a pack of cigarettes. He poked one between his lips, fired the end with a lighter from his pocket, and pulled in a chest full of smoke. "Judge Savin's boy, Billy, and dat Chuckie prick—dey're lying naked in de backseat of a Jeep belongs to de judge's girlfriend. One of 'em he even got a condom on his little pecker." I remembered Zybo tearing something with his teeth and then bending over the bodies.

"What was in..." I knew the answer. "There was carbon monoxide in the canisters. It's why you left the motor running."

"I *heard* you were smart. 'Bout time you figure out sometin' on your own."

I looked over at him. "You're an asshole. You know that?"

Zybo sucked hard on the cigarette. The ash cast a red glow across his features. "You better believe it, Tommy Boy. You better fuggin believe it."

A long shower helped. Half a bottle of good scotch helped too. None of it helped enough. I lay in bed trembling. Kai-Li lay beside me, her arms wrapped around my shoulders. She'd insisted on sleeping with me. It wasn't romantic. It was only vaguely sexual. I was freaking a little. Not crying or climbing the walls, but just a case of your basic what-the-hell-have-I-gotten-into heebie-jeebies.

Morning washed away the irrational fears but left the rational ones right where they were. I still hadn't told Kai-Li what had happened to Chuck and Billy. She wasn't happy about not knowing.

"Why is it better?"

I sipped hot coffee from an earthenware mug. "Look, this is the deal. You collected the car and picked me up along the driveway. We saw both Billy and Chuck at the ball, but they either left early or we just didn't run into them again after eight-thirty or so."

She raised an eyebrow. "And what's Judge Savin telling his dentist this fine Saturday morning?"

"Some bullshit story that won't connect him in any way to our deaths."

"But we're not . . . oh."

"Oh."

"And he can't really change his story later."

"Well," I said, "he *could*. But it'd look suspicious. And the judge's trying not to look suspicious these days. He's been fixing jury trials." I tried to smile. "You may have heard about it." I changed the subject. "Did you call Sunny when you got back last night?" I tried to sound casual, like I was only interested in a friendly way and not the least bit worried. "I hope she's having fun up north. I guess they're having a white Christmas."

Kai-Li smiled an indulgent smile. "Sunny's fine. I call every day. And, yes, I called last night. Unless they're tapping your phone, I don't think we have to worry about anyone bothering her."

She thought she was being facetious. I decided not to tell her that Joey had been regularly sweeping the phones in my home and office since I returned from Auburn.

Ten minutes later, when Kai-Li had gone for another cup of coffee, I wandered into the bathroom and looked at an old man in the mirror. Pockets of fluid puffed beneath my eyes. Plain exhaustion loosened skin and muscles and pores.

I stood bent over the sink, brushing my teeth, when Kai-Li knocked and walked in. I rinsed and spit. "A man in his thirties should *not* look like this." I pointed at the mirror.

Kai-Li smiled. She opened the shower door and turned on the hot water.

"You going to take a shower?"

Her hair was looped into a circle on the back of her neck. She reached behind her head with both hands, undid some sort of tortoiseshell clasp, and a shining black curtain fell nearly to her waist.

I turned to face her. I told her she was beautiful, and she smiled.

She worked her fingers under the tail of my red T-shirt and pulled it up and over my head; then she lifted the jazz festival T-shirt I'd loaned her over her own head and stood before me in nothing but a pair of pale blue panties. She looked like a dream, like everything I desired and maybe even needed.

Kai-Li leaned inside the shower to adjust the water. When she turned back, I said, "I'm sorry. This is the wrong morning."

She nodded and slipped her panties down and tossed them into a corner with her toes. She slipped the cool tips of her fingers inside the waistband of my shorts.

"Listen to me, Kai-Li. I'm glad to be alive. And I'm glad you're here with me. But this, what you're doing, would seem . . . I don't know . . . almost like a celebration of what happened last night.

"It's not that I mourn for their fates. Hell, they were going to kill us. It's the way it happened. It wasn't violent or vengeful. What happened was cold and . . . I don't know what, and I need to get the stink and the filth of it out of me before . . ." My voice trailed off. I'd just told her more than I'd ever intended her to know.

Kai-Li slipped her fingers out of my waistband and

placed the pad of her index finger against my lips. "It's just a shower, Thomas."

Stepping over the raised lip of the ceramic stall and leaving the door open, she stood with her back to the showerhead. She arched her back and let the steaming spray slick her hair against her shoulders and back.

She looked at me and smiled. "I promise not to ravish you."

I pulled off my shorts and stepped inside, closing the door behind me.

We stood together in the heat and steam, the hot spray washing over us, and held each other. And, right then, that seemed like enough.

Thirty-three

THE REST OF the day passed at a slow and smooth pace. I built a fire in the hearth and cooked chili for lunch. Kai-Li liked the fire. She tasted the chili and quietly retired to the kitchen, returning with a large spinach salad.

She volunteered to make dinner.

That was about it. People die every day. Nothing changes. Not usually.

I awoke Monday morning beside Kai-Li, having retained my newfound chastity. She was still sleeping when I exited the bathroom, freshly showered and shaved, and dressed by the dim light coming through curtained French doors leading out onto the deck.

Joey was due at 9:00 A.M. but arrived early. His blue Expedition was in the driveway before I finished my bowl of Cinnamon Toast Crunch. He came in and poured himself a cup of coffee.

He nodded at my cereal. "How can you eat that shit?"

I wasn't in the mood.

Joey said, "Nice eye. Kai-Li finally get enough of you?"

"Judge Savin knows we're trying to set him up."

"How?"

"Just smart, I think. He got me and Kai-Li in a back room at the Mandrake Club last night. Said he knows I'm screwing around with him. The plan was for his two gophers..."

Joey raised his coffee cup. "The two hip-hop rejects who tried to waylay you in Montgomery?"

"That's them. Or, more accurately, that *was* them."

"Huh?"

I explained what the judge had wanted them to do. I ended by saying, "And so Zybo killed both of them."

"That was nice of him." Joey drank some coffee. "How much time you figure we got before Savin finds somebody else willing to pop a cap in your head?"

"Pop a cap?"

"The Sopranos."

I nodded. "Not much. What have you got for me?"

Joey stood and retrieved his waterproof, dustproof, blastproof aluminum briefcase from the doorway. He placed it on the tabletop, popped the clasps, and opened the lid. "Here." He tossed a manila file folder in front of me. "We got financial reports on Baneberry-Cort Construction. Copies of building permits for that stack of steel they're puttin' on the beach in Gulf Shores. Even got the probate papers on Kate Baneberry."

I flipped open the folder. "She was a full partner."

"Yep."

"Damn." I quickly flipped through the rest of the documents. "What about life insurance on the partners? It's pretty common among small partnerships. One of them dies and takes their expertise with them..."

Joey shook his head. "No way to know. Now if it was a public corporation, we could find out just about anything..." His voice trailed off. He knew he was telling me things I already knew.

I stood and walked into the living room, where I picked up the phone and punched in seven numbers.

"Loutie? Good morning."

She said, "Morning."

"Joey's here. We were wondering, has your new employer filed suit in the Baneberry case?"

"Not yet."

"They prepared any pleadings?"

She was in the kitchen. I could hear her washing dishes. "Sure. They've got some first-year associate cobbling something together. What do you need to know? I can get you copies, if you need them."

Kai-Li descended the stairs into the living room. She wore jeans and a sweater. She looked great. I put my hand over the mouthpiece. "Joey's in the kitchen."

She nodded and walked on through. She didn't look fully awake yet.

"No. Thanks, Loutie. I just needed to know if Baneberry-Cort Construction is a named plaintiff."

"Yeah. I've only glanced the complaint in passing, but I'm almost certain the partnership is one of the entities suing Dr. Adderson." She paused as it sunk in. "How would they have standing?"

I walked back toward my own kitchen with the mobile receiver. "Kate Baneberry was a partner." A sharp squeak and the sound of running water went away. "You done with the dishes?"

"Yeah. Look, like I said, I can get a copy of anything they're working on."

Kai-Li leaned against the counter, drinking coffee. I sat down at the table across from Joey. "No, Loutie. The cat's out of the bag. Your career as a highly paid law-firm receptionist just ended." I waited for her to speak. She didn't. "We'll talk about it more in person."

"Sounds good." Loutie was a smart woman. Smart enough to leave it alone. "I don't think I did you much good though."

"Loutie," I said, "you'd be surprised."

I pushed the off button and dropped the receiver on the table. Joey had grabbed a bowl from the counter and was eating huge spoonfuls of Cinnamon Toast Crunch with milk. I pointed at his bowl. "I thought you didn't know how I could eat that."

"Thought I'd find out."

I leaned against the back of my chair. "Can you stay around for a little while? I'd like to set up a meeting with Sully."

"Worried about your license?"

"No. This is something else."

Joey finished the last of the cereal. He picked up the bowl and drank the milk with sugar and cinnamon in it. "Give me an hour or two. Gotta serve a summons in Foley for a buddy who couldn't get to it."

I picked up the receiver and punched in Sully's office

number. I spoke with his secretary and dropped the phone back on the table. "Right after lunch."

Joey stood, placed his bowl in the sink, and walked out. I followed him to the door, where he paused. "Tom? You know that girl in there's got a crush on you."

"She's a good person."

"So, you nailing her or what?"

I looked into his eyes. "Careful, Joey."

He laughed. Hard. "Works every time. I can always tell if you're getting laid. All I gotta do is ask the wrong way and then check out the needle on the pissed-off meter."

I said, "Why don't you kiss my ass?"

Joey looked over toward the kitchen and back down to wink at me. "I think that job's taken." He opened the door and stepped out. Over his shoulder, he added, "And it's about friggin' time."

I swung the door shut before he'd finished the last word.

Joey was back by noon. He asked Kai-Li to sit in the passenger seat of his Expedition. I climbed in back where, on the ride into Mobile, I listened to Joey question Kai-Li about whether she found it rewarding to teach undergraduates and how she had landed in Auburn after starting out life in Hong Kong. He asked all about her daughter, Sunny, and talked about spending Christmas away from family when he was in the Navy.

My giant friend really hadn't paid much attention to Dr. Kai-Li Cantil up until that morning. Now he figured she was a friend. Joey's like that. If I liked her, he liked her. If Joey liked her, nobody better *ever* cause her harm. Kai-Li was making one hell of a friend, and I doubted that she even knew it.

Sully was waiting in his office when we arrived. He asked if we'd had lunch and then sent a runner for sandwiches and soup.

I met with him first, alone. Half an hour later, Sully placed a call to Assistant District Attorney Buddy Foxglove—the man who'd arrested me for murder at the urging of his superiors. Foxglove hadn't liked the political interference at the time. Now, as Sully put the man on speaker, Foxglove paid us the courtesy of listening. We talked to him for over an hour. He said little.

For the last half hour of the phone call, we called in Joey and Kai-Li. Foxglove seemed to find my Asian-American houseguest impressive. He was right.

There were different levels of involvement and expertise among the four of us in Sully's office. Sully, our host, now knew everything I knew. The other two knew what they needed to know to stay safe and play their parts.

We all agreed, even ADA Buddy Foxglove—I was in a hell of a mess.

When the conference call had ended, Sully asked, "How do you contact this Zybo character?"

"I can't. He contacts me."

"Judge Savin's not going to let you walk around unmolested forever. So, figure out a way. You've lost your license and been indicted for murder, even if the charges were later withdrawn. A lot of people think you've lost it, Tom."

"Thank you."

He shrugged. "A suicide—let's just say *any* kind of death that even *looks* like a suicide—by someone in your position would hardly raise an eyebrow. So," he paused for emphasis, "find this damn Cajun. We've got to get moving."

We were leaving Mobile. Kai-Li sat up front again. Joey was being charming. He'd just pointed out a small alley where he once got shot through his left hand. He held the scar up to the light. "See."

I leaned forward. "This is the thug version of polite conversation."

Joey glanced in the rearview mirror. "You callin' me a thug? Go look in the mirror, bubba. Nobody's been beating me in the face with a knife and a pistol."

A mall passed by. I said, "Turn in here."

Joey braked and made the next entrance. "What're we doin' here?"

"We're looking for a music store." Kai-Li turned and gave me a strange look. I said, "I need some zydeco. I'm thinking of cranking up the stereo when we get home."

Kai-Li smiled. "Think that'll work?"

Joey glanced up again at me in the rearview mirror. "What are you talking about?" He turned to Kai-Li. "Think what'll work?"

Thirty-four

THE DOORS AND windows stood wide open. We filled the Eastern Shore with yodeled vibrato and the rhythmic twang of stringed instruments. I feared blowing my Martin Logan speakers into little pieces.

Three neighbors called. Two were almost polite. The fourth caller asked, "You lookin' for a good university psychologist?"

"That's right."

Zion Thibbodeaux said, "Same diner?"

I said, "Yeah," and he hung up.

Joey had gone back to Mobile. I quickly called him and left for the diner.

Inside the Safari, my palms sweated and slipped on the steering wheel. The sides of my stomach seemed to abrade against each other. It was a short drive that seemed long.

I found the place around dinnertime. Inside, there

was the same smell, the same waitress, and four new patrons at the counter. Zybo sat at the back table.

When I approached, he said, "Sit on down." So that's what I did. "Whatsa matter, Tommy Boy? You worried 'bout de Wagoneer? Nobody found it yet, if dat's what's botherin' you."

I leaned back and stretched out my legs. "What Wagoneer?"

"Now you talkin'." Zybo nodded. "So what's de problem?"

"Judge Savin. As soon as he figures out I'm still in the world, he's going to try again."

The Cajun looked bored. "I tol you, I got your back."

"For how long?"

He shrugged.

"That's my point," I said. "What I need is something to make him back off."

"Why you talkin' to me 'bout it?"

"I know you've got something. Something you put back to protect yourself. Listen . . ."

A man in a dirty coat stepped down off a stool at the counter and asked the waitress, "Where's the head?"

I held up a palm at Zybo as the guy made his way beside the tables and passed us. But as the dirty coat passed Zybo, he turned and placed the muzzle of an automatic pistol against the side of Zybo's head.

"Don't move. Either one of you. Keep your hands where I can see them."

Someone grabbed me from behind and yanked both of my hands behind my neck. An unseen hand clamped onto my fingers while another hand moved over my clothing. From behind, a voice said, "You can stand up and step aside, Mr. McInnes."

I looked up into Zybo's eyes. There was murder in them. I said, "Don't say anything."

He slowly shook his head at me. Then, as I stood, the front door slammed, and Zybo's line of sight shot past me. His face turned dark. I spun around and saw Joey walk in.

"What is this?"

Joey's eyes drooped. His shoulders and arms hung limp. "It's for your own good, Tom." He motioned at Zybo. "You gotta be done with this guy."

I lunged forward and swung hard at Joey's chin, just catching the tip of it as he jerked his head backward.

Two cops grabbed my arms. A third one, the man in the dirty coat, told the others to cuff me. They used nylon zip cuffs to secure my hands. I looked back. Zybo stood between the dirty coat and a second cop, his face turned to the floor.

The head cop, the one in the coat, began to read Zybo his rights as the two men holding my arms pulled me toward the door. I yelled back over my shoulder at Zybo. "Don't say a word. I'm this man's lawyer. You can't question him without me." When we reached the door, I jammed a foot against the doorframe and caught Zybo's eyes. All I could get out was, "Not a word," before the cops shoved me out into the night.

They let me go home, telling me to be at police headquarters at eight the next morning. I told them I needed to see my client. They said, "Fine. At eight in the morning."

* * *

After three phone calls the night Zion Thibbodeaux was arrested, I met Sullivan Walker in his Mobile office the next morning at seven. Sully and I were at police headquarters thirty minutes later. They let me see Zybo at 9:20, which was a few minutes after ADA Foxglove had finished rubbing my nose in the mess he thought I'd made of things.

Zybo was already in the little prisoner/attorney room when I stepped inside. His head was bowed over a small, square table made of gray metal. His hands were cuffed in front and locked to a thick chain around his waist.

I pulled out the only other chair and sat across from him. "Are you okay?"

"Fine." He didn't look up. Over his head, names and initials had been scratched into a dirty wall covered in chipped paint that, in one corner, bore the imprint of some difficult prisoner's front teeth.

"Have you said anything to them?"

He wagged his lowered head from side to side.

"Nothing?"

He mumbled. "Not even my name."

This was not the man I'd feared for weeks. "What's the matter? What'd they do to you?"

He looked up. His dark eyes were flat, almost lifeless. "Nothin'." He looked around. "I hate dese fuggin places."

I nodded. Zion Thibbodeaux's medical career had ended in a place much like this one. "Maybe we can do something about that. Look, the DA knows about Russell and Wagler. About the jury tampering. Looks like the investigation into Chris Galerina's death turned up something."

I had his attention now. "Dat why dey want me?"

"Yeah, I told you the Mobile cops got a call from Montgomery about a Louisiana hit man. Looks like they figured out who that was."

A faint spark moved behind his pupils. "Wouldn't have if you hadn' had me arrested after we tied up on de beach."

"Listen. We didn't 'tie up.' You followed me *and* harassed me *and* tried to slice my face open with a knife." I paused. "The way I look at it, the cops know who you are because you tried to kill me on the beach. And I have trouble feeling a lot of responsibility for that." I felt the anger again just talking about it, and I found myself yelling at my sort-of client.

A guard stuck his head inside. "Everything all right in here?"

I turned. "Fine. Just explaining life."

"Yeah," he said, "well, do it quieter." He closed the door.

Some silence settled between us. Zybo spoke first. "It's de way I live. Maybe I picked it. Maybe it picked me. I deal with it." He rolled his shoulders and sat up straight. He seemed to be all the way with me again. "So. De cops dey tink dey got sometin' on Russell and Wagler. What 'bout de judge?"

I smiled. "Smart boy. That's exactly what you've got that they don't. Also, you need to realize that, once the DA starts in on the law firm, they're going to start yelling your name, blaming everything on you." I stopped and waited for him to speak. He didn't. "Anyway, if we come forward first, I think we can make Wagler admit that you were just hired to make people sick—not to kill them."

"Dat'll help dem too."

I nodded. "Right. They just hired you to make a few jurors sick. That way, they're not accessories to murder."

"What 'bout de Baneberry woman?"

"Did you kill her?"

"Hell, no. I tol you." He looked down again. "Damnit!"

"Well, I guess I don't have much choice but to believe you. And—whether I believe you or not—if you can give the cops enough hard information on Savin and his ties to Russell and Wagler, I think the DA's going to be willing to go along with Jim Baneberry claiming his wife died as a result of medical malpractice. Basically, I'm thinking the DA's going to take a statewide jury-rigging case over a possible, probably unprovable, death by poisoning. One is better press and better politics. *And* I'm thinking Jim Baneberry is going to believe the story that puts money in his pocket. Malpractice does that. Murder doesn't." I paused to let Zybo absorb what he'd heard. But I didn't want him thinking too long. I wasn't sure that I believed all of it myself. "You don't know everything, but there are a lot of complicating circumstances surrounding Kate Baneberry's death. And, Zybo, we'd be talking about immunity for all acts committed in connection with this case. That would include Mrs. Baneberry."

"What 'bout Savin's boys?"

"No. Not them."

He shrugged. "Can' have everyting."

"Don't get ahead of yourself. We may get nothing. But I've got something to sweeten the deal a little." He raised his eyebrows. "Dr. Cantil—the Chinese psychologist?" He nodded. "She's got this study she did. She can show—without any doubt at all—that Russell and Wagler has been fixing jury trials."

"Good. But why she gonna use it to help me?"

"She's not," I said. "She's going to use it to help herself and maybe me. After the other night, neither she nor I are ever going to be safe until Judge Luther Savin is behind bars or dead. *And* I'll never practice law anywhere ever again until Savin is ruined."

Zybo nodded. He started to say something and stopped. Seconds passed. He tried again. "What now?"

"It's your turn."

"To do what?"

"You're too smart to've worked for people like these and not have figured out some way to protect yourself." I stood up. I had too much energy to sit. "I want to make a deal with the DA. I get my license back. You get a reduced sentence. Maybe even immunity."

His eyes bounced around the room. "Screw reduced sentence. I ain't doin' anyting without immunity." He looked around. "I'm tellin' you. I can' stand dese fuggin places."

"You got something that's worth immunity?"

Zybo sat up straight. For the first time that morning, he looked like the same scary bastard who'd been ruining my life for a month. "Dey want de judge? I can give 'em de judge."

"How fast can you get the information here?"

"Make de deal," he said. "I get it here fast. Jus' make de deal."

An hour later, Zybo was ushered back into the room. This time ADA Buddy Foxglove had joined us in the tiny room.

I nodded at Foxglove. "Zybo. The DA says he needs to see what you've got."

"Hell, no. He see what I got, why he need to make a deal?"

Foxglove said, "Fine," and walked out.

I spent another hour cajoling Zybo. While I was at it, my lawyer, Sully, stroked the DA. A few minutes past eleven that morning, we had a meeting of the minds. Zybo gave me a website address, a list of exceedingly strange instructions, and a string of mixed letters and numbers to use as a password.

"Tell 'em. If dey try to print it, de site it'll shut down. De password it'll change. Look, don' print. You got it?"

I said, "You're kidding."

He didn't answer. I guess he wasn't. Two guards escorted the Cajun back to his cell.

All the government computers had firewalls designed to keep our law enforcement officials out of the porno sites. We couldn't raise Zybo's site on Foxglove's computer. Ditto for his secretary's unit.

We stood around. Foxglove mumbled under his breath. I asked, "You got anybody who investigates Internet crime?"

The DA cussed. He banged open a door and jogged down the hallway. We followed him to Vice, where he butted some clerk out of the way and logged on to a computer labeled FOR VICE USE ONLY, which struck me as something that could, without fear of contradiction, be printed on most computers with Internet access.

In the address window, he typed Zybo's World Wide Web address. Detailed specs for an old Luxman stereo receiver filled the screen.

Foxglove said, "Okay, what now?"

I reviewed Zybo's instructions. "Count down to the twentieth word."

"Count the title?"

"Beats me."

Foxglove used the cursor to jump from word to word. The clerk and Sully stood behind him. Their lips moved as the cursor bounced along the lines of text. He said, "harmonic."

"Click it."

He did. A picture of the receiver's innards popped up. I said, "Find something labeled 'THD Switch' and click on that."

It took a while. When he had it, a one-line text box popped up on screen. I said, "Type in what I tell you," and read off the jumbled password Zybo had given me.

And there it was: SERVICES PERFORMED FOR JUDGE LUTHER SAVIN.

There were dates, names, payments, and contacts at Russell & Wagler, as well as jobs for firms in Birmingham and Huntsville. Foxglove used the arrows on the right of the screen to scroll down through what looked like twenty or thirty pages of data.

Foxglove said, "Jeez," and moved the cursor up to the print icon.

Sully and I yelled almost in unison, "No!"

The befuddled clerk said, "What? What's wrong?"

Foxglove said, "Bullshit. I'm printing this out." He clicked on print. The screen disappeared into a swirl, like water spinning down a drain, and filled again with a picture of two women. They were naked and engaged in a private recreational activity. We could only see one of their faces. Foxglove cussed.

I wanted to say, "I told you so," but kept quiet. The prosecutor at the keyboard was red-faced. We gave him some time.

Finally he said, "Now what?"

"Do we have a deal?"

"Not unless we can get this back and print it."

I stepped around to the other side of the computer to face him. "You screwed it up. And you're saying, because it's screwed up now, we don't have a deal?"

Sully put his hand on my shoulder. "Tom."

Foxglove leaned back in the clerk's chair and exhaled loudly. "Fine. I fucked up. Now what do we do about it? I gotta have this stuff *and* it's gotta check out before your guy walks. It's that simple."

I said, "Let me go talk to him."

Zybo smiled. "I knew somebody'd do it. What a dumbass."

"Congratulations. What do we do now?"

"He gonna give me de immunity?"

"If they can verify any of the stuff on your site. Enough of it to nail the judge and Wagler. Then, yeah, you're going to walk away from this, Zybo."

I could almost feel the tension leaving the man across from me. He said, "I need a piece of paper and a calculator."

I reached into my briefcase and put what he needed on the table.

As Zybo worked, he explained. "De password it

only works once. It gets generated new each time with a formula. Letters represent numbers. I gotta transpose 'em, run de formula with de old password, and get de new string. Den I advance by two each number dat used to be a letter and make dat new number a letter."

"Thanks for clearing that up."

He punched and scribbled. "Jus' like a spreadsheet. Change one value and it roll throughout the cells, changin' all de other values."

"Yeah. That's really fascinating. You know we've got to let him make copies this time."

The Cajun dropped his pencil on the table and shoved the paper with the new password at me. "Okay. Here's what you do. Go 'bout halfway down de report to a place where you see a bold 'P' off by itself..."

I started taking notes.

I stood beside a conference table strewn with printouts. Kai-Li's jury research was stacked neatly in one corner. "Well?"

Sully was smiling. Foxglove wasn't. The sourpuss spoke first. "Looks like we've got most of the top partners at Russell and Wagler, as well as Luther Savin and maybe half a dozen other lawyers around the state." He looked up at Sully. "I know you're grinning because you got your client off, but this is not a happy day."

I said, "Crooked lawyers are still crooks."

He just nodded, stood up, and left the room.

Sully pushed back from the table and stretched. "He won't let Zybo out until he gets something to verify all this. I guess you need to tell Zybo that."

"How long before they execute search warrants?"

Sully stood and walked around the table. "They don't share stuff like that with civilians, but my guess is Foxglove is applying for warrants as we speak. As connected as Savin is, they won't wait to execute on them."

"Tonight?"

"Probably. Look. Go talk with your client, or whatever he is. Tell him what's going on, and let's get the hell out of here." He glanced around the room. "This fucking place is depressing."

Thirty-five

SULLY AND I had hit the Bienville Club to celebrate. Now, as we drove across steely saltwater flats toward Point Clear, I melted into the seat. Good scotch flowed through my veins. Relief flowed over my brain and swept down my body like a woman's touch, soothing aches and pains and smoothing tense muscles.

It was only midafternoon.

Sully broke the silence. "You drunk?"

"Nope. Just relaxed for the first time in God knows when."

Up on the right, two old men fished from a flat-bottom boat. I pointed. One of them was reeling in a fish. "Those same two guys were out there fishing a few days ago when I came this way. Looks like they caught something."

Sully smiled. As we got closer, the one whose line was empty stood and leaned out over the gunwale. He held a net ready for his friend's fish. Something round and dark came up out of the water. Suddenly, the man with the net straightened up and snatched his head to the side. Dropping the net, the old man pulled a knife from his trousers, unfolded the blade, and sliced through the line.

I pointed. "See that?"

"Yeah. Looked like they hooked into a dead turtle." Sully glanced over at me. "It happens."

"I guess." Twisting in my seat to look back, I asked, "Why do you think they're the only ones out there?"

"Beats me." A few seconds passed. "I guess maybe because it's cold as hell. That'd keep me home. Or maybe they're breaking the law. Is this even fishing season?"

I told him I didn't know.

"I've been thinking about something," he said. "What the hell was all that with Thibbodeaux and his website? I mean, what ever happened to safe-deposit boxes? Tom, *that* was some strange shit."

"I thought about it too."

"Decide anything?"

"Yeah. Smart and weird as hell with too much time on his hands."

Sully glanced over at me. "How long it take you to come up with that?"

"Not long," I said.

Sully dropped me at home before three. *It's a Wonderful Life* was playing on the television screen when I walked in. The sound was off. Instead, Nat King Cole sang about chestnuts through my stereo speakers.

"Hello?"

"We're in here." It was Kai-Li's voice. I hardly noticed the British accent anymore.

I walked through to the kitchen. Kai-Li stood at the stove, cooking something. Joey sat at the table, drinking my beer. He had a pink Band-aid on his chin.

I walked over behind Kai-Li and kissed the back of her neck. She said, "Someone's been drinking."

"Yep."

Joey looked up at me. "Is it done?"

I pulled open the refrigerator door and grabbed a Foster's. "They're probably raiding Judge Savin's house and Russell and Wagler's offices as we speak."

Kai-Li turned to face me. "I was afraid to ask."

"I should've called."

She stepped forward, wrapped her arms around my rib cage, and buried her face in my chest. The bruise Zybo had put there twinged a little when she hugged me. "I'm just glad it's over," she said.

I stroked her hair. It felt like silk. "Yeah," I said, "me too."

Joey drained his beer and stood. "If you two are gonna stand around gooin' on each other, I'm goin' home." He pointed at the bandage on his chin. "I owe you for this by the way."

"I had to make it look good. You should've ducked."

He grinned. "I did. Truth is, you're kinda fast for a pansy-ass lawyer."

Kai-Li let go and turned back to the stove. I caught Joey's eye and nodded at her. "Thanks for keeping an eye on things here. We're dealing with crazy people."

"Any time." Joey stopped in the kitchen door. "You sure y'all are gonna be fine now?"

"I think so. Go tell Loutie Blue hello for me."

"The hell with that," he said. "I'm gonna go tell her hello from *me*."

And he left.

I stepped up behind Kai-Li and circled her waist with my left forearm. When I pulled her against me, her breathing felt labored and jerky. I reached up. Her cheeks were wet with tears.

"What is it?"

"I don't know." She took in a deep breath. "Partly relief, I imagine." She shook her hair. "Lots of things. Saturday's Christmas Eve. Sunny's a thousand miles away." She motioned over her shoulder at the living room. "Could be the music. Who knows?"

Three or four days after Kai-Li first arrived on my doorstep, I'd noticed that the phone tended to be busy when she was in my office "doing research." It had taken me a few days more to realize she was talking to her daughter in Iowa. I suppose you don't think of those things unless you have a kid of your own. At least, I didn't.

"Have you called Sunny today?"

She nodded.

Placing my hands on her shoulders, I turned her toward me and gently kissed her lips. "Bad timing." I put my arms around her waist. "I wonder if we'll ever feel...you know, at the same time. Just a couple of emotional wrecks, huh?"

Kai-Li reached up and wiped the tears from her cheeks. She hooked her hands over my shoulders and leaned back to focus on my eyes. "Speak for yourself, Thomas. I'm sad, not dead."

And, with that, she turned off the stove and led me by the hand through the living room, up the stairs, and into the bedroom, where holding each other was only the beginning.

★ ★ ★

I stood before the beachside windows in the living room, wishing it were warm enough to step out onto the deck. Broad strokes of purple and lavender, blended with a thousand shades of blue and gray, swept the glass square of sky before me. It was amazing. Outside, standing at the edge of the deck, it would have been something like a religious experience. Or maybe it just would have been nice. I was in an expansive mood. Not, apparently, expansive enough to walk out in thirty-degree weather in gym shorts.

Kai-Li's bare feet made swishing sounds on the stairs. She came up behind me and circled my stomach with her arms, resting her chin on my shoulder from behind.

"Nice."

"Yes," I said, "it is."

"What are you thinking about?"

I turned and slipped my arm around her waist. She stood next to me now. "Is this where I get in trouble if I say 'nothing'?"

"Jerk."

I smiled. "I was thinking it was too easy today."

She pulled away. "I beg your pardon?"

"No, no. I don't mean that. The thing with Zybo. That was too easy."

"Oh." She walked toward the kitchen. "I'm thirsty. You want something?"

I shook my head. She came back bringing me a Foster's. I guess she didn't believe me.

She took a sip of something brown from a tea glass. "You really are not a well man. Think about it, Thomas. You lost your license, almost got killed three times, and were dragged off by a Cajun murderer—I gather to witness his extermination of two law clerks."

"You don't know that. And only one of them was a law clerk. Young Billy was Savin's demonic seed."

"Colorful."

"Thank you."

She looked out at the sky. "Let's see. You planted Loutie in the law firm, put Joey on this pretty much full-time, and engaged one of the finest psychologists in the country..." Kai-Li turned back to face me.

I held up my hand, palm down, and wiggled it from side to side.

"So," she said, "just what in Hades was *too easy* for you."

"Well, not the whole thing. Just the end."

"The end is always easy. It's how you know the problem is solved." She poked my shoulder with her index finger. "Think about it." Her eyes moved over my face, as thoughts dodged around in her skull. "But there's something's bothering me, too. Something you know and I don't."

I started to tell her not to bring up Chuck and Billy, but she anticipated my objection and waved it off.

"No. It's not what you're thinking. I'm just not sure I have a complete understanding of what you and Joey did here." She took a sip of her drink. "I know you set Zybo up to be arrested, but I don't understand why you'd take the chance. You couldn't know he had information on the judge and Russell and Wagler. And you couldn't know he'd turn state's evidence."

I turned the last few weeks over in my mind, deciding how much to tell her. Finally, I said, "Okay. You understand that I needed to get somebody—the judge, the law firm, or Zybo—to turn on their partners?"

She nodded.

"Well, I asked Sheri to fire me so I could get her into the law firm's camp. That didn't do us much good. Some, but not much. Loutie Blue got us almost everything we needed there—you know, the routing envelope and various bits of information. So that left Judge Savin and Zybo, and I started out trying to work both of them.

"When I first met with Judge Savin at the Mandrake Club, Zybo showed up the next day demanding to know what we had talked about. So, I knew then that he didn't trust the judge. *Then*, when you and I had dinner with Judge Savin and Dr. Adderson, somebody who was *not* Zybo broke into my house and tried way too hard to make it look like another visit from the Cajun."

She nodded. "Right. So then you knew that the judge was setting up Zybo to take the fall in case things went south for him."

"Yeah. At least, I think it was the judge. I'd be surprised to learn that it wasn't Billy Savin who bashed in the back window of the Land Rover that night."

"No finesse."

I agreed. "None, except maybe for the word IOWA scratched into the Safari's paint job. That showed some level of thought. But it was still too heavy-handed for Zybo, and I figure that whoever did it—probably Billy or maybe Chuck, no way to know—was following the judge's instructions. So, anyway, that's where we stood. Zybo didn't trust the judge, and the judge was beginning to set up Zybo. Unfortunately, Judge Savin figured out what I was up to, which I should have anticipated. Whatever else he is, the man's very smart.

"At any rate, once the judge was onto us, we had to move fast before he either hired someone else to finish what Chuck and Billy started or figured out a way to frame me for everything that had happened."

Kai-Li's bright eyes shot around the room as her mind worked over the chain of events. "So you manipulated Zybo—using the routing envelope from Russell and Wagler and his arrest record with Judge Savin's fingerprints all over it..."

I interrupted. "I doubt he checked for fingerprints, but making sure the judge had his literal, as well as his figurative, prints all over the arrest record was a nice added detail.

"So," I said, "getting back to why we set up Zybo for the arrest..."

"You didn't have much choice."

She was right. "Not much. But Joey had a friend with the ABI in Montgomery call the Mobile cops about a 'Cajun hit man' so, number one, the cops would have someone besides us raising Zybo's name and, number two, it helped to put Zybo under more pressure. The fact that the ABI tip came from Montgomery— where Judge Savin lives—was just a little added push for Zybo.

"In the end, we set up a meeting with Foxglove in the DA's office to work all this out before Zybo was even arrested. So the only real chance we were taking was that Zybo might not cooperate for immunity." I drank some beer. "The computer records were great, but we could have done the same thing with his testimony. It just would've taken longer."

Kai-Li seemed to relax.

I asked, "Anything else?"

She shook her head. "I've got it."

Outside, through the window, purple and lavender haze had fallen beneath the soft black blanket of night. I took a swallow of beer and felt a chill run along my spine. "It's been a long day." I turned toward the staircase. "I think I'll go up and get a shower before dinner."

"You aren't getting depressed now that this is all over, are you, Thomas?"

"No. Just cold."

She trotted after me. "Good. I'd say, after the other night, you owe me a good frolic in the shower."

As she passed and jogged up carpeted stairs ahead of me, I said, "I hope you're talking about sex. 'Cause I'm not sure I actually know how to frolic."

Thirty-six

I'VE ALWAYS LIKED courthouses, especially the ancient ones with dark shellac, worn marble floors, ceiling fans, and courtroom balconies. In every county in America, citizens stream through dusty courthouses, buying licenses to fish and hunt, to get married or drive a car. People fight over wills and ice on driveways and who'll get the kids after the divorce. Sometimes they even get married there, in some judge's chambers between summary judgment arguments. It's like somebody boiled life down to all the important stuff and built a creaky old building to hold it.

Now it was just after lunch, and we stood before the Honorable Toby Pithway. He was not a happy man. Lawyers had been indicted. The Chief Judge of the State Court of Criminal Appeals had disappeared driving home from his office the night before—he'd vanished just fifteen minutes before he would have been pushed into the back of a police car, his hands cuffed, his humiliation taped for the morning news.

Judge Luther Savin had dodged the handcuffs and, with his contacts and resources, was probably halfway to Brazil by now. Not much he could do about the morning news programs, though. He was a star—his embarrassment exacerbated by a report that his only son had been found asphyxiated, lying nude in the backseat of a car with his father's law clerk.

Now the cops would have to do something about finding who called Luther Savin to warn him away. Sooner or later, Judge Pithway would have to do something about all of it. For the present, he was called upon to grant prosecutorial immunity to a hired killer while fellow members of the bar sat weeping on metal cots in the county jail.

Pithway glared at ADA Buddy Foxglove. "Is this your idea of good public policy?" The judge looked down to shuffle through papers stacked haphazardly on the bench in front of him. "According to the immunity agreement you've executed with Mr. Thibbodeaux here," he moistened his thumb and flipped a page, "he admits to poisoning eighteen jurors over the past three years. Can that be right?"

Foxglove cleared his throat. "We believe it's a correct number, your honor. My office has analyzed the cases. In every case cited by Mr. Thibbodeaux, a juror left service due to illness and was replaced by an alternate. We are in the process of interviewing the parties and jurors on those cases."

"And one of them, a Mrs. Kate Baneberry, later died?"

"Yes, Your Honor. But we are unable to establish any nexus..."

The judge waved an open mitt in the air as if shooing flies. "And still your office is comfortable enough to let," he motioned at Zybo with the same relaxed, open hand, "this admitted felon with a previous conviction for..."

Foxglove filled in the blank. "Assault, attempted murder, and manslaughter."

Pithway turned his massive head and trained his eyes on Zybo. "Quite a life you've carved out for yourself, Mr. Thibbodeaux."

I stood. "His conviction stemmed from an act of self-defense, which the parole board took into account in cutting short Mr. Thibbodeaux's sentence. If I may, I'd like to point out..."

"Mr. McInnes?"

"Yes, Your Honor?"

"You may not."

"Yes, Your Honor." I sat down.

"Stand back up, Mr. McInnes." I stood. "Are you admitted to practice before this court?"

This was not the fun part. "My license has been temporarily suspended by the State Bar. However, we have already received notice that I'll be reinstated as soon as the disciplinary committee meets. In the interim, I've asked my own attorney, Sullivan Walker, to sit..."

Judge Pithway glanced at his watch. "Mr. McInnes? It is now one twenty-three in the afternoon. Do you, at one twenty-three in the afternoon, on this date, have a license to practice before this court?"

"No, Your Honor."

"Then sit down, Mr. McInnes."

"Yes, Your Honor."

"Mr. Foxglove?" All eyes turned to the DA. His face was red; his eyes watered with suppressed laughter. "You enjoying yourself?"

"No, Your Honor."

"Stand up!"

And so it went. The lawyers got reamed, and Zybo got his immunity. Just another day in the Mobile County Courthouse.

Maybe I didn't like the place as much as I thought.

On the sidewalk outside, Zybo reached out to shake hands. We were not friends; everything was not in the past; I hoped a bus would run over him.

I shook his hand. "Joey's a friend."

Zybo withdrew his hand and just looked at me.

"He thought he was doing the right thing when he brought the cops to our meeting at the diner."

Nothing.

"It turned out right, Zybo. That's what's important, and I don't want anything to happen to Joey. I'm serious."

"I owe him, your friend."

"Let it go. Take a swing at him if you want. Just don't do anything permanent." I paused while a gaggle of young lawyers strode past, discussing some slip-and-fall like it was the trial at Nuremberg. When they had passed, I asked, "Are we straight on this?"

The Cajun nodded. "We're straight." He turned and walked away down the sidewalk. He hailed a cab.

On my flip phone, I punched in Sheri Baneberry's

work number. Just as before, she answered her own phone. I told her we needed to meet.

She had heard about the arrests at Russell & Wagler.

"That's part of what we need to discuss."

Seconds ticked by. "Not today. I can't. Call back tomorrow. We'll set something up." She hung up.

I held the phone out and looked at it. That didn't help. I called my office and spoke with Kelly. "We're back in business. At least we will be after the first of the year."

"I heard. Congrats."

"Thanks. There's still not much I'm allowed to do before the disciplinary committee meets. What's going on there?"

"Sorry, it's dead here. You do have a message, though. Dr. Laurel Adderson's office manager called— a girl named Naja. The doctor wants you to stop by her house tonight after dinner. Around eight, she said. I have a number."

"I'm standing out on the street. How about calling her back for me? Tell her I'll be there. That it?"

She said, "That's it."

"Fine. Why don't you close the place up and go home. We've got voice mail. No need staying around just to answer the phone."

"You read my mind."

"See you January second."

"Really?"

"Really. Merry Christmas."

I got home around three. Kai-Li borrowed the Safari to run in to Fairhope. She said she wanted something to read.

Upstairs, I shucked off my suit and put on jeans, hiking boots, and a long-sleeved polo. After grabbing a canvas hunting coat from the hall closet and locking the door behind me, I struck out along the beach. It had been a while; my thighs and calves felt taut and sore. I walked until my body felt like a whole thing again, instead of the random collection of bones, joints, and muscles I'd had when I first stepped off the deck.

I was home in an hour. Kai-Li wasn't.

Reading didn't take. An old Bogart mystery on TV sucked up the afternoon. I had dozed off on the sofa by the time Kai-Li reentered the house a few minutes before six.

"You've been busy."

I sat up and stretched. "I should've gone with you."

"You weren't invited. I was getting a little stir crazy. Needed some time to myself." She smiled. "No offense."

"None taken." In fact, as much as I liked Kai-Li, I was pretty sure I'd like her even better if she lived somewhere else. I wanted to see her. But neither one of us had really asked for this practically living-together thing we'd gotten ourselves into. "I'm going out tonight."

She smiled.

"I've got to meet with Dr. Adderson."

"I didn't ask."

"I know."

She picked up a large grocery sack. "I picked up a deli tray, some rye, and pumpernickel." I followed her into the kitchen, where we each built sandwiches and scooped potato salad onto plates. We ate that night in front of the television like an old married couple.

Thirty-seven

DR. ADDERSON HAD been uncharacteristically imprecise about the time for our meeting. I left home at 7:30 and made the now familiar nighttime drive to her home. The shining traces of ice and snow were memories. The air had warmed during the afternoon, and distant lightning flashes glowed inside thick cloudcover, preceding distant rolling thunder.

When I pulled up at the farmhouse, a new bronze Land Cruiser, complete with brush guard, roof rack, and heavy-duty winch, was parked by her walkway. It was a nice vehicle for a hunter type like Adderson.

I wouldn't have wanted the Wagoneer back either.

The lightning was closer now. I jogged through light rain to reach the protected alcove that held the front door. I pushed an ivory button, and chimes like the ones in my grandmother's house played a tune somewhere deep inside the house. I waited, then pushed the doorbell again. This time, the faint gonging was accompanied by the quick beat of shoes on hardwood floors.

The door opened. "Tom," was all she said.

I stood there. "May I come in?"

She stepped back to make room. I walked into the warmth of her dimly lit foyer and removed my coat. Dr. Adderson let me stand there and hold it.

I tossed the coat over an umbrella stand. "I guess you've seen the news."

"I have." She looked off in the distance over my shoulder and cleared her throat. "I suppose I owe you an apology."

Something was wrong. I listened for someone else in the house. "That's not necessary."

She nodded. The skin creased between her eyebrows. "Then why are you here?"

"You invited me."

"No, Tom. I didn't."

My heart trembled. "Do you have an office manager named Naja?"

"Yes." Dr. Adderson stepped forward quickly and locked the door. "But I did not invite you here or ask anyone else to."

The chimes of St. Michael's played on a grandfather clock somewhere in the old house, and a small hammer began to beat out the hour. *Pong . . . pong . . . pong . . .* With each note, my heart struck harder in my chest. "I'm a little concerned here, doctor."

She said, "Don't be silly," but I saw her swallow before she said it. "You're certainly free to leave."

"Who else is here?"

"No one. I can assure . . ."

My voice grew sharp. "Who else is here, Laurel?"

"No one. I promise. No one is here but us." She turned and motioned for me to follow. "This is ridiculous. Standing around snapping at each other. Come this way. We need to sit down and talk about this."

I wanted to leave. But if Dr. Adderson was telling the truth, then leaving could be deserting her to face Luther Savin or Zion Thibbodeaux or God-knows-who alone. I really did want to leave. Instead, I followed her along an L-shaped hallway to a sitting room—the one with the thing she'd called a breakfront.

Dr. Adderson motioned at a chair, then left without comment and returned minutes later holding a silver tray. Two blue-and-ivory china cups sat on either side of a silver service. She placed the tray on a coffee table. She poured coffee into one delicate cup and held it out.

As I reached for the lip of the saucer, the room went black. The china cup and saucer hit the tabletop with an outsized crash. Steaming coffee splattered over my jeans. Someone yelled, "Shit!" I think it was me.

"Did I burn you?" Dr. Adderson was using her physician's voice. Calm. Self-assured. Mildly interested in others' pain.

I brushed at the drops of coffee burning through my blue jeans. "I'm fine. Sorry I cussed."

Lightning flashed, casting Dr. Adderson, the walls, and furnishings in shades of silver on black. "I'll survive." Her shadow raised up before me. "Stay here. I'll go try the switch breaker. Maybe they're not out."

"I should come with you."

"No." She leaned down to level her head with mine. "You'll trip over something, and I'll have to look after you *and* the house." Her shadow moved across the room, her shoes beginning to click when she reached the edge of the carpet.

I just sat there, trying not to be a burden.

The tinkle of broken glass filtered in from another room.

"Dr. Adderson?"

Nothing.

I tried again, louder. Furniture squeaked against floorboards as someone bumped into a breakfront or a sideboard or maybe a chiffarobe—the woman didn't have any simple furniture. "Laurel? Answer me. Are you all right? I heard glass breaking."

The static sizzle of falling rain, muffled by closed doors and windows, filled the darkness. Against the background of white noise, floorboards creaked in the hallway.

Rising slowly, stepping carefully to avoid the crunch of broken china beneath my boots, I moved across the rug, feeling my way around hand-carved furniture and antique knickknacks. Someone's weight shifted just outside the sitting room door, and I stepped next to the wall. I flattened my back beside the doorframe and waited. Nothing happened. Someone in the hall waited for me, as I waited for him or her.

Fear disciplines. I stayed put. Seconds turned to minutes. Minutes piled on top of each other, and still no one moved or spoke. My legs quivered with the strain of tensed muscles held immobile. Sweat trickled down between the cords of muscle on either side of my spine, bringing the skin-crawling sensation of an insect roaming inside my clothes.

Lightning. A hard shadow, the shadow of a gun barrel, flashed on the opposite door jamb. I waited. There was no noise. The person on the other end of the gun shadow had gotten past the creaking floorboards and now moved silently. The dark form of the barrels slid into sight through the doorway. It was a double-barrel, like the ones hung in the Mandrake Club Gun Room and, I thought, like the ones hung on the wall of Dr. Adderson's study.

The double-barrel penetrated the room slowly and deliberately. First, just a couple of inches of steel. Then a foot.

Pivoting on my left foot, I made a grab and clamped onto the barrels with my right fist. Yanking hard, I felt someone on the other end lose balance. A bulk of shadow fell forward through the doorway as a thunderous *boom* sounded like thunder in the small sitting room. The shot sent a scalding flash of heat through the barrels. I lost my hold on the hot, slick metal and spun sideways as a shattered window cranked up the volume on falling rain.

Bounding up onto my feet, I'd taken only one step when lightning flashed again. Judge Luther Savin stood across the room, leaning painfully against an antique hunk of walnut. His hands held a twelve-gauge double-barrel. The twin black barrels pointed directly at my chest.

In the brief flash of light, I could see his features— features twisted into a mixture of pain and pleasure. He was hurt, but he was going to kill me. I held both hands out in front of me, palms down. I didn't speak. It wouldn't have done any good.

A blinding flash filled the room, exploding like a flashbulb, tingling the small hairs on my arms and neck. Thunder followed with such speed and force that the boom seemed to originate inside my chest.

I spun hard and ducked into the hallway.

A second boom sounded in the small room as I cleared the doorway. A dozen wasps stung my shoulder and the back of my head. I kept pumping hard, into the second hall and right to the front door. I snatched at the chain, twisted the dead bolt, and grabbed the brass knob. Labored footsteps knocked a shuffling rhythm on the hardwood floor behind me, and time slowed to a series of snapshots, like the stuttered movements of pictures on flipcards. I remember the brass feeling cool in my hand. I remember the gush of cold, wet air as the door swung wide. I lunged forward and lost balance, skidding on my chest over the brownstone landing and over the sharp edges of stone steps.

The night swam in a bath of freezing rain. My shoulder throbbed. Sharp, jarring streaks of pain shot across my scalp from the back of my head, ending in a metallic jab at the backs of my eye sockets.

I planted both hands in the mud and pushed up, arching my back and craning my neck to look back at the doorway. But she was in front of me.

Dr. Laurel Adderson stood on the walkway eight or ten feet from my nose. The front door had been locked; she'd walked through pouring rain from the back of the house. Wet, dark hair plastered her head. Silk and wool hung on her body like soaked laundry. In her hands and mounted against her right shoulder, Dr. Adderson held her ten-thousand-dollar Krieghoff shotgun. Rainwater ran down the ventilated rib and fell in a tiny waterfall from the muzzle.

Still on my stomach in the mud, I pushed hard with my right palm and spun left. The woman could shoot. I knew that. I knew too that I was dead, but damn if I was just going to lie there and take it.

I hit on my knees, stumbled onto my feet, and had taken the first step of a hard sprint when the shotgun fired. And I felt nothing. Nothing but freezing rain and the cold burn of wet December air in my lungs. Mud, grass, and leaves spun and slipped beneath my feet, and I was in the pecan grove. I cut right and glanced back. No one was following. Ten more yards and I stopped to listen. Still there was nothing.

Seconds passed, and I worked forward to the edge of the grove.

Dr. Adderson knelt before the front steps as if praying at an altar. Her extraordinary shotgun lay in the mud at her side. I moved forward, using the doctor's new Land Cruiser for cover. As I neared, she lowered her thighs onto her heels and bent her face forward into open hands.

I saw him.

Judge Luther Savin lay in the doorway, his shoes sticking through the opening at an awkward and unnatural angle. I breathed deeply. I reached up to touch the back of my neck and came away with a hand smeared thick with blood.

Not knowing how much longer I'd be conscious, I walked forward through the winter storm to stand beside the doctor. I reached down and picked up her shotgun. Through the door, I could see the judge's round, slack body. Half his neck had been chewed away by a load from his lover's gun. A black halo of blood spread around his head.

I stepped beneath the sheltered alcove and pushed numb fingers through the mud and grit caked across the top of my hip pocket. The cell phone came out streaked with mud, but the small screen lighted when I flipped open the keypad with my thumb. I dialed 911 and gave the address. "There's been a double shooting," I said. "We need an ambulance and the police." I asked them to hurry.

I had a shoulder blade full of nine shot. Three stray pellets had punctured skin on the back of my head but hadn't penetrated skull. Judge Savin had never been an outdoorsman, and he'd made a bad choice. The judge had pilfered shells from Dr. Adderson's skeet bag. He'd stolen low-brass shells loaded with bird shot that was never designed to bring down a large mammal. By contrast, Dr. Adderson had not made the same mistake. She knew guns, and she'd known where she kept the buckshot.

Nobody—not the police or the doctors, especially not me—told Dr. Adderson that her lover had planned to murder me with *her* gun and then frame her for the crime, likely snapping her neck or something equally unpleasant, in a staged fight with some imagined partner of mine. No one mentioned this to Dr. Adderson for obvious reasons, even though that scenario seemed pretty obvious to everyone involved. No one told Dr. Adderson any of this, but they didn't need to. She was not a stupid woman.

When I was released from the hospital just before midnight, the nurse told me that Dr. Laurel Adderson had been admitted to the psyche floor. "Just for observation." But I was pretty sure she wouldn't be practicing medicine for a while. I thought it'd be longer than that before she found another afternoon's pleasure firing her Krieghoff masterpiece at flying bits of clay.

Thirty-eight

KAI-LI PICKED ME up at the hospital in Daphne, but she did not share my bed that night. She understood that the gash Zybo had cut into my nose had been an unfortunate side effect of our plan to capture him. She understood that the mouse over my eye had resulted from being cornered by Judge Savin, Chuck, and Billy at the Mandrake Club. She even understood that I had no control over what had happened to Chuck and Billy later that night. Kai-Li said she *really had* understood these things. The shotgun pellets in my back, however, had been too much—the straw that broke the camel's back. Her narrow Asian eyes had grown narrower. A white line had formed around her lips.

I pointed out that Judge Savin's death meant we no longer had to worry about her daughter in Iowa. It meant that she, herself, no longer had to watch for frightening shadows in the night.

Kai-Li had tried to smile. Then she'd gone to sleep in the guest room.

By the next morning, the tension had melted a bit. But it would be Christmas in three days, and I expected now to spend it alone.

"I need to talk to Sheri Baneberry."

Kai-Li nodded and probed scrambled eggs with her fork. "Time to tie up loose ends."

"She's my client."

Kai-Li glanced up. "You know, Sheri has other problems besides her mother's death. This is not judgmental. At least, I hope it's not. But she really should speak to someone about her drinking."

"Probably," I said. "But not her attorney."

Kai-Li ate some eggs and took a small sip of hot coffee.

Might as well ask. "Will you be here when I get back?"

She gave me a wan smile. "Of course. I've been thinking about catching a plane to Iowa, but . . ."

"Can you do that? I mean, will your . . . your ex-husband . . . is that okay with him?"

"No." She pushed back from the table. "It's not going to happen. I'm just thinking about it."

I stood and cleared the table of dishes. As I raked leftovers into the disposal, Kai-Li pulled open the dishwasher and waited for me to hand her the plates and glasses. "This is over, Kai-Li. I'll make it up to you."

She turned and locked onto my eyes with hers. "Go see your client. I'll be here when you get back." She leaned over to close the dishwasher door, then looked up to smile. "Promise."

★   ★   ★

Maritime Mutual Assurance occupied a somber brick rectangle only a dozen blocks from my office in the Oswyn Israel Building. I parked on the street. A uniformed guard buzzed me in through a glass-and-steel door.

"Tom McInnes. I'm here to see Sheri Baneberry."

He scanned a computer printout on a clipboard. "Ms. Baneberry expecting you?"

"Yes. Well, probably not this minute. But she knows I wanted to meet."

The guard nodded and picked up a phone on his desk. He couldn't have cared less whether Ms. Baneberry was expecting me or not. He was asking what they'd told him to ask. "Ms. Baneberry. Jerry up front. Yeah. Got a fella here . . ."

"Tom McInnes."

"A fella here named Tom McIntosh says you're expecting him." He nodded, said, "Yes ma'am," and hung up. "She'll be right down." He pointed with one hand as he picked up a newspaper with the other. "Sit over there."

I sat over there.

Eighteen minutes passed before the elevator dinged and Sheri Baneberry stepped out into the industrial-decor lobby. She looked ticked. She was wearing that pissed-off smile of hers.

"Tom. I thought I made it clear about meeting with you here."

"We needed to meet. You didn't call me back. I knew you'd be here."

"Well, can this wait? Because . . ."

"No. It can't. We need to talk."

She sighed deeply and turned her back. "There's an

office down here nobody uses." She walked away, and I followed her down a narrow hall to a plain particleboard door. When we were inside and Sheri had closed the cardboard behind us, she motioned at one of four metal chairs around a cheap table. "Have a seat." I did. Sheri sat across from me, tucking her navy skirt tightly around her thighs as she perched on the plastic cushion. "Okay," she said, "what is it?"

"Have you heard about Judge Savin?"

"Yes."

"I don't mean about the indictment. I'm talking about last night."

"Yes, Tom. I know he's dead. I know Dr. Adderson killed him, and I know you were in the middle of it somehow."

I felt sorry for her, but I'd also had enough of this. "You put me there, Sheri."

She flushed red, but her features softened a bit. "I know. I'm sorry."

"What happened to Bobbi Mactans?"

She squinted at me. "What do you mean?"

"I mean, where is she? The last I heard, Bobbi had come to my house making threats when you were there, and Joey ran her off."

"Oh. Well, Bobbi called me a couple of times after that. I, uh, didn't get back with her. She's fine. There was a message yesterday from her on my answering machine at home." Sheri hesitated. "It *was* strange, though."

I waited for Sheri to decide to tell me.

"Bobbi said she was going to take care of things last night, that everything would be like it was."

My head pounded. My shoulder ached. "Sheri, the

night Bobbi told you she was going to 'take care of things' is the same night Judge Savin tried to murder me."

She shook her head. "That's ridiculous. She could have meant a thousand things . . ."

"She could have." I shifted in the chair to see if a different position would help. "And I'm not accusing her. It's just, the cops don't know how Savin got to Doctor Adderson's farmhouse. Somebody—they don't know who—drove him there. And they think from footprints in the mud that an accomplice cut the power lines." I fidgeted some more to find a comfortable place in the ache. "Obviously, that doesn't mean it was Bobbi. I was just wondering . . ." Some time passed. "I'd still like to help you, Sheri. I told you from the first that I'm not a plaintiff's lawyer, but even I know you've got the mother of all lawsuits against Russell and Wagler."

Her eyes rounded above bright red cheeks. "But they're out of business."

"Yep. And every one of them is worth a few million bucks. You get in line first, and I think you could wind up with four or five times the money you could've ever gotten from Dr. Adderson. And," I said, "unlike Laurel Adderson, these bastards have it coming. Let me set up a meeting with Sullivan Walker. By the time he's done, you'll own Russell and Wagler."

Sheri looked at the floor. "I heard you helped get off that awful man who poisoned Mom. Is that true, Tom?" And there it was. She was hating me big time for that one.

"His name is Zion Thibbodeaux, and he gave your mom something in her dinner to give her food poisoning. I don't know what happened at the hospital, but . . ."

She glanced up.

I took the opportunity to lean forward and hold her gaze. "I wish I'd been able to wrap up everything in a pink bow, Sheri. I had to make choices. The choice I made was to get Russell and Wagler, to get the people who hired Zybo to make your mother sick."

"It wasn't your choice to make."

I nodded. "Maybe. And maybe I'm just trying to make myself feel better, but I don't think Zion Thibbodeaux ever intended to murder your mother."

"Yes he did!" She was yelling. "Jonathan Cort saw him . . ."

"What?"

Sheri stood and reached for the door.

"Sit down."

She ignored me.

"Sheri, you put me in this. I've been knifed, pistol-whipped, disbarred, and pumped full of bird shot. Now sit the hell down and talk to me!"

She sat. "They told us not to say anything. The law firm." She chewed her nail. Her eyes made designs on the plastic woodgrain tabletop. "I guess it's okay *now*. The lawyers were probably just protecting their own person who did their killing for them."

"What did Cort see?"

"The night Mom died. Mr. Cort came by to take Dad to dinner and saw that Zion whazisname leaving Mom's room."

"And Wagler told you not to mention it to anyone?"

"Yes, well, he told me to keep quiet after Dad mentioned, you know, in front of me, what Mr. Cort had seen. I guess it was really more Mr. Cort telling me to keep it a secret than it was Bill Wagler. Mr. Cort threw a fit. He was mad at Dad for talking about it in front of me. Anyway both he and Wagler told me not to tell anyone what he'd seen. Wagler said it was their ace in the hole."

I needed to think. Sheri said something and I held up a hand. Thoughts swirled in my birdshot-pelted skull. Somebody was lying—either Zybo or Cort—and I didn't know which. I asked, "Have you been in on the discussions of your mother's life insurance?"

"What?" Lines formed across her pale forehead. "Well, yes. I'm an actuary. Dad wanted me to look at everything."

"What about the construction company? Did the partnership have life insurance on your mother?"

"How'd you know that?" She leaned back and studied my face. "I thought that was strange at first. But it's not. I never knew that the company was started with some money Mom inherited from her grandfather. And Dad said she worked there getting it started right along with him and Mr. Cort. So she was a full partner."

"How much insurance did they have on your mother?"

"Two-point-four million."

My head spun from a collision of thoughts. I'd lost enough blood from the shotgun hit to wiggle things around some when I tried to concentrate. "And so what you were saying about your mother being a full partner—does that mean your parents had two-thirds of the business?"

"Until she died, yes."

"What do you mean until she died?"

"The living partners get the partnership interest of any deceased partner in equal shares."

"So your mother dies. The next day the partnership gets two-million-four-hundred-thousand dollars, and Cort goes from a one-third partner to owning a full half?"

"Well, yes. But . . ."

"And Cort's the only witness that someone other than him killed your mother?"

Sheri stared off into a distance that wasn't there. Tears pooled along her bottom lashes and ran down flushed cheeks. "That's *not* it. That *can't* be it, Tom. That can't be it." She sounded less sure with each word.

I stood, and the cheap metal chair banged sharply into the wall. "I'm going to set up a meeting between you and Sullivan Walker, Sheri. He'll take care of you. He'll do the lawsuit against Russell and Wagler right. Can I do that for you?"

She nodded.

"Good." I said. "Now, where can I find Jonathan Cort?" She didn't answer. "Sheri!" She startled. "I asked you where I can find Cort."

"Oh, yes. He's out on a job. The company's been having problems with a condo project in Gulf Shores. He's starting the work up again." Her voice trailed off as she realized what she'd said.

"The insurance money?"

My young client leaned forward and cupped her eyes in both hands. She nodded her head. Her arms moved up and down. "Yes," she said, "I guess that must be it."

Thirty-nine

I WAS ANGRY. I also was so beat up, cut up, and shot up that I was starting to walk funny. I stopped by Loutie Blue's house and picked up Joey before leaving for Gulf Shores.

I drove for the first hour, until a ghost hunkered down behind me and proceeded to pound my head with his ghost mallet in a steady rhythm that seemed to echo my heartbeat. Pulling over at a quick mart, I found a bottle of Excedrin Migraine on the shelf and washed down a few with a cold Coke. Back outside, Joey was already in the driver's seat. I thanked him, and he put the Safari in drive.

Just west of Gulf Shores, Joey spoke for the first time. "We gonna mess this guy up?"

"I couldn't mess up a ten-year-old girl right now."

Joey let some time pass. "Be glad to do it for you."

I can't say I didn't give the suggestion serious consideration. In the end, I said, "No. I want to confront him. See what he says. What he does. But, if he tries to get tough—well, I'm too banged up already. So, if he starts something, I would very much appreciate your beating the living shit out of him."

Joey nodded. "You got it."

Minutes later, Joey pulled the Safari onto the Baneberry-Cort Construction work site, and I stepped out. Cort spotted me. He didn't run, but he didn't quite walk either as he beat a path for a red pickup truck. I was already out. I banged on the door to get Joey's attention and pointed at the pickup.

Joey floored the gas pedal, sending a rooster tail of sand and gravel into the air. He charged Cort's pickup and, maybe three yards before collision, slammed on brakes and slid with a loud bang into the pickup's front grille.

Cort bounced back and forth inside the cab, shook his head, and dropped the transmission into reverse. Joey was ready. He floored the accelerator once again, knowing his forward gear would produce more acceleration than Cort's reverse.

Nose to nose, Joey pushed the pickup across the construction site in a wavering line that filled the air with rock and dust and sand. The trucks smashed through stacks of plywood and insulation, over a trough of fresh cement, and across the sugar-white beach on the other side. Twenty feet from the high-tide mark, Joey locked up his brakes and shot Cort's pickup out into the Gulf of Mexico.

I followed on foot, arriving on the beach in time to see Cort climbing through the driver's side window of his truck and falling head-first into the Gulf. I looked over at Joey, and he shot me with his index finger.

Someone behind me yelled, "What the hell you doin'?"

I turned to see three construction workers running at me. The door on the Safari slammed, and Joey stepped between me and the laborers. He held a Colt .45 automatic at his side. All he said was, "Stop." That's what they did. He turned to me. "Go have your talk."

I walked to the water's edge. Jonathan Cort stood in the shallow surf, catching his breath. Waves slapped the backs of his knees. He looked up and took a step forward.

I said, "Don't."

"You can't tell me what to do. I'm going to kick your..." His eyes wandered past me and spotted the gun in Joey's hand. He stopped. "What is this?"

"We need to talk."

"Fine. Let me come up there and..."

"No. You're going to stand there. I got shot last night."

Cort's eyes seemed to acquire an added twinkle at the thought. "I heard."

"So I'm not going to fight you. You're going to keep your distance." I walked down to where the water lapped the wet sand only inches from my shoes. "I just met with Sheri. She told me you saw Zion Thibbodeaux at the hospital the night Kate Baneberry died."

"That's right."

"Why didn't you tell someone?"

"I did. Told my lawyer."

"You told a lawyer who was representing you and your partner in a civil action for money. Why didn't you tell the police?"

"Attorney's advice." He glanced over my shoulder again at Joey. "So it's none of your fucking business what I did."

"I think what you did was kill Kate Baneberry for the insurance money. I also think you found out about Zion Thibbodeaux after Judge Savin and his minions at Russell and Wagler hung him out to dry. When you did, you planted the story with your lawyer about Zybo in case anyone ever got suspicious about how you killed her."

The man actually smiled, and there was something like pride in it. "Yeah, well, that all sounds real good. But, tell me, how do you think I did something like that?"

"Probably a potassium push. Maybe a drug like Pavulon ahead of time to paralyze her so your partner's pretty wife wouldn't put up a fuss about dying."

Cort stopped smiling. He looked at the water, then leaned down and picked up something off the sandy bottom. After glancing at Joey, he held up a gray-green sand dollar between his thumb and index finger. "Guess I'm gonna have good luck."

"I wouldn't count on it."

He smiled again and threw the sand dollar at me with a sidearm toss. It missed. Joey glanced back and then returned to his job of watching Cort's men. "Boy, all you're doing is telling bedtime stories. *If* this happened and *if* that happened. Shit, McInnes, last time I looked they didn't convict people in this state on *ifs* and *maybes* and bullshit theories."

I tried to bore into his conceited eyes. "But you killed her just the same, didn't you?"

He smiled and shrugged. "What difference does it

make? Nobody'll ever prove it. Nobody'll ever even believe it."

"Sheri believes it. So do I."

"Big fucking deal. So little Sheri hates me. I'll learn to live with it. Hell, Sheri's old man already thinks she's gone off the deep end." The man smiled. It was almost friendly. "No, no. Even saying for argument's sake that I killed Kate Baneberry," he shook his head, "nobody will *ever* prove it." The bastard actually winked at me. "Face it, McInnes. *Whoever* did the job, it was a clean kill."

Acid burned inside my gut. The afternoon sky moved and blurred behind Cort's head. The soft, repetitive sloshing of the Gulf at my feet grew loud and grating. I needed to get out of there. I needed not to murder this piece of shit in front of three witnesses.

"Joey!"

"Yeah."

"Time to go."

"Yeah."

I turned and walked to the Safari, where I stepped inside and shut the passenger door. As I moved, I could feel Cort walking behind me, coming up out of the water.

I never looked back.

Epilogue

CHRISTMAS EVE TURNED out to be the warmest day of December. Kai-Li spent an hour on the phone with Sunny and hung up with some new kind of peace or happiness. I seemed to be forgiven. She wanted to go shopping for presents in Fairhope later in the day, to "do something normal" and make it feel like a holiday. We had something to celebrate, she said.

Around ten, Sheri Baneberry stopped by with Christmas cookies. I smiled. It seemed unlike her. She smiled too. A shy and genuine smile. "Mom always baked cookies for friends at Christmas. I wanted to do it this year." She paused. "I wanted to do it for you."

I thanked her. I felt as though I'd been kicked in the stomach.

Kai-Li went to the kitchen to make coffee and to leave me alone with my client. Unfortunately, neither Sheri nor I seemed able to say much.

Finally, I asked, "You heard from Bobbi?"

Her blonde hair moved against her face as she shook her head no. "I think she's gone. The police came by asking about her." Some time passed. Then Sheri walked to one of the beachside windows as if something had caught her eye. "Who's that?"

I walked over to stand beside her. Out on the beach, seemingly hovering on the sand like a Halloween raven cut from black construction paper, stood Zion Thibbodeaux. I glanced over at Sheri. She looked frightened. "Stay here."

"Is that him?"

I nodded. "He's not someone you want to confront, Sheri." I turned to look full in her face. "Can you stay here and let me go talk to him?"

"Can I . . ."

"You know what I mean."

She turned and walked away from the window. "I'll stay."

I stuck my head in the kitchen and told Kai-Li what was happening. She hurried into the living room, where she sat beside Sheri on the sofa.

I left by the back door—the one Chris Galerina had watched with trepidation the night he shot himself—crossed the deck, and stepped down into the yard. Zybo didn't move. I kept walking until I was standing on the shore, five feet from him.

The Cajun stared at me.

I said, "You got my message."

He nodded slowly with a small ducking motion, but his eyes never left mine.

"Bad timing. Sheri Baneberry's inside."

"So what you want?"

"I ran into Jonathan Cort yesterday over in Gulf Shores."

He nodded again, and I filled him in on my conversation with Cort. I didn't add anything. I tried not to emphasize anything. It was a report, and it included Cort's claim that Zybo had killed Kate Baneberry.

When I finished, Zybo said, "Dat what he say? He ready to finger me anytime it look like trouble?"

"I think that's a fair interpretation."

"Unh-huh." Zybo's eyes grazed across the sand at his feet. "A clean kill, huh?"

"Yeah. He sounded proud of it."

The dark man turned his back to me—something like a sign of complete trust in his world. Time passed. He was thinking. "Tommy? You ever clean a empty swimmin' pool? A big old cement one?" He kept his eyes on the horizon, his back to me and my guests.

I studied the black leather stretched across his back. "I was a life-guard one summer in high school."

"What you use to clean it?"

"Why?"

"Go a minute here. Answer de question I'm askin'."

"I think . . ." I looked up at the house. Sheri and Kai-Li stood at the window watching. "We used bleach. Ten or twenty gallons of Clorox."

"Cort, he got a pool in his backyard. Did you know dat?"

"No."

"Yeah. He got a big un." He pushed his hands deep inside the pockets of his coat and rolled his shoulders like he had in the diner. "What you tink ah dis, Tommy Boy? Let tings calm down round heah for a few month. Get on back to normal. Den sometime in

March, maybe early April, Cort he decide to get his pool ready for warm weather." He paused and then spoke the next sentence with no accent at all, mimicking a television reporter. "Apparently overcome by the fumes." He went back to his roots. "Dats what I'm tinkin'." Zybo turned his profile to me now and smiled. "Let him lie there in a couple feet ah bleach and fuggin marinade over de weekend," he kicked a puff of sand into the water, "turn de man as white as dis." He turned to face me. He glanced up at the house and then back into my face. "Now, Tommy Boy, *dat* would be a clean kill."

"It's Christmas Eve."

He grinned. "Merry Christmas."

"I can't talk about this today. Not any day." I turned and walked back across the sand, over dead winter grass, and up onto the deck before glancing over my shoulder.

Zybo had disappeared. Other than the slow drift of clouds and the lapping of water at the shoreline, the only movement was the gentle rocking of the floating Christmas tree—its lights painting colored trails in the late-morning mist.

Sheri met me as I stepped back inside the house. "What'd he want?"

"We needed to wrap some things up."

Her eyes were wide, her skin tight and pale. "Is he going away?"

"Yeah. I think he's going away for now."

Kai-Li put her arm around Sheri's shoulders. "What do you mean 'for now'?"

I looked out at the beach, at the sand and water and

the impossibility of the lonely lighted tree floating on the bay.

Sheri asked, "Is there somebody we should tell? I mean, a man like that—are we safe?"

I nodded. "We're safe, Sheri."

I turned to look at my frightened client. I pictured her at ten years old, standing on a kitchen chair while her mother—tired but smiling after a long day at the construction company—hemmed a Dracula cape for a Halloween costume that would never be worn. I thought of Kate Baneberry lying dead in a hospital room, of two dead punks in a Jeep Wagoneer, of Judge Luther Savin with half his neck blown away, and of Laurel Adderson sitting in the psyche wing of her own hospital. I thought of Jonathan Cort standing in the surf at Gulf Shores, grinning at me.

Kai-Li's voice broke the chain of nightmare visions. "Talk to us, Thomas. Are you going to do anything about him coming back? Are you going to warn anyone?"

I turned to look back out at Mobile Bay. "No," I said, "I don't think I am."

About the Author

MIKE STEWART is an attorney who lives and writes in Birmingham, Alabama.